Anders Flagstad's

Thad Says
Parts Is Parts
(and Thad Is Right)

Book Two
of
Principal
Parts

ALSO BY
ANDERS FLAGSTAD

Spare Parts (Book One of Principal Parts)

Circles and Wheels

The Chaotic Pendulum

A San Francisco policeman, dark blue short sleeves and a blue baseball cap barrels towards Eddie. He's been running alongside Eddie and **his putt-putting yellow Vespa (which Eddie calls The Great Banana)** for a block now. Rush hour traffic has all but ground to a halt and Eddie's been forced to thread his way between jostling cars. A lane to Eddie's right breaks free. Space! Movement! Eddie's wild to hide someplace. He points his bike through a tiny gap between bumpers, in the direction of the distant sidewalk and bravely accelerates.

Thad Says
Parts Is Parts
(and Thad Is Right)

Book Two
of
Principal
Parts

A Novel by

Anders Flagstad

Bubble Eyes Publishing
www.BubbleEyesPublishing.com

Bubble Eyes Publishing
San Diego, Ca
www.BubbleEyesPublishing.com

www.AndersFlagstad.com

Library of Congress Control Number: 2013935688

ISBN: 0-615-78109-8
ISBN-13: 978-0-615-78109-9

Illustrations and Design by K.P. Anderson

for

L. S.

CONTENTS

INTRODUCTION

The following is an adaptation of the Roman playwright Plautus's comedy *Epidicus*. Except for the setting, which is San Francisco, and not Athens or Thebes (or Rome for that matter), and the characters, who are mostly LGBT folk, and the fact there are no slaves, war booty, female courtesans, sacrifices, or public flogging in my novel, a great deal of what Plautus wrote made it into what I have written, only slightly and somewhat transmogrified by the cultural changes of the last 2,200 years.

At least that's my opinion, but I'm a tad biased, having just spent many, many months of my life working on/with both. You'll have to decide, of course, what your opinion is of *Parts is Parts* and *Epidicus* for yourself.

Also – this is the BETA version of my novel. It hasn't turned out exactly, or even inexactly the way I thought it would (but, really what in life ever does?) - so maybe I'll change it in the future. Or maybe I won't. I just figure that if BETA mode was good enough for Gmail for 5 years, it's good enough for my novel too.

Thad Says Parts Is Parts (And Thad Is Right) is Book Two of Principal Parts, a set of stories about people who live or come to live in The City, San Francisco (as San Franciscans refer to the place they live in, or at least the editors of the San Francisco Examiner always spell it - always capitalized – i.e. The City). The characters in this novel continue the lives of some of the characters of the book of short stories *Spare Parts*. Either book can be read on its own. I would encourage you to do so. Read them on your own, that is.

You could also choose to live in The City and find out for yourself what your life would look like, were you to experience San Francisco 24-7, as these characters do – but stay on your toes – things on the edge of the continent are often not quite what you were led to expect,

…at least, that's the way it was for me, in The City – the city by the bay.

xi

Thad Says
Parts Is Parts
(and Thad Is Right)

PROLOGUE
(A Few Weeks Before,
Eddie by a Body Shop in the Bayview District)

Edward "Eddie" Stone is running from the law, and he's finding he's not very good at it. His Vespa's not nearly as fast as he thought it was.

A San Francisco policeman, dark blue short sleeves and a blue baseball cap barrels towards Eddie. He's been running alongside Eddie and his putt-putting yellow Vespa (which Eddie calls The Great Banana) for a block now. Rush hour traffic has all but ground to a halt and Eddie's been forced to thread his way between jostling cars. A lane to Eddie's right breaks free. Space! Movement! Eddie's wild to hide someplace. He points his bike through a tiny gap between bumpers, in the direction of the distant sidewalk and bravely accelerates.

Eddie wheezes and gasps, pulls and parks his bike on the curb, unclips his helmet and promptly trips on his Vespa's kickstand. Shit. Shit. Shit. He grabs his helmet, which he notices is rolling towards the curb, twists and jumps over the bike, and tries to escape into the nearest building. As he makes the leap it registers in his adrenalin-hopped brain that this, the nearest building, is turning out to be Alice's Garage and Body Shop in the Bayview. Not actually the biggest surprise to Eddie, as this, Alice's, was the very place Eddie had been zigzagging to get to, through angry drivers for at least the last hour or two.

Eddie lands on two feet this time and slows and stops and thinks - he's forgetting something, he knows he is.

No, not the rain. It's been raining on Eddie lackadaisically, on and off for hours. And yes, it's now started raining on him again, deliberately, with a definite purposefulness and an impressive depth of feeling, which Eddie can't help but admire. In fact, it's pouring Olympic size swimming pools of pure unadulterated wet on Eddie enthusiastically right at this very moment. But no, the rain, that's not it, that's not what Eddie's forgetting.

And no, it's not the Law. He looks up and over his shoulder and sees the officer has almost caught up to Eddie and to his bike, and Eddie's mind blazes into a firestorm of panic - "Fuck me. What in the hell am I doing? Why am I doing it? Why here? And who do I think I am?" But, no, surprisingly, it's not the police he's forgetting. He's forgetting, what? Something or someone else. It's...

Bam! It hits him, of course, a solid punch to his gut - the money! Where's the money! He 's lost the money!

No, he hasn't. Eddie fumbles and unstraps his favorite briefcase from the luggage rack, which, incidentally, is packed chock-full of bundles of well-used twenties (not technically his own property – the twenties that is, not the luggage), all the while expecting wet policeman's hands on his shoulders any second - two hands dragging him off, bringing Eddie to judgment and to justice and to a well-deserved retribution. But that doesn't happen to Eddie. At least, not yet.

Eddie, by the way, dearly loves this ancient piece of leather – his briefcase. He's had it for decades. It is a lumpy, scuffed, brass-bound box with a handle on it which has a tendency to pop open and disgorge itself and its contents at random intervals. Eddie however has outwitted it this time. Anticipating its deviant ways, Eddie's tied it up with copious amounts of multi-colored string. It's been popping all day, but nothing's been disgorging. So far.

But it tries again. It's relentless. The briefcase pops in a disgruntled, defeated kind of way and Eddie steps backward as it snaps at him. He tangles and untangles himself from the kickstand again, balances, teetering on the curb for a second, then slips and falls into the street. He misses a passing bus by inches. Thinking quickly - as he tumbles in front of tons of diesel powered steel steam-rolling its way towards him - he hurls his briefcase to safety, up and over the bike, holds on to his helmet, and manages to rip open the seam of the seat of his suit pants in the process of not killing himself.

And no, Eddie's not wearing his old pair today, of course not, Eddie's just ripped the seam out of the expensive new pearl-gray pants he'd seen in GQ 2 weeks ago – that special-ordered, tailored, credit card-destroying pair he'd purchased just 7 days ago, taken possession of 2 days ago, and worn for the first time today. Worn, of course, in honor of his criminal agenda this morning. Now they flip and flap around his bare thighs as would a Savile Row hula skirt, and the contents of his pants pockets litter the gutter in colorful and embarrassingly personal profusion.

While unsuccessfully trying to cover his exposed derriere, and swatting at his bike, Eddie regains his balance in time to dodge a glint of something silver flying through the air in front of him. It's a tarnished piece of Eddie's front fender trim - a scimitar of pitted chrome that just knifed him in the butt, and it whirls and dances off past his face and into oncoming traffic. Horns honk, cars brake and squeal, Eddie ignores it all, hoping everyone else won't extrapolate the trajectory of the spinning metal sliver back to its origin and to this half-naked man standing in the rain assaulting his very yellow Vespa.

Eddie wonders if things could get worse. He wonders if it is possible there could be an even higher ratio of water to air in the space around him, in his immediate vicinity. Eddie finds that, yes, it can, and yes, there could. The rain becomes massy walls of water moving horizontally straight at him. They flatten him against the parked car he's standing next to.

Meanwhile, his briefcase slides with a mind of its own across the flowing mountain stream which is the sidewalk now, farther and farther away from him. It spins and stops at the feet of the running officer. Eddie pushes his glasses back up onto his nose, pulls himself off the car trunk he's been plastered to, takes a long, shallow asthma-stunted breath, and listens to his lungs whistle. His once-pressed suit hangs on him in moist bag-like folds, and expensive, soggy rips. The officer, equally soggy, stops in front of Eddie.

Eddie mentally braces himself. There's going to be a lot of rights-reciting and behind-the-back handcuffing occurring in the near future. He puts on his helmet, to keep from dropping it, to try and keep his head dry, and also because he figures - thinking and planning ahead – the helmet ought to give him sorely-needed protection should the officer decide to beat Eddie into submission.

So, Eddie begins again. He moves carefully this time over the bike, succeeds in exiting the Vespa, and looks up to see the officer saying something to him. Eddie can't hear a thing. He smiles at the guy, who's breathing heavily – the uniformed man is a severe, professionally concerned, but dramatically dripping face frowning at him as Eddie pulls and yanks to get his helmet off. It's a gigantic suction cup now on his very wet skull. The officer finally helps him, and they unscrew it painfully off of Eddie's head.

Alice is there. Alice is waiting. In her garage-repair shop, in a wide door, 10 feet away, hands on her hips, standing under some dented, what looks like military-ballistic-grade garage doors, Alice is watching. She's watching Eddie. As Eddie struggles towards her. Her eyes are half-closed. She is motionless. Unreadable expressions are passing over her face.

The officer yells through the monsoon right into Eddie's ear. It's the only way you can hear somebody out here. They are both leaning at a 45 degree angle into the wind.

"Are you all right? Feeling O.K.? You aren't on any kind of medication, are you?" screams the officer, "Drugs? You aren't…" then he gives it up, stops speaking, slowly and carefully hands back the briefcase bundle in the gusting wind. Both Eddie and the officer stare at it. – the briefcase - the exterior of which is mostly crazy-wrapped cord and fist-sized knots, obviously not boy-scout caliber tying, more like what a bored cat would do with a ball of twine and a long afternoon ahead of it. Eddie finally gets a hold of it, it burps and pops once or twice, the officer lets go of it like it's a thing alive.

The officer looks at Eddie for a long moment after Eddie gets it back, and even more closely as Eddie hugs it to his chest. Eddie smiles encouragingly. He can't think of a thing to say. He forgets to thank him. The rain smashes the two of them together, then drags them apart. By the time Eddie thinks to shake his head - no, he is not on drugs - the officer is gone, jogging madly down the street through the rain, plunging calf-deep into puddles, bouncing off of walls, heading around the corner, and then it's just Eddie, Alice, the suitcase and the rain.

Eddie blinks for a second or two, trying to figure out how he got free and why he remains free. He senses movement out of the sides of his eyes. Alice is motioning him to get in out of this downpour. He goes.

"So, do you have the money?" says Alice as Eddie finally makes it over to her and the dry, oil-stained concrete inside. It smells like honest work in here, grease and metal, everything out in the open, it smells like Alice. His glasses fog up immediately.

"Not exactly" says Eddie.

Eddie ducks before Alice can land a punch on his shoulder. He takes off his glasses, cleans them badly with the front of his shirt, which is also waterlogged, puts them back on, yanks them back off again.

He takes in as big a breath as he can, which isn't very big. He lets it out. He takes in an even smaller one.

"Alice..."

He blinks. Water's dripping into his eyes. He doesn't want to say anything. He knows he's got to say something. He can feel her standing there, even though he can't see her. He busies himself rubbing and buffing at his glasses. It's good for a person to have something to do with his hands. He blinks and rubs and buffs.

"Alice…"

A million fists drum the metal roof of the garage. It's going to tear this garage off its foundations. But Eddie doesn't want to move. Ever again. He wants to stand here. Watch it happen. Be with Alice to the end. Wouldn't that be great? Just standing and being able to breathe and dying? He blinks, and then he starts talking, saying something, even though he doesn't want to.

"Alice, I'm so close this time. So close. I can taste it, I'm so close. The Yuba City land deal, well, it's going to make us all rich."

Eddie stops. He realizes he's been massaging gravel and mud into his lenses. His shirt is splattered with it. He's probably destroyed them, he's probably holding precision-ground glass splinters in his hand now. As he tries to inhale, through his ever-tightening chest, he wonders if they issue new glasses to you when they put you in prison. Probably not.

"So, Alice, what I'm trying to say is…"

"What you're trying to say is, you don't have the money."

"Well, not exactly."

It's always "not exactly" with Eddie. Eddie's life is not an exact science. It's not Art either. It's more a continuous comedic improvisation with a consistently tragic ending. Repeated nightly. With a matinee on Sundays.

Eddie has stolen many thousands of dollars from his employer. It's all in the knotted briefcase. He was going to pay back Alice with it, but now, on the way over, he got a phone call. Now, he has to pay it back to someone else. Someone he can't refuse. Someone by the name of Ace.

Eddie rubs his fingertips together, feeling for flakes of glass.

You know what? It is *never* like those posters Eddie has all over his office – "Dream Big" "Work Hard" "Opportunities Abound" "Dare to Succeed" – hah! Dare! Those posters never mention doing jail time, and watching friend's faces as you lie to them and riding Vespas in the rain on dangerously slick city streets transporting stolen goods in psychotic briefcases. They never mention that, do they? No. It's always the sunsets, and the pine trees and the blue, blue lakes, and the achingly capable young men walking beaches, pointing at mountains, climbing cliffs and hang-gliding. Hang-gliding? Hang-gliding? Where the fuck is Eddie's hang glider? Eddie wants to know. Where is it? Eddie should have had dozens of them by now. His flat should be *full* to the ceiling with them.

Eddie does a poor imitation of inhaling. Then he does it again. And then he exhales.

But, still Eddie believes in it. Success. It's his drug of choice. He believes in its unlimited happiness-generating powers, in the fact that Success (and it's always capitalized in Eddie's mind) is the solution to every problem, the medicine for every ill. Success succeeds. Eddie believes in it. With all his strength, with his whole heart, with every particle of willpower he has. Eddie believes. He believes it works.

It's just that, apparently, it's always worked for other people over the last 20 years, and never for Eddie, at least that's been Eddie's experience. But Eddie's turn is coming up. He knows it. It has to be. It's time. The time is now.

"Do you hear that, universe?", he directs an earnest inquiry towards the ceiling, where the universe lives. Eddie is probably mumbling to himself again, he does that quite a bit, but he doesn't care all that much. Usually. And especially now. He's too wet and too broke to care. "Universe? You hear that? Now. This year. It's Eddie's year this year. It's hang glider time. If there is any leftover luck out there…."

Eddie ruffles his hair back and forth with one hand and tries to get some more of the water out of it. He sees Alice eyeballing his briefcase on the floor. Eddie scoots it and its knots between and behind his feet. At the same time, he ruffles his hair some more, hoping he's distracting her. Then he pauses, biting his lip.

He's wet, cold, depressed, and can't breathe. What is he doing here at Alice's? This is never going to work. Why did he come? He's such an idiot. What would Mr. Periphanitides, his soon-to-be-former boss, do in Eddie's situation? What? What would the fabulously rich Mr. P., the man he's just stolen from, what would he do?

The more Eddie ponders this, the more Eddie starts getting the uncomfortable sensation he's being examined. He's being evaluated and he's being watched. The way a plump lemming munching a grass stem in the morning sunshine knows somehow it's being watched by an invisible hovering hawk.

It's Alice. Alice is watching him. Alice is patient that way. She's going to give him time, she's going to let him think. She's going to let him stew and brew and boil and eventually blab everything to her. She knows Eddie. She knows she just has to give him enough space and time and Eddie will self-destruct all on his own. That's Eddie's forte.

Eddie decides to grab the bull, or in this case, the cow by the horns. So to speak. That doesn't sound right somehow, no matter how he re-phrases it. He hopes he's not muttering out loud again. He sucks in as much breath as much as he can, which isn't much, and starts talking.

"But, uh, Alice. Alice, that land and the mobile home by the reservoir, the one I was wanting for myself, if you could help me with that money, if you could see your way clear and give me some more time and maybe then possibly, if there was a way to…" He runs out of breath before he can really finish. His sentence ends unexpectedly with a dying sigh.

Alice is silent. Maybe the slightest hint of disgust in her eyes now. Or maybe she's squinting because it's so dark in here. And loud. The storm is getting worse.

He puts on his glasses again. Nothing but streaks. And scratches. He looks to the left and to the right, at cars in various states of disrepair, at benches and shelves, there's no tools out really, they're all put away, Alice is very organized. Eddie likes that about her. Eddie looks here and there, he examines a dusty Pepsi machine, the ceiling light fixtures, anywhere, everywhere but Alice's eyes again. And Alice is so quiet, he can't tell if she's in the same room with him still.

He waits for a period of time – he estimates it conservatively at a few hours. Then, tries to clear a bucket-load of phlegm out of his lungs, inhales, and in a scratchy, husky voice he says "So what are you thinking?" This uses up all the breath he'd just pulled in.

Alice looks him over, up and down, from soggy Italian loafers to the top of his thinning blond hair, up and back down again. She even shakes her head at his ripped pants flapping in the breeze.

Eddie meanwhile, pats down all his pockets, remembering now he just got a new inhaler. He better find it soon, or he'll collapse right here, into a big pile of gasping Eddie and let 911 take care of the aftermath. Which actually, the more Eddie thinks about it, seems like one of his better ideas. It would feel so good to lie down right now, just for a second. He's so tired. Eddie looks around the floor for a likely spot.

"Well, Eddie..."

He snaps his neck back and jumps a few steps when Alice's voice booms out into the garage. .

"Eddie, helping you depends on what 'not exactly' means. So, why'd you show up at all?"

He's so grateful to hear her speak, so grateful for a little human companionship, that it all tumbles out of him, before he can stop it, before he can close his mouth. It's a torrent of words tumbling and running over each other, pouring out into the empty air between them. Eddie tries, but it's just no good. He spills it all. Alice brings that out in him. He's gasping for air at the end.

"Alice, give me a break. I spent it. I spent the money. What I needed for the down payment on the land – well, I spent it on Ace. My boss, Mr. Periphanitides' son – yeah, I know that you know who Ace Periphanitides is, and I know you know I know you know."

"Hey, c'mon, Alice. We all know. Listen, Alice, this time, he really needed the money. This time it was an honest-to-God emergency. This time his dad, Mr. P. is fed up with him. He's sick of him. He won't help Ace. He wouldn't piss on Ace if Ace were on fire right in front of him. Well, maybe he'd piss on him. I don't know. Mr. P. can be pretty severe. But…"

Eddie pauses, Alice's face is a masterpiece of blankness. Alice is great at poker. Eddie's wallet has been emptied many a night because of it.

"Look, Alice. Alice, please, I had to do it. Someone has to do it. You know I practically raised Ace myself. God knows his mother and father didn't exert much time or energy in Ace's direction. Left Ace up to me. Yes, me, Alice. Ace comes to me with his messes."

Eddie stops and carefully surveys Alice's face for emotion. It is a less than useless effort. He sighs. He continues. First, he sucks in more air.

"Ace says he'll pay me back. Quick. No, really. I know he will, Alice. This time, he promised. Fast. Quick. This time I believe him. Alice? Alice? Hey, Alice?"

Eddie slows down and stops and concentrates on trying to breathe and watches again, wheezing, for Alice's reaction. But Alice is too quick for him. She's already walking away towards her back office, motioning Eddie to follow. Eddie can't see her face. And now she's using her businesswoman voice on him. Which could mean anything or nothing. It drives him crazy. She knows it too.

"When are you ever going to learn, Eddie? Well, I think this time, you're up shit creek without a paddle, my boy."

Eddie waits, knowing there's more. He stays outside her office. He tries to cough, tries to breathe. He looks around for a soft place to fall.

"I'm going to have to put a stop-payment on my check, Eddie." Her voice torpedoes out her open door.

Eddie bites his lip, wills himself to silence, doesn't move forward.

"I'm picking up the phone, Eddie, I'm dialing my 24-hour courtesy services line, the check will be no good in a matter of seconds."

Eddie shuffles forward, dripping, gripping his helmet, brandishing his briefcase, to find Alice leaning back in her chair, feet on her desk, her hands nowhere near her phone.

"Why should I bail out that spoiled, stuck-up, good-fer-nothing one more time? Just because you like him doesn't mean I have to.

Eddie, this has got to stop."

"Maybe Alice, because, you know, I'd do the same for you, if you needed me to, without thinking twice."

Alice glares at him, but Eddie can see she's working at it, the glare isn't coming easy. She's shaking her head. Eddie closes his eyes. He's miserable. He's wet. He's a bad friend. When he draws his breath in, it's like he's breathing through the lungs of a hamster.

"Yeah. Yeah. Well, next week, Eddie. Next week. At the latest. But this is the last time, you hear? The well is dry now Eddie, dry as a bone. You hearing me? Eddie?"

Eddie's looking down, concentrating on pumping oxygen around the few bronchial tubes that are still bothering to inflate and feels something small and sharp hit him in the chest. It's his inhaler. Alice is closing her top desk drawer. She's smiling her small, satisfied smile. It's a ray of sunshine to Eddie, a blast of sunlight after a violent storm.

"Next week, thanks, Alice. Thanks."

"Help each other through it, it's why we're here Eddie. It's why we're here." .

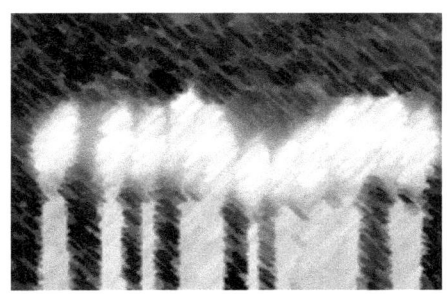

CHAPTER 1
(Saturday Morning 9:15 A.M.,
Eddie in The Castro)

"Hey Alice." Eddie speaks into his cell. His voice is clipped, tense, and whiny. He hates it when he sounds like that, he just can't help himself.

"Hey right back at you, Eddie. Eddie, what's wrong? You sound like someone just sat on your birthday cake."

"Well, it *is* my birthday."

"Forty-two isn't all that old, buddy. My girlfriend's forty-three. She's still wet behind the ears."

"So, how's Janey doing, Alice? She found a job yet?"

"Good, and no, and don't try and change the subject, birthday boy. 'Fess up, Eddie, what's eating you?"

"Oh Alice…" Eddie slides into a whine before he can stop himself.

"Don't 'oh Alice' me, C'mon, Eddie. Stop teasing. Tell me everything, boy."

"Jesus. Well, Alice, it's just the same old same old. Ace and his father. It's not a job. It's a vocation, like joining a monastery. I may be Mr. P.'s personal assistant, but since his wife died, it's like, well, like I'm the glue that's holding that family together. And it's not even my family. And it's not even holding together all that well. I'm just worried about Ace, is all it is."

"What you see in that boy baffles me."

"Alice, I don't know who I am anymore. I don't know what I am, anymore. I thought I'd be rich by now, working for the Periphanitides. Hah! They treat me like shit. I'm going to wake up when I'm 65 Alice, and be used up. Then I'll be thrown away. Trashed. I'm trash, Alice, just trash.

"Eddie, you're working, that's something at least."

What do I have to show for all these years of work? What? Who am I kidding? It could happen tomorrow. Pink slip. Trash. Then what?"

"And you wonder when you'll ever get the time to get yourself a family of your own?"

"Yes, Alice. I do wonder sometimes.

"Well, stop wondering, Eddie, and start dating. You're going out with us for your birthday tonight, come hell or high water. We'll get you a boyfriend. Or at the very least get you laid. You in? Eddie? Eddie?"

"Eddie?"

"Yeah, I'm here."

"So what else? C'mon… spill, Eddie."

"Yeah, I not only used my own money, I had to steal even more money from Mr. Periphanitides to get Ace out of his troubles. I'm going to jail this time. It's more than little. It's a lot. So it's jail. I know it. Jail. Oh, crap. Wait a second, Jesus! I've got to grab my inhaler. There. Sorry.

Eddie can hear Alice waiting, a companionable silence on the phone. He tries to smile, even though she can't see it. Eddie has to admit, it's not a very convincing smile.

"Alice, I'll never get some land and a trailer and a creek and a dog and oh it's all just getting farther and farther away. Some days, I just don't know Alice. I just fucking don't know. What am I going to do, Alice?"

"Now you listen here, Eddie Stone, and you listen good. No, no pissing and moaning. Nah, just pipe down and listen. Farm land's not going anywhere. The country's full of it. You'll get there. You'll get that rancho, or whatever it is they call a farm here in California. You will, you'll see. You just listen to momma Alice."

"I'm at the end of my fucking rope, Alice."

"I know, Eddie, I know. Eddie, you're one of the most stubborn people I've ever met - no, there's more, just be quiet, I'm not done yet - and one of the smartest people. If anyone can get from San Francisco to wrestling cows in central California, or wrestling men or whatever the hell it is you're setting your eyes on wrestling, well, you can Mr. Stone. I believe in you."

"Well, that makes one person."

"Self pity isn't going to get you a mortgage. Or a dog."

"And no one remembers my birthday either, Alice. It's like I don't exist."

"This is just your day for complaining isn't it, Eddie? Well, listen real careful to what I'm about to say to you, Edward. Happy birthday Ed. Happy birthday to you."

"Yeah, happy birthday to me."

"That's better. Now, Eddie, listen up! You are not allowed to forget this – we *will* be going out tonight celebrating. You're dead meat if you cancel on all of us again. You hear me, Eddie? Dead meat."

Eddie doesn't say anything, he doesn't have to. He knows Alice. She doesn't make empty threats. Alice gallops on.

"Now, go out and have yourself one hell of a nice day. Forget the Tragic Endings. Make yourself a Rosy Beginning, for a change. You can do it Eddie. I know you can."

Eddie smiles at the phone again. He makes the smile count. He figures Alice can see it this time, on the other end of the line.

"Hell, it's your birthday, Eddie, and it's your life. Goddammit, if you don't do something with it, who's a gonna?"

CHAPTER 2
(Saturday Night 9:03 P.M.,
Eddie on the Corner of Castro and Market)

Eddie's been hanging out in the Castro all day. He's sick of it. Eddie tries to call Alice again, but her cell's charging or some shit like that. Eddie swipes his cell off for the fourteenth time and slouches back into a waiting posture. Eddie frowns at the San Francisco crowds ebbing and flowing past the corner of Castro and Market. Eddie's not a happy guy right now. His stomach is doing flip-flops. Something's about to happen. Something bad. Eddie knows it. His stomach never lies.

A police car rolls by Eddie. It slows down. Eddie's heart skips a couple of beats and he holds his breath, trying to become as small as possible. Eddie pushes himself nonchalantly away from the street, backing deeper and deeper into the shadowy entrance alcove he's waiting in front of. The police car turns, drives slowly down Castro, disappears. Eddie exhales.

It's the fifth one he's seen this afternoon, well, now it's evening. And the cars always slow down. Almost to a crawl. Of course, they *are* making a left turn onto a neighborhood street. You don't make left turns on two wheels at sixty miles an hour. At least, Eddie doesn't. But maybe the reason they're turning onto Castro all the time today, maybe, just maybe the reason they're turning is because they're very, very interested in this suspicious guy in black (Eddie) who's been loitering on the corner all afternoon, doing nothing but make dozens of phone calls, for hours and hours. Eddie looks like a drug dealer. It all makes sense. Terrible sense. Eddie's in trouble.

Someone squeezes and pushes past Eddie to look at the hours on the closed doors of the closed and darkened shop Eddie is using as his shadowy hideout. The guy bumps and pushes at Eddie. The guy doesn't apologize for it, even though Eddie scurries back and forth to get out of his way. Eddie's amazed at people sometimes. The guy seems so angry.

Eddie can't tell anymore — what's real, what isn't. He can't remember a time when he wasn't stressed and nervous and a little crazy and feeling like he was tightened and thinned and way too taut — an old stretched-out rubber band about to snap in two, rip apart, rupture and disintegrate. Eddie works all the time now. Office and home, day and night. He's even thinking of himself as office supplies. He needs help. He needs to talk to someone. A real person. A real voice. Interface with something other than a spreadsheet, or a website. His heart starts beating faster again.

He feels his chest tightening. He feels his breath getting shallower and weaker. He moves his hands over his pants and shirt feeling for his inhaler. It turns out the inhaler's tucked away in his inner coat pocket. Good. Good. He'll puff himself in a minute, although he's already had to do it once today, early this morning. He tries to slow his breathing down, do it by willpower alone and it just makes him dizzy.

He calls Alice, but hangs up before the call is connected. He closes his cell phone and hits it hard against his forehead a couple of times. This is ridiculous. He's a grown man. Acting like a teenager.

He calls Alice again, but gets the same out-of-service junk. He's lonelier than ever. He blinks and watches the stoplights change. He's scared. He watches for police cars. He thinks of texting, but Alice never looks at her texts. She barely remembers to look at her new messages. Eddie on the other hand, always looks at his messages. He even answers Alice's phone for her, to keep it from ringing endlessly when they're out together. Alice thinks it's cute. Eddie does it to preserve his sanity.

Ace Periphanitides sent Eddie one of his mysterious text

messages this afternoon: to meet him on "The Corner" - one of their code phrases for Castro and Market - so Ace's father can't discover where Ace is hiding out. Eddie has to be crazy to be doing this cloak and dagger bullshit still, for so many years now – is it twenty? No, it has to be twenty two if it's a day. Eddie can remember covering up for Ace's stealing cookies - now what's Eddie going to be covering up for? Grand Larceny? Kidnapping? Murder? Although with Ace it's usually man troubles. Ace has a good heart, but bad instincts when it comes to finding boyfriends. Real bad. It frightens Eddie how poor Ace's judgment is sometimes.

Eddie shakes his head. Having Ace in his life - it's holding one grenade after another in your hand and watching the pins falling to the ground. The next explosion is always on its way. Following right behind the previous explosion. It's never a matter of *if* with Ace's commotions and disorders – it's always a matter of *when*. Ace's problems detonate in Eddie's face with disturbing regularity. Eddie's not sure how many more last minute rescues he has left in him. He tries to inhale.

His breathing is getting no better. In fact, it's worse. Eddie pulls out the inhaler and blasts himself. There's the familiar rush, and a flush of anger and aggressiveness, he feels warm all over. Then his lungs begin to open up. Eddie has his eyes closed. Breathing is so pleasurable. Eddie loves the first few moments of the inhaler when everything and anything seems possible in his life. This must be what hope feels like.

When he opens his eyes, someone walking by is looking at Eddie strangely. Eddie feels his jaws snap shut. He's been talking to himself again. Eddie gives the guy a blindingly harmless smile and waves his hand in a friendly way. He can afford to be friendly, now that he has a supply of oxygen again. The guy quickly moves off. Ah well. Maybe the wave was a little much. Maybe he's mumbling all the time now. Maybe he's falling apart. Piece by piece. Right here on a public sidewalk. Who would care if he did? Would anyone collect all the Eddie-pieces and put them back together again? Eddie wonders.

Anyways, these are the cheerful thoughts Eddie's experiencing now that Eddie's been trapped on the corner of Castro and Market, pinned down next to the entrance to the underground, for most of a Saturday afternoon. And, Eddie reminds himself, the better part of the evening. In fact, soon it will be night, then it will be morning. Amazing how that happens. Would Eddie wait that long? Will he be waiting here weeks from now, a long beard covering his face, stretching towards his shoes, his clothes in shreds? Who would feed him?

Then Eddie has an epiphany. Of sorts. He hears two guys talking as they exit the Muni – one says "Never?" the other says "Not in my lifetime", and Eddie knows, knows with a certainty beamed down into his head from the perfect, ideal heavens above, that not only has there been no sign of Ace this afternoon, there will be no sign of Ace this evening either. Ace is not coming. Ace was never going to come. Eddie's beginning to put two and two together. And for once he's not coming up with five. Ace has done it to him again. Ace has set him up.

Well. Fuck Ace. Fuck Ace and his bag upon bag of troubles and suffering and mayhem. Eddie's been helping Ace with his baggage all his adult life. And guess what? Eddie's tired. It's been a little too much lately. Too much with the baggage. Way too much.

Eddie may have been fooled up till now. But he doesn't have to stay fooled. It's his fucking birthday. Like Alice said. Eddie's punching out. He's off duty. He'll get together with someone and the two of them will head over to see Alice. After all, Eddie promised Alice he'd come. And while the wrath of Alice is one of the Seven Wonders of the World - truly a marvel to behold - Eddie would rather it was directed at someone else. No, he'd rather not be on the receiving end of Alice this time.

Eddie gets a strange, painful grin on his face. He'll call Thad. It's Eddie's birthday. Even the evil Thad will be nice to him today. Right? Eddie tries to get Thad. He has to call three numbers. Only the third one works. He gets Thad's voice mail. Thad is in Los Angeles. Duh!

Thad's gone down there to be with Ace, Thad's best friend. Besides, what was Eddie thinking? Thad is handsome and rough and slick and sleazy as a used car salesman, and, oh yeah, twenty years younger than Eddie. The last thing Eddie needs is to be tailing Thad all Saturday night, whining and wide-eyed and grinning vacuously and lousy with infatuation. He's done it before. Thad just pushes him away. Literally. Into the gutter.

Get a grip, Eddie. Besides, Thad's safely in Los Angeles. Far from Eddie. Too far to be of any help to Eddie tonight. Eddie will just have to find some other way to humiliate himself on his birthday.

Eddie taps his foot and clicks his tongue against his teeth and scares a few more pedestrians with his muffled murmurings.

Eddie pulls out his cell phone again. He'll call Derrick. It rings and rings and Eddie gets a message. When did Derrick fly down to Australia for training for a new job? What new job? It hasn't been that long, has it? No, they just talked. Eddie and Derrick, you wouldn't exactly call it dating, but Eddie thinks about him all the time. Every day. That counts for something, doesn't it? Eddie feels close to Derrick. Yeah, yeah, yeah, so how long exactly Eddie? It had to be last week. They were laughing on the phone last week. Or at the most, the week before that. Eddie looks back in his saved messages - the last one, Derrick mad about Eddie cancelling on seeing a movie – it turns out to be over four months old.

Well… what about Joe? That was last summer. Or was it two summers ago? Joe's number is on his phone, but when he calls it, a girl's voice answers, someone who's never heard of Joe, and Eddie hangs up. Eddie's chest is getting tight again. It's getting hard to breathe. And Jose? Wait, Jose has a boyfriend now. He'd found that out a year ago Christmas. And Jose hates Eddie. Eddie never kept their dates. Who did that leave? Well, there was Robbie. But Eddie didn't even have a number for Robbie. Robbie didn't believe in telephones. He made pots for a living and had ten roommates, or something like that. Did Eddie even have Robbie's address? Let's see… Brad and Tim moved to Phoenix. Georgie moved to a commune in Oregon. Bob just disappeared – that happened a year ago. Eleven dates in eleven days and Eddie has never heard from Bob again. Who did that leave? Eddie doesn't want to look anymore.

Eddie sighs. But what if Ace *is* coming? What if he's just very, very late? What if Ace really, really needs him this time? Eddie feels himself sinking into a familiar, habitual feeling of dead-tired, helpless responsibility.

Yes, he has to help Ace. Who else would do it? Not his dad, that's for sure. And Thad's a follower not a leader, even though Thad thinks he's the star, center, hub and quarterback of every social gathering he's a part of. But Thad's no good at helping. He's much better at mooching. The helping part, that's Eddie's specialty in the Periphanitides family. For the last twenty years. No twenty-two years. God, Eddie feels old.

The fog, which has been hanging high above over the Castro all day, has begun to descend, block by block down the steep slope of 17th Street. It's just starting to hit Eddie and the sidewalks of the Castro. Eddie feels like he's slowly drowning in it. He swats at it and punches at it, knowing he looks like a psycho case. He pretends he's pummeling Ace. Passersby pretend that Eddie's not there.

Ace was supposed to be driving the Tesla - so Eddie's been looking for a low-slung silver something (or was it red? Eddie can't remember worth shit anymore). At any rate, Eddie's been looking diligently both on Market and on Castro. He puts his phone away. He settles back into his search pattern. And a very efficient pattern it is, if he doesn't say so himself. Look up one street, Look up the other. He watches and he watches. He watches stoplights cycle endlessly through green to yellow to red, until Eddie thinks he's going to go colorblind. He finds himself counting the seconds for each color. His head feels as tight as a drum.

And, of course, no Tesla, no Ace. But who knows what trouble Ace could be in now? Certainly not Eddie. He'll be the last to know. But he'll be the first to have to make it all go away. Yes, he will. The stoplight changes again, Eddie lets out a moan, more of a groan really. It's the sound of someone being sucker-punched, for the umpteenth time.

Then, out of the corner of his eye, he sees something familiar, and adrenalin hits his brain with the force of an ice pick jammed into the back of one of his eye sockets.

Finally. There. Right there. Eddie spies Ace's 23 year-old, blond crew cut, on his six foot eight body. It's bobbing around on top of the crowds boiling up out of the station entrance, the selfsame entrance and staircase that Eddie's been standing in front of for most of the day. Hah! No Tesla! Ace is using the friggin' Muni. Fucking Ace.

Eddie's brow furrows. Eddie's mouth compresses into two firm lines of outraged determination. But only for a second or two.

Eddie launches himself towards that very blond head like a heat-seeking missile. Fucking drama queen Ace William Periphanitides. Eddie's not babysitting Ace all night again. Not on his own fucking birthday. Alice is right. No one's watching out for Eddie, but Eddie. Well, Eddie thinks again, maybe Eddie and Alice are watching out for Eddie. That's one. That's one more than no one. And Alice's friend Adam asks about Eddie. Sometimes. That's two. And Ace's friend Charley thinks about Eddie. So…come to think of it, there are some people who do think about Eddie. A few. Just none of the eligible gay bachelors, of which there are tens of thousands in this city. They don't think of Eddie. They won't give Eddie the time of day.

All Eddie can see in his mind's eye is Ace's crew cut, getting away. Unfortunately, Eddie's new shoes have slick leather soles. A guy bumps Eddie, just as Eddie approaches the stairs, and Eddie starts sliding, skating on red paver blocks in the sidewalk. But the sliding, it doesn't stop Eddie – it helps him. Eddie is going to get Ace if it's the last thing he does - he's a hockey player accelerating down the ice for the game-winning goal now. Success is in his reach. Eddie's mind is focused. Eddie's determined. Eddie's thinking about what he's going to say when he gets to grab Ace's shoulder and spin him around and settle this face to face. He should probably calm down a bit first. Yes, and take some deep breaths. And think a little. Before he throttles the living shit out of Ace.

Eddie feels himself stumbling over the first step, and he knows, he knows right then and there, in his heart of hearts, that he's done it again, he's up for some serious pain, and he's not avoiding it this time.

When will he learn to keep his mind on his feet? Especially on staircases. Especially in this city of staircases. He trips, and in the slippery mist falling over the plaza, the cavernous entrance to the Muni station yawns wide before him. It welcomes him - and obligingly swallows him whole.

Eddie disappears. He's history. Looking like a slightly overweight, moon-faced, middle-aged magician in his black shirt and long black pants and black coat thrown over his shoulders (hey! It's cold out tonight – it's friggin' San Francisco, man). A magician, that is, with an odd, unadulterated terror in his pale blue eyes. Eddie exits in a puff of smoke. And, poof!. He's gone.

Eddie reaches for a railing and misses. He tries to keep one eye on the blond head in front of him. He looks for the next railing.

Eddie looks down, as he reaches for a second railing along the wall and misses that too. He looks up again and Ace is gone.

Eddie can see fog rolling in above him. Time seems to be

slowing down. Is his whole life going to flash before his eyes now? Is he going to crack his head open like a dropped egg and end up a one line obituary in the San Francisco Examiner – Edward Stone, professional patsy, dead at 42? Really, how much more trouble could Ace make for Eddie today? How much?

No, universe, says Eddie to himself and the cosmos, I am asking you to please not answer that last question. Please no. Just ignore it. I don't want to know. Really. As much as you'd like to answer. Please. Just skip it. Thanks all the same.

Eddie floats, for a second, and time seems to slow even more and then to stop. This has to be death. Eddie composes himself. He's lived a good life. Maybe not as fulfilling as he would have liked. But good. And he guesses Ace isn't all that bad. He can be a really sweet kid at times. It's good. It's all good.

And the fog, Why has he never noticed it before? It's mesmerizing. It rolls down gently upon him, a benediction for the terminally uncoordinated. It falls in glowing, fuzzy clumps onto his already limp blond hair. It caresses his spastically tumbling limbs. It wreaths his body artistically in ribbons of iridescent moisture, each time he jerks forward. It cools his face and wets his lips, and drips into his eyes, making it difficult for him to see the hard surfaces rising before him that promise to break his teeth and skull into pointy, splintered bits. He twists, he tumbles, he rolls - head over heels - down and down and down.

Above him, Eddie thinks, on the now empty corner of Castro and Market the air brightens and blurs, pink and orange blazes of reflected streetlight burn the dark away, the teeming streets of the Castro lie expectant, waiting, spotlighted and shadow-filled – a carnaval playground of alcohol-sodden bodies, dramas set to house music, yearnings, fulfillments, and hopefully a few future satisfactions.

In other words, thinks Eddie, it's a typical weekend evening.

Yes, the Castro waits, but, unfortunately, it no longer waits for Eddie. Eddie has vanished, leaving only a whimsical void in this young Saturday night, where once a mysterious man was standing, leaning decoratively against the curving beige walls of the neighborhood club clothing store.

At least that's the way Eddie would like to imagine he will be remembered, not only as a faceless employee of the Periphanitides, but also as a man who loved and lost in this foggy gay wonderland, in this city by the bay. Yes, that's how he'd like to be remembered, Eddie thinks, as he swan dives into the subway.

CHAPTER 3
(Saturday Night 9:08 P.M.,
Eddie on a Staircase Leading Down)

"Damn! Shit! Fuck!"

Eddie's lost his imperturbability. His Minnesota calm has evaporated. Now his thinking is – maybe he doesn't want to split his head open. Maybe there's an alternative. Splitting sounds very inconvenient. Not to mention, messy. Eddie's not much for messes. He's much more about orderliness and neatness. Much more.

And he's fairly certain he's mumbling his thoughts again to everyone around him, probably speaking loudly this time and enunciating precisely.

But Eddie's missing step after step now, and splitting his head open seems more and more likely and so doesn't give a rat's ass who he's talking out loud to – let 'em stare. But he tries to keep his voice down anyway, at least down at the level of a manly yell rather than a hysterical scream. He also tries to appear cool and collected on the off chance that maybe he'll be (literally) bumping into Mr. Right. Mr. Right, right on these stairs. Admittedly vain and improbable, but it could happen. Eddie has to have an intact skull, for the whole meeting-of-Mr.-Right scenario to work. Otherwise, how will either of them know that they've met the other? Eddie thinks that's logical. Keeping vertical is job one for Eddie, for a number of reasons.

Shit, there goes another one. Eddie's actually rotating in space, moving downward – he's a felled redwood, a diminutive redwood, a surprised but calm redwood, heading to the sawmill to be cut into pieces.

Yes, Eddie is calm. Outwardly. Inwardly, his thought processes resemble tapioca pudding in a wildly out of control cement mixer, but outwardly, well, that's a different story. People often tell Eddie that his face doesn't readily exhibit a wealth of expression. Eddie thinks what they're hinting at is that Eddie's boring, and unemotional. And you know what? Eddie's O.K. with that. He's from Minnesota - well, Minnesota on his mother's side and New Jersey on his father's. But, Minnesotans, well, Minnesotans can't be contorting their lips and wrinkling their noses, throwing their arms in the air and wiggling their eyebrows every time another three feet of snow falls on them, or the rivers flood, or spring forgets to come and May begins in icy, windswept darkness that blankets the state.

What good would it do? What would be the use of all that expressing? It wouldn't change anything in Minnesota. No, it wouldn't. Not a darned thing. So Eddie doesn't. Express that is. At least not very much. Well, maybe when he's stressed. Then he does do it a little. But he's half New Jersey boy, so he figure's, he's entitled, he figures he's allowed.

This mob that Eddie's plowing through with the professional efficiency of an ice breaker on Lake Superior heading in to Duluth (Eddie's actually seen this, the ice breaker, with his grandpa Schmidt, growing up in northern Minnesota), well, anyways, this mob is basically ignoring him. All of which is fine by Eddie, because Eddie's basically ignoring the mob. It's hard concentrating on any mob, however interesting just now, what with him trying *so* hard to keep his head from being split open, and with him dodging the pitted, poured-concrete floors, steps, railings, and walls that keep lunging out at him, intent on bashing his extremities into bruised bags of mush.

Eddie thinks if anyone thinks he's snubbing them, well, they should cut him a little slack, for Chrissakes let him do a little ignoring for the time being.

However, a piece of Eddie's mind (admittedly, a small one, but still a piece) wanders over each face in the crowd, stubbornly looking for a certain blond head, a certain self-satisfied, self-absorbed, devilish, calculating look, a wide and tall linebacker's physique which would signal to Eddie's very preoccupied brain that Ace is nearby. Ace. Where *is* he?

Eddie can't help searching. His mind is like that. Give it a problem, and it does the bloodhound thing, loyally sniffing and snuffling its way towards its quarry, trotting indefatigably, nose-down over hill and dale. It irritates some people, his constant thinking. But not Eddie. Eddie's accustomed to it by now. After all, he's had forty-some-odd years to get used to it himself. But he understands, others may not take a liking to his scheming and his plans. To each his own, that's what Eddie says. But Eddie respects thinking. Eddie has a long history with thinking.

Eddie ponders the mob, the shit-load of bodies shoving their way upwards towards and past him. They keep coming, and shoving. He keeps falling, and bouncing. Eddie thinks about it. If pressed, he'd probably say this particular mob was most likely disembarking from an inbound tram say, just arrived from the Sunset District. That's what Eddie might say. If pressed. You see, Eddie's just a thinker. He's a ponderer. Like he's mentioned before, he's an analyzer. It's just the way he is.

So, Eddie misses the third-to-last step (Eddie's also a compulsive counter, he likes to count things, especially when he's anxious and upset and, yes, frightened out of his wits about the near future, like, for instance, right now, this very minute). So, the step comes and goes and Eddie can see it, but Eddie's foot doesn't even touch it and Eddie proceeds to take a header directly towards the substantial-looking cement buttress at the back of the station. The one at the bottom of the stairs. Not the smartest move Eddie's ever made. It's his face that's going to stop his fall. He could have picked a better body part to land on. When, Eddie thinks to himself, when will Eddie ever start to keep Eddie's mind on what's in front of Eddie?

Yet, true to form, his mind keeps on analyzing. Even as Eddie's death (or lengthy hospital stay and reconstructive surgery) approaches in the form of a large, solid wall made of concrete, this does not faze the ever-rotating gears of his finely-meshed mind.

You see, the thing of it is, well, Eddie's no bragger. No, not

Eddie. He's not. But he *is* a problem solver. Everyone says that. No one accuses Eddie of not being a bright guy. They may not sometimes give Eddie all the respect that's due him, but hey, they maintain a cordial admiration for him. And his thinking. They do. He senses it. It's an unspoken thing. He knows this to be true.

All of which is fascinating, Eddie admits that. Thinking always interests him.

But right this minute, nobody's asking for his thoughts. Nobody's pressing for his opinion. Right now, what people are doing mostly around Eddie is avoiding. Avoiding and a lot of shoving and sidestepping and cursing. And Eddie's doing all those things too. But it's not really solving anything, Eddie keeps finding himself repeating - "Do something!" and "Do anything!" and "For crying out loud, Eddie, at least do something else!"

So, Eddie comes to a decision point. Eddie's a decisive guy. He feels the immediate need to be stationary.

Eddie comes to a competent stop by colliding successively with three anonymous public transit patrons who are both dodging and ascending while he is so rapidly descending. Then, at the bottom of the stairs, on the wide, flat stretch of floor, Eddie stumbles and skids, bouncing across the yellow, bumpy safety rubber mats that the city of San Francisco helpfully covers key patches of its walkways with.

He slides, slips, slides again off his feet, and inadvertently grabs the clothing of an unfortunate body squeezing past him. Eddie grazes hard against the steel gates at the opening of the station tunnel. He hits even harder with his right shoulder against the wall, and at the end of his slipping and grazing he finds he's holding onto a pair of limbs. Lower limbs. Limbs that aren't excited about having Eddie around.

Clinging to this newly-found squirming set of legs in a blind instinct for survival, he allows himself to pour downwards and to the left and slides the side of his chest and legs against the damp of the concrete wall. He flips over and there's a padlock and some chains cutting into his back as he sinks bonelessly onto the floor. With a deep and abiding sense of surprise, he begins to understand that he's come to a rest. And that he's still conscious.

Blinking, shaking his head, and re-focusing his eyes, Eddie attempts to look up. It's then that he notices certain, very specific details about these legs that he's so enthusiastically fastened himself onto, legs that aren't very happy to have an Eddie coming along for a free ride.

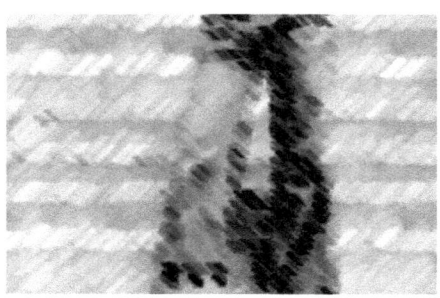

CHAPTER 4
(Saturday Night 9:09 P.M.,
Eddie on the Floor of the Castro Muni Station)

Eddie looks up. Time seems to speed up. It's kind of an unpleasant sensation. Mainly because it involves a lot of pain. Pain he hadn't been aware of so much, just a few moments before. They were right. Ignorance is bliss. Eddie moans.

And apparently his moment of death has been postponed. Now he has to see what parts of his body still want to move, and what parts won't. But first he notices the fancy material, the really expensive fabric, not 2 inches away from his nose.

"Hey, dude", Eddie says, "Nice pants."

"Don't 'dude' me. I'm not your dude. I'm not anyone's dude, dude. Who the hell are you?"

"Me?" Eddie can't think. Is that blood all over his arms? What's that on his hands? Why oh why did he choose a short-sleeved shirt to wear today? He looks like he crawled naked through barbed wire. And where the hell is his coat? Eddie remembers the guy is waiting for him to answer when the guy tries to shove his knee into Eddie's teeth.

"I'm nobody. Nobody in particular. Just a guy. A friend. A friend in need." Eddie fakes a short, barking laugh to show it's a joke, but stops when he realizes the laughing is making his chest hurt like a… . Fuck, what did he do to himself? The guy starts kicking at Eddie, shaking Eddie around, all over the landing of the staircase, the way you'd shake off a dog intent on doing a certain activity on your leg.

So, Eddie silently paws his way up one ankle, then on to a knee, then higher, trying to pull himself back up on his feet. The guy is obviously not going to assist Eddie much. No helping hand. No encouraging word. Just violent self-righteous wriggling and writhing.

Eddie can barely see a close-shaved head with black spiky hair far above him. There's a lot of frowning going on up there. The unhappy face floats over yards and yards of brilliantly white silk material. That part must be a shirt. Below that is the beautiful pants. In the crazy glare of the station, in the buzzing fluorescent overhead lights, it all looks dangerously irradiated to Eddie though. Every bit of it. The shirt, the guy, the haircut, the pants, Eddie's blood on the pants. All of it. The guy is kicking harder at Eddie, trying to get away. He talks down at Eddie in a violent whisper.

"Yeah, I believe it Mr. Nobody; you're getting friendlier by the moment. Easy on the cuffs, man. Those are designer jeans, Dencellini's man."

Eddie stops. He has a sinking feeling. All this seems strangely, well, like he's done all this before. There's a French phrase for it, isn't there? He can't think of it. He absentmindedly starts smoothing out the pants, pleat by pleat as he ponders this. French. A sinking feeling. Pants. He kind of caresses the material as he smoothes. It's so soft. He leaves reddish smears every time he touches them. The guy above him rattles on in a hissing whisper, which grows more and more energetic with each word.

"They probably cost me more than you make in a week. Before taxes. Hey! I said, fucking let it go, man! Ah, c'mon, stop trying to make them flat, they're *supposed* to be wrinkled and stained like that. They're designed that way. Get it? Designer jeans? Ah crap, just let 'em go. "

Eddie feels dizzy again. Which is no surprise, since he just tried to force his head through a steel gate, by running at it and ramming it, at a high rate of speed. Understandable. Logical. But what, what does this remind him of? It's just there, just below the surface of his mind. He can feel it. He can touch it, if he pushes hard enough.

Eddie, why are you so depressed and agitated at the same time? Why? And why in the hell, Eddie, are you holding onto this guy's leg?

Eddie shakes his head, which is a mistake. Now his head is pounding. And how does Eddie know, how can Eddie tell, that even though he can't see it, this guy with the leg he's glommed onto, this guy is smiling a 1000 Kilowatt smile at everyone that passes by. How does Eddie know that? That this guy's trying to pretend like Eddie's not there. That this guy's going to treat Eddie as if Eddie were a piece of trash that happened to blow between his ankles, that's entangled in his shoes? How does Eddie know this? How does Eddie know this about a total stranger?

And all the while, as Eddie tries single-mindedly to re-boot his addled brain, this guy with the beautiful pants is doing his best, his level best, to give Eddie enough kicks in the face to persuade Eddie to unfasten himself and find something more docile to attach himself to. But it's not working. Eddie smiles to himself. No, it's not working on Eddie. Abuse just makes him more stubborn. If this guy knew Eddie, he'd know - kick Eddie and he'll hold on tighter, longer, more vigilantly. If this guy knew Eddie at all...

Eddie feels his brain itching. It's like tiny cogged thinking wheels are slowly breaking free, coming unstuck, starting to spin in familiar ways. Gears mesh with gears, fly belts fly, rods rotate, assembly lines lurch and then there's motion, and then suddenly Eddie's suspicious. He's seen these Dencellini's before. And not just in the shop window upstairs. They've got these huge monograms on the bottom cuffs – "TTT". Who monograms denim? Yes, indeed. Who? And he's sure he's heard that bleating whine one too many times before. The bleating. It's coming. It's coming. He doesn't remember the kicking, though. But maybe the rest of it. What? Somewhere? Some-when? And then…

It dawns on him.

Thaddeus Tucker Tavoularis, the man himself. Ace's insufferable sidekick. The evil, impossibly hot, absolutely uninterested (in Eddie) Thad. How? How could Eddie not have known? Except for the fact he'd just had a strong blow to the head, and was subsequently kicked in the same spot over and over again by said Thad. Yes, all that's true. But Eddie should have known, right?

Maybe Eddie's just never looked up into Thad's crotch from

shoe-level before with blood and fog dripping into his eyes. No, that's not true, he did do that once before. When Thad threw him into the gutter, after Eddie had consumed seven shots of Tequila in one hour and attacked Thad, Eddie being the dangerous sexual predator that he is. He remembers this vantage point. The crotch. The pants. Eddie admits, it's a memorable view. Thad's a sight to behold.

Eddie had a crush on Thad. Well, present tense, Eddie still has a crush on Thad, but that's his own private purgatory, at least for right now, and probably (if Eddie's being honest with himself) far off into the distant future. But anyway, the Night of the Gutter, as Eddie now remembers that night, well, that night Eddie tried to give Thad some tips on wrestling, and that's all. Really. If you examine it disinterestedly, it was all very simple and proceeded from the most innocent of motives. You just have to look at it in the right way. Really.

So… they were outside of a dance club, after last call, in the middle of the street (it was a cul de sac, so there weren't a lot of cars – it wasn't as dangerous as it sounds – really, it wasn't), and… since they'd both been on college wrestling teams, well, admittedly, Eddie had been on a team a couple of decades before Thad, but still… they'd chatted about wrestling. Eddie at least remembers that part. Eddie offered to show Thad some neck locks. Eddie was sure Thad had seemed interested, talkative, even excited. And Eddie was also sure he hadn't said anything about lip locks. Well, pretty sure. At least he hoped he hadn't said anything out loud. But, anywho, Thad had seemed open, very open to a wrestling demonstration.

Thad finished by throwing Eddie against the curb. It must have looked spectacular. After flipping Eddie over his shoulder like a rag doll and snapping him like a whip. He'd started to laugh, seeing Eddie sprawled in a cubist, angular pose – you know, the position they sketch those chalk figures in, on the street after there's been an accident – kind of like an Egyptian painting, all elbows and knees. Well, anyways, Eddie didn't' say a word. He'd just looked up at Thad. And then, the strangest thing happened. In a gesture that was very much out of character for Thad, Thad had stopped laughing, cocked his head, almost looked concerned and pulled Eddie back onto his feet. Maybe they would have had a chance to talk, get to know one another, even (who knows?) gone home together, but at that moment, Eddie's stomach decided to unload all of its remaining alcoholic contents onto Thad's shirt. Thad was not happy. Eddie went home alone that night.

And now, here Eddie was, hugging Thad's ankles, trying to get another lock on him. Who'd have thought it? A second chance at wrestling Thad?

And what about Ace?

"Well" thinks Eddie, not daring to hope too much, considering everything that's happened so far tonight, "well, where there is a Thad Tavoularis, could an Ace Periphanitides be very far behind?"

Maybe this night will be something other than a total train wreck. Maybe. Maybe, if he plays his cards right, well, who knows what might happen? Who knows where he might end up? Yes, Eddie, who knows? It is your birthday after all.

Eddie smiles to himself, and winces almost immediately - feeling his smile lines crack the bloody scratches on his face. Thad, feeling neglected, tries to gouge out Eddie's eyebrows with the heel of one shoe and Eddie twines himself around the other foot to get to Thad's other side to get the hell out of range.

But something else still doesn't make sense. What is it? He feels more pieces clicking into place somewhere in the back of his mind. Piles of it. Eddie senses troubles. Ace troubles.

Now why would Thad be taking public transportation? A man who won't take a taxi if he can find a Town Car? And sneaking around on the subway? Thad?

Before Eddie can ponder this any more deeply, his eyes start to sting and he rubs this junk– whatever it is – off of his face and out of his eyeballs. It turns out to be blood. He starts to wipe the blood (where'd all that come from?) off his forehead, but only ends up depositing the gore that's on the back of his right hand in a long smear all across the central part of his face. His head must resemble a red lava lamp that's boiled over.

He realizes, too late, that he's also making dark streaks up and down the lower third of Thad's pants. Then the gunk starts dripping into his eyes again. Squinting and blinking Eddie mutters to himself "Fuck it" and pulls his once black knit shirt up and over one of his arms (keeping one of Thad's leg in a wrestling grip he learned on the Varsity team in High School) and smears and daubs and rubs until he can see again.

He gives Thad's pants a few brisk wipes halfheartedly and tries to blend the blood into the overall pattern of artful crinkles and streaks and stains that Thad paid so much money for. Eddie talks while he blends. To distract Thad, before Thad kicks some of Eddie's teeth loose.

"Hey, just give a gander, earthwards, Thad, and stop trying to work the crowd." Eddie yells this as loudly as he can upwards, as his face is buried deep in his own muffling shirt. He gives up trying to not look like crash victim. It's a lost cause. Eddie wriggles and writhes to hold onto Thad and get his shirt back on at the same time, and just manages to push his bare hand and arm through the neck hole.

"Yeah, look just a little lower. A little lower and to the right. There. Yeah, it's me talking. The guy grabbing your feet. Thad, it's me. Eddie." Eddie pulls his reeking, clot-covered shirt on his back as he pushes his hand through the empty sleeve and waits. The knit shirt is stretched all out of shape. Eddie looks like he's wearing a black trash bag that once held dripping scraps from a Butcher's shop. Thad's not looking down. He's shaking Eddie again and cussing. Eddie yells louder.

"Thad. Eddie. It's Eddie. Thad. Look down, Goddammit. It's Eddie." Thad finally glances down at the stairs.

"It's Thaddeus, to you. How do you know my name, huh? Who is that anyway? What are you doing down there bleeding and slobbering on my genuine alligator skin sneakers - sneakers I might add that I haven't even had waterproofed yet? And if you…

Thad stops in mid sentence.

"Wait. Hold it just a friggin' second. You really Eddie? Eddie Stone? No shit? I can't believe it. Eddie. Just my luck. Eddie? Is that really you? You aren't going to throw up on me again, are you?"

Thad stops struggling, chuckles a little pathetically, his brown, limpid, beady eyes darting about in the crowd surging around them. Keeping an eye out for something… or someone… Eddie scrutinizes the crowd also from his low vantage point, trying to see what Thad is looking for. Eddie identifies a great number of footwear of various types and brands. Big help that. Eddie yells up at Thad again.

"One and the same, Thad, in the flesh, or what's left of it - I've been leaving pieces of myself all over the San Francisco Municipal Railway's property lately. So what are we looking for Thad?"

Thad has no response for that. He's still searching, but slyly, like he doesn't want to be noticed. "Eddie. Well. Well. Eddie. Well. If it isn't Eddie... Eddie..."

"Yup, it's me, Thad, Eddie." Apparently the novelty of Eddie bleeding at his feet has worn off. Something else is taking its place. Thad watches Eddie silently for a half minute, biting his lip, obviously thinking hard, looking at people to the left, looking at people to the right. Eddie can almost smell Thad's transmission grinding, his belts burning, his pistons pumping with too little oil. Thad's scheming. Eddie's beginning to get worried Thad might not speak again, not at all tonight. He grabs on tightly to Thad's legs, a little higher this time, up by the thighs, pulls himself up onto his knees (fuck, that hurts) and yells up through the crowd "Thad? Thad? Thad?"

In a lightning-quick move, a blitzkrieg move, really, Thad makes a sudden, unexpected, gymnastic leap for the upper steps and freedom – a strategy that would have borne more fruit if Eddie hadn't been crawling up Thad's legs. But still, a brilliant tactical maneuver, Eddie has to admit. Thad bounces straight back, however, into Eddie's lap.

Eddie rests his back against a railing. Thad's sitting on top of him. You know, Eddie's head is hurting in a funny way. Like he has a two small headaches, one set behind each of his ears. And sometimes he thinks he's seeing double. Then it gets dark and misty. Of course, that could be the fog - it is, after all, a staircase in San Francisco, Eddie. And the night's turned hazy. Or it could just be the blood drying and gumming up his eyelids. Or it could be the new drips hitting the corners of his eyes, and making his eyes itch. He's rubbing at his eyes all the time now. He squeezes one eye shut, then the other. They feel sticky and gritty. It's really annoying. Or...

Eddie shakes his head, endures the throbbing aching that follows, and concentrates. Eddie's got bigger fish to fry at the moment.

Thad's off his lap and moving again. Thad's not giving up on the leaping. Thad doesn't have to. He's 23 and six foot six. He can leap all night if necessary, and he will. Eddie knows that. Thad works out seven days a week. Eddie, on the other hand, has a gym membership he punctually pays too much money for every month – but it's a gym he hasn't seen the inside of since before Ace finished up college. Eddie doesn't want to figure out how many years ago that was. He feels old. And fat. And on top of it now, bruised and broken and dazed. He's in no mood for all these Thad shenanigans.

Thad pulls him bodily up the stairwell. Thad kicks at him. For Thad, it's easy. He's obviously used to it. To Thad it's like training at the running track with Eddie-weights on his ankles. He makes steady progress jerking Eddie upwards, one step at a time.

"For Fuck's sake, Eddie. Let go." Eddie trips him with one leg as he leaps up another step. Eddie holds on tighter.

Thad falls flat on his face. He quickly gets up, checking to see if anyone's noticed him licking the concrete stairs. He turns towards Eddie with a look a tiger might have if you just pissed on its whiskers. He reaches for Eddie with muscular, capable hands.

But then he stops. He closes his eyes and Eddie can swear, he sees Thad counting out loud to ten. Thad's lips are moving, he's almost chanting. When he mouths "ten" Thad opens his eyes and he smiles at Eddie. Eddie is intrigued. More blood drips into Eddie's eyes. His head pounds. Now his ears hurt too.

"We can do this the easy way, Eddie, or the hard way. I'll tell you what…I'm going to count till three, and then you're going to let me go, awright, Ed?"

"One."

"It's not going to happen Thad. I'm not letting go."

"Two."

"Hey, what the hell are you doing on Muni at 9 PM on a Saturday night? Huh? It just doesn't add up man."

"Uh… Uh…"

"And why are you giving me all these chances? You always punch first and ask questions later. You're kind of stupid that way. No, don't bother punching me now. It's a waste of your time. I wouldn't even notice a couple more bruises in my present condition. I mean, just look at me. So. Thad. You in trouble or something, big guy? Something maybe you can't handle? Huh? Thad?"

"Uh… Ah, crap! Eddie! Me, stupid! Who you calling stupid? Shit. Fuck. Fucking hell. Just. Let. Go." Thad pulls but Eddie pulls back. They go nowhere.

"I knew it was something, Thad. Something's up, right?"

Then Thad gets that evil smile on his face again, fluffs out his white silk shirt collars, smoothes out his expensive pants, adjusts his oversize belt with the huge buckle. Eddie has to admit it. Thad is a handsome guy. Thad's eyes soften. His eyebrows rise. He almost looks interested in Eddie. With a shock, Eddie realizes Thad is flirting with him. Thad stops kicking. He pats Eddie on the head. It's even a gentle pat, not a vicious backslap. All the same, Eddie can see him planning, or possibly just plain panicking. He can see it in Thad's eyes. There's a touching desperation to each of Thad's reactions. Eddie's drawn in, despite himself. And the patting on the head isn't so bad either. Eddie relaxes the tiniest bit.

"Yeah. Yeah. Eddie. Eddie. What can I say? It's been real. But uh, I'm, uh, you know, seriously late, man. Whoa, look at the time! Gotta boogey, as the saying goes. Been real good seeing you Eddie. Real good. Let's do lunch some time? Yeah? Hasta, Eddie. Bye, Eddie. Bye. Bye."

But Eddie's still not letting go. Thad's just plain pathetic. The pats stop.

"Hey Thad? Wait a sec. You should be happy, shouldn't you?"

Thad glares, then closes his eyes and responds. "Why? Why the fuck should I be happy? And what am I waiting for, exactly, Ed?" Thad starts pulling grimly on Eddie. He manages to drag him a couple of feet across a concrete landing towards the last flight of stairs.

"You're back home, Thad. Back home from Los Angeles, right? I just wanted to say welcome back, Thad."

Thad slows down slightly and with a puzzled look says "Thanks, Eddie, I guess."

"And... We'll take you out for the traditional Welcome-Back-To-Civilization-Bar-Crawl-And-Tapas-Night in the Mission when you have time. And by we, I mean it's all on us, Periphanitides LLC of course. Ace's dad wouldn't have it any other way."

Thad, with a worried look grabs onto a handrail and starts pulling again, harder this time. He pauses, almost says something, stops himself, then methodically drags Eddie up towards the plaza, one painful step at a time, keeping his eyes fixed on the top of the stairs - the alpine professional with low oxygen doggedly trudging towards the top of Everest. He's desperately silent.

"So, Thad, Ouch! That hurt. Thad, how does... Uh, wait a second, my legs caught in the banister here. There. So how does this Tuesday sound?"

"Tuesday? What in the fuck are we talking about?" Thad drags some more. "Oh yeah. Ace's dad. Dinner." Thad stops for a moment to consider whether or not he'd accept a free meal. He would. He starts dragging again.

"Well, Edward." Jerk. Drag. Pull. Jerk. Drag. Pull. "Edward, you know what? You've convinced me - if you're offering, I'm accepting." Eddie notes how the mention of the family Periphanitides improves Thad's manners towards Eddie tremendously.

"So." Jerk. Jerk. "If that's all, Edward…"

Eddie wedges his torso into the railing and forces Thad to stop. Eddie's figured it out. Something's rotten in Los Angeles.

Los Angeles. Thad. Ace. Eddie. Mr. P. Eddie gets the sinking feeling he'll be blamed for something. Like he always is. Periphanitides employee Eddie leads a dangerous, exciting life. Despite all his efforts to make it smooth and boring. It always turns out career-threatening. Or life-threatening. Or both. And it never stops.

When will it stop, Eddie? Eddie sighs. He's whining again. Alice would be punching his shoulder about now. She'd be punching right there. Right where the rip is, right where it's bleeding through the knit fabric. The answer, Eddie replies to himself, is of course - it all stops when you make it stop, Eddie. A no-brainer, plain as the nose on your face - as Alice would say.

Thad tugs on him, one long belligerent jerk and interrupts these happy thoughts with a kick to Eddie's mouth, which fortunately misses his mouth, but unfortunately hits his shoulder. Right where it's ripped.

CHAPTER 5
(Saturday Night 9:26 P.M.,
Eddie Almost Back on the Corner of Castro and Market)

Eddie holds on more tightly to Thad's knees, and yells up Thad's torso in the direction of Thad's face.

"So, Thad, how'd it go? How was L.A. Thad? You guys make it back in one piece?"

Thad kicks, trying to improve his aim. Eddie dodges.

"So, hostile takeovers can be a bitch, huh? Thad?. Guess the internship at the law firm is over? Thad? For both you and Ace?" Thad tries a new move on Eddie, involving hopping on one foot, kicking with the other, but quickly gives up with a grunt and a whispered "Fuck this" and a yelled "Fuck you" and a raised hand – which he slowly lowers as an amazed expression of disgust blossoms across his entire face.

"Wait a friggin' minute – is that blood all over your face Eddie? It that shit on my pants too? Jesus! It better not be on my fucking shirt."

"L.A.? Thad?"

"It's blood, Eddie, it's blood. Blood doesn't come out Eddie, not out of silk. Shit! How the hell do you think it's turned out, Eddie? Just look at me. Use your famous brain. And for fuck's sake call me Thaddeus, you bleeding freak."

"Well, Thaddie, let's see then" Eddie yells up his leg. "Tanned. Check. Buff. Check. Expensive clothes. Check. Looking good so far..." Eddie peels back Thad's socks while Thad kicks and struggles like a madman to get loose. "And no police bracelet on your ankle either. And you always bragging about how you can steal a man blind." Eddie had forgotten how muscular Thad's calves were. They were bigger than ripe cantaloupes and hard as rocks. And now they had some bloody Eddie-fingerprints all over them. Eddie gets easily distracted by athlete's calves.

"Hey! Fucking hell, dude," Thad gasps and moans as he pulls at his pants leg and drags Eddie up the final three stairs, in an insane spurt of heroic jerking and throws them both out of the station and into the fog and the streets of the Castro.

"It's not stealing Eddie, if you have a contract. And besides, I haven't had one of those ankle things on for months and months. At least a year, man. It was all bogus anyways."

"Yeah?"

"I wasn't breaking parole, I was doing a bicycle marathon. I just forgot to tell them."

"I, for one, believe you. But where's the car, Thad? The Tesla you and Ace drove to L.A.? You forget that too? Maybe leave that on the train?"

"Ho ho. Very funny. It is to laugh." Eddie has a horrible sinking feeling. So this is it. So, the car is wrecked. Ace is in an Intensive Care ward, lost somewhere down south in the L.A. basin. It's all turned to shit. Eddie's going to have to tell Mr. P. Thad sure as hell won't. Thad's running away. Eddie's left holding the Ace-bag, once again.

Mr. P. told Eddie he was responsible for Ace. And the car. And the lawsuit. And the money. The money Mr. P. was spending on Ace during his internship with that big international law firm down there. He may as well have added responsibility for the Federal Budget Deficit for all the control Eddie has over Ace and Ace's various projects in the pursuit of Ace-happiness.

Basically, Eddie's professional life is over. And he's broke. And he doesn't have a boyfriend. He doesn't even have a dog.

Eddie pulls himself to his knees, groans and blinks and realizes Thad is just standing there looking at him. No more escaping. No more running off. Now Eddie is really frightened.

"But no, really, Thad. Where is he, Ace? And where's the car?
"Ace?"

"Ace. Ace Periphanitides. Chairman of the Board's son. My employer's son. Your best friend. The guy you went down to L.A. with. Part of the takeover team. Junior legal guy. Ace. You remember Ace. Too handsome for his own good. Built like a Raider Defensive Lineman. Ace. You went to Elementary School with him. That guy."

"Uh… Ace…"

"Yes, Ace. He's O.K. right? Not in a heart and lung machine? Not incarcerated? Not forced to swim the Pacific with concrete Nike's on? Not crippled for life. You guys weren't taking on the Teamsters Retirement Fund or anything down there, were you?"

"Uh… no. Ace…"

"Ace. Yes, Ace? How's he doing?"

"Give me minute, will you, Eddie? Ace. How is Ace? Well let me see. Ace. You'll be glad to know, Eddie, Ace is good. In fact, Eddie, he's better than good. Ace is fucking amazing. Ace is bench pressing, literally, I'd say, 370 last time I saw him. Oh, man if you could've fuckin' been there. Whole place just stopped and watched. Must've been 10, 20 guys. Cheering him on. That was this afternoon, Eddie. At Gold's in Hollywood. He is, uh, taking a, uh, later flight. Yeah, Eddie. Today, a later flight. Last I saw him. Hollywood. Today. Bench pressing. Later flight. Yup, Eddie, that's it. That's Ace. That's all I know."

"And…"

"And, Eddie, that's it. Your ears not working? Let go. That's all I know. For fuck's sake, stop leaning on me, you're bleeding on my pants."

"And…"

"And… Yes, that's it, Eduardo. That is, as they say in the movies, all she wrote. I'm done. Finito. This is part where the music gets louder, the credits roll and a big 'The End' appears floating in mid air in front of my face."

Eddie doesn't say anything. Thad throws his impressively muscled, white silk covered arms up in the air.

"Look, what the hell gives anyways? What gives a little shit like you the right to give me the third degree? And for God's sake, why don't you get up off your knees and drip your bodily fluids on someone else?"

Eddie can tell, he's wearing Thad down. He can feel it. Just a little more, and…

"Which question do you want me to answer first, Thad?"

"You listen, and listen good Personal Assistant Edward. I don't care if you do work for Ace's pop. You just better watch your back, little man. You grow eyes in the back of your head, cuz, I am watching you. From now on. Watching you. All the time. And I don't know how you found out, I mean about the ankle-bracelet shit – jeez, I limped in a fake cast for months covering for that thing – I better hear nothing, you hear? No blabbing it all over the place. Nada. Or you'll be very, very sorry. We communicating here? And let me go, for Chrissake. Stop it. This is embarrassing, Eddie."

"For both of us. And I get it, Thad. I understand. Perfectly. Just one more thing. Mr. Periphanitides is very interested in the car. What about the car, Thad?"

Thad motions with his eyes at the people walking past. It's a very strange gesture. It's what a cartoon Thad would do if he were knocked on the head with a hammer and was about to keel over, knocked out cold. Eddie looks around the two of them. People everywhere. The Castro. Saturday night. What? There must be some logical reason for Thad's wayward eye acrobatics –but for the life of him Eddie can't figure out what it is.

"Eddie, dude, can't talk here. Too many ears." Thad crosses his arms and leans back, staring up at the top of a nearby building with a wide-eyed, curious expression on his face. At least his eyes have stopped going in circles. Now he looks like a lost puppy. A sly, twisted, pathologically lying puppy, with 18 inch biceps. He speaks to Eddie out of the side of his mouth. With his mouth closed. It's a disturbing lisping hiss - a few vowels, no consonants, mostly a lot of air leaking. It must be exhausting to do.

"Later." He looks significantly off into the middle distance. Eddie looks to see what he's peering at, but all there is, as far as Eddie can see, is fog out there, dripping on everybody and everything. Eddie looks back at Thad. He waits. Thad finally groans, rolls his eyes again, looks up at the banks of fog blowing over them, sighs, shrugs his shoulders and finally speaks.

"Eddie, it was a casualty of war, man, a casualty of war. Just the nature of the beast." Thad nods his head sagely, and looks carefully out of the side of his eyes at Eddie to gauge Eddie's reaction.

Eddie waits again - for what he assumes will be the real

explanation - but a long silence begins. Eddie raises one hand and places it on Thad's shoulder, to get his attention. He puts it on the shoulder of the expensive silk shirt, and instantly pulls it off, but too late, too late. He leaves a pinkish palm-sized Eddie-mark on the material. Thad's still looking up at the sky. Eddie speaks, quickly, in a sharp whisper directly into Thad's ear.

"So, Thad - how does a very junior lawyer-intern lose his own car doing grunt work for someone else in a lawsuit against a Russian mining company? Huh? Thad? How?"

Thad jerks his eyes and face back towards the skyline and talks to the whole corner of Castro and Market, sweeping his arms out in a large, cautionary gesture, flinging Eddie's hand off his clothes in the process. When he realizes what he was feeling on his shoulder, he examines his ruined shirt, squeezes his eyes shut and pretends not to see the handprint there. Then he waves his hands again. People waiting for the light to change, and the tramway car to turn the corner stare at the both of them.

"Meddle not in things beyond your ken, dude. A word to the wise. A stitch in time saves nine. *De gustibus non est disputandum* and all that crap. You know, ignorance is bliss, baby. And not too shabby an alibi in a court of law. Except in the actual case of ignorance of the law of course."

The onlookers at the corner are unimpressed. They continue to stare. Thad makes a fist at them.

"What you looking at, fuckers, huh! What you looking at? Waddya want? You want some of this? I said, motherfuckers, do you want some of this?"

Thad, under his breath, hisses out of the side of his mouth at Eddie again - a deranged tea kettle. "And you fucker, you're going to pay for this shirt. Every penny. You hear?"

Thad stands and glares, in the misty illumination under the lamp post, shaking his fist and watches the herd of trendy, observant men waiting to cross at the light. The men watch back. They're bored. And Thad is nice to look at, even if he appears to be more than slightly deranged. The silk shirt, in the wet, foggy air, clings cleanly to his bulbous pecs. So, they watch.

Then the light changes. They walk on. All but two, who are talking and shivering in the mist. Why are those two guys wearing only short sleeve shirts? Tourists. Eddie shakes his head, and looks back at Thad. Thad, however, looks like he has run out of conversational gambits. He's silent. He's staring at the two shivering guys also. Eddie can see a long silence developing again. He doesn't have time for this.

"O.K. Right. Good enough. Well, Thad, maybe I'll just ask Ace when he gets here. By the way, his dad, as always, says hello. Although he doesn't know you're here yet. But he'll be interested to know. Very interested. And, Mr. P. , well, he wants to see Ace as soon as possible. Tell Ace to go see his father when he gets in town."

"Uh…Eddie. The thing of it is. Well, Eddie, Ace doesn't want, uh that is, he can't, uh, Ace can't meet his father yet." Then, once again, Thad lapses into silence.

"And he can't, Thad, because…"

Thad re-crosses his arms and starts looking up at the corner of the building again. Eddie has had enough of the spy stuff. "Look, Thad, I'm going to find out one way or the other. It may as well be now. Besides, you look like you're in trouble. Maybe I can help, huh?"

Thad continues to peruse the interesting architectural details of the third story of a building in front of them. He watches the two guys and speaks out of the side of his mouth again. It makes him look like he's just had a stroke. It's all slurs and slushy noises. It's also painfully obvious to everyone on the corner that he's trying to hide something.

"All right, Eddie. All right, already. O.K. So you forced it out of me. Here it is. I'll level with you. Ace sold the car. But that's not the thing of it. The thing of it is, Ace is in big trouble. Ace wasn't only talking to Russian mine owners. He was talking to some other Russians. Maybe ones he shouldn't have been talking to. But I wasn't the one who told you Eddie. You didn't hear it from me. I didn't say nothing to you. O.K. Eddie?"

CHAPTER 6
(Saturday Night 9:42 P.M.,
Eddie by the Lamp Post on the Corner of Castro and Market)

"Sold the car?" Eddie can hardly understand him, with the side-of-the-mouth spitting and whispering Thad's doing - it's listening to a leaky inner tube trying to speak English. Thankfully, Thad is getting tired of it too. He gives it up.

"Sold it. Yeah, Ace sold it. And used the money to post bail for a guy he met in L.A., a guy who kind of got mixed up in crap he had no business being around – what a dumbshit, this guy Ace likes so much, name of Jay, and not too smart I'm telling you, but don't say a word to Ace – so the dipshit Jay in jail needed dinero quick and Ace stepped up to the plate. And he posted bail, like I said."

"And he did this, he bailed a guy named Jay out of jail because…"

"He had an itch for this guy. So he scratched."

"Does Ace scratch every single itch he gets?"

"You're asking me? I say, a guy itches, a guy scratches. What's the big deal? Parts is parts. One guy's as good as another, if you know what I'm saying, huh? Eddie? Huh? You know what I'm talking about, Eddie, huh?…" Thad tries to nudge Eddie with his elbow, and raises his eyebrows significantly, but remembers his white silk shirt and Eddie's ruined bloody shirt and pulls back his silk-enclosed elbow just in time. Thad settles for a knowing nod in Eddie's direction.

Thad re-opens his mouth, and Eddie makes the quick tactical decision to interrupt Thad before Thad can wander off on what will probably be another deviously sly tangent meant only to dazzle and distract Eddie. He talks over Thad's booming voice, and Thad eventually and reluctantly quiets down.

"Well, Thad, maybe it doesn't make sense, maybe it sounds crazy, because Ace just had me bail out another guy, only that guy was up here in San Francisco. That was just a few weeks ago, Thad. So, maybe that's the big deal, to me. Maybe that's why it's so hard for me to understand. Do you know who I'm talking about, Thad? Do you know, Thad? Do you?"

Thad looks on at Eddie in wide-eyed innocence and points at his chest with both hands, shaking his head no.

"Well maybe, Thad, you might have heard of him, one Dakota Johnson, a.k.a. Dak? Dark hair. Slim. Kind of a wise-ass. Sweet smile though, and not a bad kid. Just forgot to make his car payments for a couple of years, and in a couple of states. Stop shaking your head, Thad, I know you know him. You know everybody Ace knows. You were there, Thad. I'd lay even money you were there when they met. Before Dak got arrested. Huh? Thad?"

Thad makes his eyes look even wider. It has no effect on Eddie. Well, maybe some effect. He doesn't believe Thad. But he'd sure like to go out with him. Thad can be devastatingly handsome without even trying. Now he's trying. Thad's working it like there's no tomorrow. He's tilted his head down, looking at Eddie out of half-closed eyes, through his eyelashes. Whatever kind of look he's trying to achieve, Eddie has to say, it's effective. But it's not getting Thad anywhere. Eddie's not giving up.

"O.K., Thad, have it your way. So, anyways, Ace gave the same reasons. Itching. Scratching. He said this was the big one, the real thing, the one he'd been waiting for. I spent a fortune springing him. Typical Ace melodrama. I suppose you don't know about that either, huh? All the money that's been spent on Dak, me getting Dak out of jail? Paying off his debts? I spent my own money, Thad. And I spent Mr. P.'s money, without his knowing. All of it on

Dak. You wouldn't know anything about all that, would you? Thad? Thad? Hello? Thad?

Eddie watches Thad for some sign of intelligence, for some small reaction. But... nothing. Even though Eddie's stopped talking, Thad doesn't say a thing. He's moving his tongue around inside his mouth, getting a seed or something out from between his teeth. He's humming to himself. He's drumming his fingers against the side of his pants. His eyes don't even register Eddie's presence.

Eddie glares at him. Eddie knows Thad too well. Eddie thinks Thad's probably going over items on a grocery list in his head, or trying to remember if he needs to pick up his laundry, or maybe, it being a Saturday night and all, he's mentally running over guys' names in his mind in his little black book, and thinking of which one(s) he will be gracing with his own sexy presence later on tonight.

The silence lengthens. Eddie's tired, all of a sudden. And he's in pain. His chest feels like it's tightening up, which he doesn't need right now. And he's grilling a lunatic who happens to look like a Renaissance bronze statue. Mist falls upon the two of them. People pass. There's laughter and yelling and conversations all around them, but between the two of them there's nada, no connection, no communication.

At least Thad's trying to pretend that's what's going on, all this nothing. Eddie's not fooled. Thad can't really expect that just being quiet will save him? Can he? Eddie inhales, and it's deep and good. So the tightness wasn't asthma and all this moist air, Eddie's just raw and irritable and tired. That or God help him, Eddie's in lust.

Man, it feels good to inhale and exhale though. Eddie pulls in another decent lungful of air. Excellent. Thad still ignores him. He's looking off at the corner. Eddie glares at him. It has no effect. Eddie's being the straight man in Thad's comedy routine. O.K. All righty, then, Two can play at this game. So. Eddie will feed Thad some lines. Prime the pump. Get this party started.

"So, Thad. Thad? Ace said he'd pay me back. For what I spent up here in San Francisco. And now you're telling me he's spent a fortune down there. Down in L.A. I'm done for Thaddie, aren't I? How much was the bail bond in L.A. for? Huh, Thad? How much? Thad?"

"Sorry, bro. You say something, Eddie?"

Eddie maintains his purposeful glaring. The glaring bounces

harmlessly off of Thad – it's water rebounding off of freshly applied Teflon. But Eddie continues glaring. Then Eddie glares around some more. Eddie can see Thad watches out of the side of his eyes.

But something has changed, or rather not changed. No matter how many times the stoplight endlessly cycles, the two beefy tourists shivering in hilariously thin summer clothing remain. Eddie looks over at them, and looks back. He forgets to glare. Thad stares at them too.

This time, Thad looks nervously around him, at the corner, at the street, and he fidgets and fusses, waiting for Eddie and Eddie's questions to walk away and disappear. He tries to help Eddie understand it's time to leave – Thad does this by getting ready to leave himself. Thad fluffs his collar. He pulls in his belt, straightens out the big buckle, shines it a little with his sleeve. Checks his sleeve (probably for Eddie-blood). Stretches his shirt and runs his palm over his buzz-cut side burns.

Eddie watches the whole performance. Finally Thad gives up. Thad looks around the corner one last time. His eyes find their way back to Eddie's bloody forehead. Then to Eddie's eyes. Then to Eddie's shirt. Thad manages to look really handsome, unhappy and very inconvenienced, all at the same time It's a gift he has.

Eddie nods his head at Thad, and opens his eyes wide at him.

"What? What? Why do you keep on staring at me? What? So you want to know how much? How much Ace spent? Well, Ed my man, now, that's a good question, Eddie. Really, a very good question.

"And it's Thaddeus, Eddie, Thaddeus. I keep on telling people, but no one listens. Thaddeus. Say it with me. Is it that hard to say? I don't think so. Three syllables. Easy. Anyways… What were we talking about? Oh, we could only sell the car for fifty thou, so..."

"Fifty thousand? Dollars? Sell? Did you say sell?"

"Yeah, fifty. Who'd a thunk it? I'd have said eighty, seventy minimum, but he only got a measly fifty. Surprising, no? So he had to get the last twenty thou…"

"Twenty thousand?"

"Twenty. Yes. Twenty. Do you always repeat the last words you hear? It's a very annoying habit, Eddie, not becoming at all. Not at all. And I'll never get finished if you keep on interrupting me. You're a goddamn echo, Eddie, an echo. So. What was I fucking saying? I can't remember what I was saying…"

"Yeah, twenty? Nah, no interruptions, man. Good, you done now? So, yeah, for the last *twenty* we had to take a short term loan out under Ace's name from a private family that offers that kind of uncollateralized lending on short notice. The family was related to the guys that owned the mine in Russia. Yeah, Russians. Moscow. Siberia. Vodka. You got it, Eddie, you got it. And I have to tell you, Eddie, I really don't think Ace got the best terms on this loan. Not good terms at all, Eddie. In fact, Eddie it's a very strict loan. So strict, a few associates of this family, well, the truth is, they flew back here to San Francisco with me. With me, Thad. Me, Eddie.

Thad stops, waits. He's waiting for Eddie to ask a question. Eddie has no idea what he's supposed to ask. Thad sighs, shakes his head, slaps his hand against his thigh for emphasis.

"And then, well, Eddie, you might ask, if you were inquisitive and following what I've been saying to you at all. You might ask, Eddie… Why, Eddie, why are the Russian *associates* following Thad around, huh, Eddie? And not Ace? You might ask that, Eddie. Waddya think?

Eddie shrugs his shoulders. Thad starts with the gloomy staring again, looking all around the corner.

"Well, I'll tell you, Eddie. Here's the story. Ace ditched us in Los Angeles, and now I've got them. The two associates. They're not very happy with Ace. I'm not very happy with Ace. I've got Russian hit men following me around. Talking their secret Russian talk. Who knows what they're planning? Probably were in the KGB or their uncles were or shit like that. And now Ace has got them mad at me too. Only Ace isn't here. Thad's here. And those two guys are tailing me. They're hot on Thad's ass, my ass, like white on rice. I'm the one with my behind on the line. Me. Thad. Not the guy who borrowed the money. Me.

Thad winds down, looks at the sidewalk, frowns. Eddie clears his throat. Thad looks up. Thad nods with his head over his shoulder.

"O.K. So. Just look. Over there. Not like that, not obvious-like. Just look. Yeah, that's them, those two slabs of beef shivering with their 3% body fat. Up there. By the stoplight. The two big galoots turning blue in their short sleeve polo shirts. They could break me in two as fast as you could break an olive toothpick in a martini. Faster even. Fuckin' Ace just better show up sometime soon.

Anyways, I told 'em it'd be cold, but did they listen? No. They did not. It's summer, they said. Never been to San Francisco in the summer, that's sure as shit what I said to them. I'm hoping they get sick up here. Right on that corner. Sick and end up in the hospital. Pneumonia, that's probably the only way Ace is going to survive this week. Nah, make it double pneumonia. Only way he, and probably me, are going to stay alive and unbroken, come Monday morning. Them dead, both with double pneumonia. Fuck."

Thad looks really sad all of a sudden. Eddie wants to hug him. But even more, Eddie wants to hit him.

And, Eddie realizes, if he's going to get Ace out of this predicament or rather predicaments (in the plural - predicaments are always in the plural with Ace), Eddie's probably going to have to ask for Thad's help. At some point. And Thad, well, Thad is the kind of guy who uses words Eddie has only heard in movies before. Who uses "galoots" in everyday conversation?

Now Eddie has a reason for being depressed. As Thad might say "this aint going to be fucking easy, is it? No, thinks Eddie, no, it is not.

"Look, this is all maximum confidentiality, right?" says Thad glaring at Eddie. But all the oomph has gone out of Thad's glare. Now it's kind of plaintive. And worried. And needy. Yet still very adorable. All of which is not helping Eddie's mood, not at all.

Thad keeps staring at the two Russians talking under the street light.

"Eddie, you got some ideas, I know you got some ideas. You're always thinking, Eddie. Always figuring out some angle."

Thad motions with his head that they should get going. Go? Go where? Thad starts off. Eddie starts walking, but one of his ankles is tender when he puts weight on it. He stops and rubs it. It doesn't feel swollen. But you can never tell. He can walk, but he walks like an old man. Thad's ahead of him already, of course, but he looks back. Then surprisingly he waits.

"You can help, right, Eddie? You can help me and Ace?"

Eddie feels Thad hook his arm under Eddie's. He doesn't even check for blood this time on his shirt, at least not so noticeably that anyone else can see him doing it. Eddie gets more worried. Things must be worse than Thad's letting on. But Eddie doesn't say anything. Eddie holds on to Thad as they walk. He's still a little unsteady on his feet. And his head hurts. And he's covered in gore.

But he's holding on to Thad's arm, and it's a little like holding onto the trunk of a tree. A trunk of a tree that's flexing. Actually, it's not so bad. Eddie's not complaining. Not one bit.

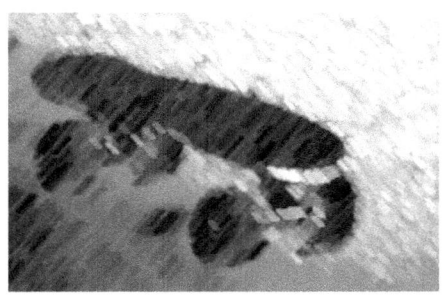

CHAPTER 7
(Saturday Night 10:04 P.M.,
Eddie Going Down Seventeenth Street)

They both start walking downhill, cross Castro, hit 17ᵗʰ, pass all the F-Line Tramcars waiting in a row, and keep on walking. The two muscle men behind them shrug their shoulders trying uselessly to get some body heat flowing and follow at a discreet distance, working at being as inconspicuous as possible. Of course, two body builders in damp, skin-tight shirts with erect nipples on a cold Saturday night at gay Ground Zero in San Francisco go about as unnoticed as pair of matching twin nuclear explosions. At each street they cross, the murmuring and appreciative crowd parts before them like the Red Sea before Moses and his staff.

The muscle guys may glance around at the Saturday night crowd from time to time, but they sure keep up with Thad and Eddie. Eddie can hear Slavic expressions of dismay hanging in the air. They must be freezing, with no coats. Eddie sure is. At one point it sounds like they're having a long conversation on their cells. First one, then the other. But for the most part, they're invisible, and quiet and after a while, Eddie even forgets they're there. Thad on the other hand, keeps glancing back at them, calculating something, following their every move.

Eddie lists his troubles. He's lost Ace. He's lost all his savings. He owes Alice big-time. He's stolen a ton of money from Mr. P. His life is going nowhere. His career is over. He doesn't have a boyfriend. And he's chilled to the bone. And he's lost a lot of blood. And he has no coat. And Eddie's night is just beginning. And... And... And... Well, it's a long list. This shit never stops, and it's always flowing down towards Eddie, and more keeps on coming, and there's no sign of it stopping, not anytime soon.

Eddie slows his walking pace down some. And then some more. What does Eddie have in front of him that Eddie is in such a friggin' rush to get to? What?

Eddie limps along at Thad's side, trying to keep up, pulled by Thad's strong arm and his relentless, muscular legs, pumping away, pounding at the sidewalk. The corner of Castro and Market is left rapidly behind them. Eddie hobbles and thinks. Eddie's life is quicksand - every time he tries to struggle, every time he tries to get loose, the Periphanitides make sure Eddie's sucked in even deeper than he was before. Problem, struggle, solve, sink. That's Eddie's life. That's been his life for two decades. That will be his life two decades from now. What a pleasant thought.

But on the upside, a very temporary upside, he's getting to surreptitiously massage Thad's oversized arm as they walk. And Thad's pretending not to notice. That's something. A little something unexpected for Eddie today.

Well, what about Thad? Maybe Thad can help after all. He seems to be in a helping mood these last few minutes or so. Maybe. So, Eddie starts talking to the air in front of him. Thad looks ahead, looks back over his shoulder, looks ahead in a steady rhythm. Eddie assumes the Slavic hit guys are keeping up nicely.

"I'm a dead man, Thad, a dead man. Ace was writing me these emails and I spent all this money, some of it my own savings, money I owed to other people, and... oh, it's just no use explaining it."

Thad turns his head towards Eddie, but Eddie can see Thad's just looking over Eddie's shoulder.

"Thad, no one cares what happens to me. I'm a walking catastrophe. I am the plague. Stay away, everyone, stay away. One touch from me and your lives will turn to shit. Run, run while you have the chance."

"Sorry, Eddie, are you talking to me again? I didn't really catch all that."

"Ah, just fuck the hell off, Thad. Fuck it." Eddie tries to pull away, Thad pulls him closer.

"Whoa! Eddie, whoa. Stop a second. Hey, for the record, Eddie, I was trying to be decent. Civil. I'm trying to do the right thing and help you, Eddie. Look, trying to help."

Thad points significantly at his arm, and then at Eddie's arm, and then he looks Eddie in the eye, questioning. Eddie pulls away, and stands to one side. Thad shrugs and shakes his head, looks back at the guys following and talks directly into Eddie's ear.

"Try to do the right thing. Look where it gets you. So, Eddie, I can take a hint. Adios, my muchacho. Good luck with rest of your life." Thad disengages, walks more quickly downhill, the two guys move quickly to follow, they start to jog after Thad. Thad starts to jog, thinks better of it, hears their footsteps, and slows down.

Thad turns around and yells back at Eddie "Don't forget about me. Me and Ace here." Then he starts walking rapidly downhill.

Eddie yells out at Thad's retreating back. "Thad, does Ace say he's in love with this guy down in L.A.?"

Thad yells back over his shoulder, "Love? It's actually sickening hearing him go on and on for hours and hours about this guy Jay."

"I'm a walking corpse, Thad, I'm done for."

"Look who's talking. Always thinking about yourself, Eddie. Always about yourself. Hey, what about me? And what about old Ace? Remember we're counting on you."

Eddie thinks - so much for maximum confidentiality. Thad gets louder and louder, and keeps walking farther and farther away. Everyone in the Castro knows Eddie's and Thad's and Ace's business tonight.

"So, Thad, where the hell are you going, anyways?"

Eddie starts following Thad downhill. Actually his ankle isn't so bad. As long as he watches where he steps. He tries to catch up with the three men ahead of him. He doesn't make much progress. Thad looks back, waits. You could've knocked Eddie over with a feather.

"Hey, Eddie. Yeah, Eddie, over here. Oh, so now, you're following me. Now, I'm O.K. Now you want to be around me." Thad shrugs and frowns. "Make up your fucking mind, man. We don't have all night."

Eddie doesn't comment, Thad extends his arm out again, Eddie takes it.

"So, Eddie, so I got to get these guys over to Charley's flat. I figure Ace is there waiting for 'em. Well, he doesn't know he's waiting for 'em, but he is. He better be."

Thad lowers his voice. The two big guys are about ten feet behind them, making comments back and forth to themselves in staccato bursts of musical grousing.

"Ace only has two days to get them their money plus interest back (100% interest I might add – I don't think that's legal? Is it? But who the hell cares now) – it's the money, or they're going to take it out of him the hard way. So before he sees Dad, he wants to get straight with them. So to speak. Not straight. Even, I mean even. You know what I mean. Shit."

"You bastard, Thad! You said Ace was still in L.A."

"Well you know Ace. He's quick. And maybe I lied. Just a little."

"Yeah, yeah."

"So, Eddie, my man. Here's my stop – our stop - Charley's flat, I mean. You know Charley, right? So. You and that famous thinking organ of yours. Work it, Eddie boy, work it."

Eddie won't reply to that. The two guys are caught up with everyone, and now Eddie stands aside. The three men move past him and towards a steep staircase - not the most surprising architectural feature in San Francisco.

The sidewalks are on and off crowded. People press past the four of them. Lots of people out tonight. Apparently all on this sidewalk. Mostly they're headed uphill. Headed towards the Castro. Eddie stands back against a cracked retaining wall - cold, cut-up hands warming up in his front pockets.

He steps further out of the wind behind one of a pair of spiral-trimmed cypress trees in big glazed pots. Something cold starts dribbling down the back of his neck. He scrunches up his neck, and hopes he's not starting to bleed again.

So.

What is he going to do? He watches Thad and the two guys climb the long steps to the middle of three front doors on the flat, and then with a ring and a click of a locks being triggered, they whisk inside, the locks click again, their hollow clomping up another long flight of stairs gets fainter and fainter and he hears a distant "Charley! Ace!" and something rough and uncomplimentary in Russian and then a lot of talking for a few minutes, all at once, and then all is fairly quiet.

Eddie takes in a deep, deep breath. Slowly Eddie lets it out. Then he does it again. It's maybe a little self-indulgent, but Eddie likes the feeling of having his breathing apparatus in something like good working order. It's scrumptiously satisfying. If Eddie could sell this feeling of freely breathing in a retail environment, why, Eddie'd make a fortune, he'd be rich. As he lets his breathing get deeper and slower, deeper and slower, he also tries to empty his mind, and just be. Be the wall. Be the spiky, uncomfortable cypresses.

Eddie has to think. He can't go back home, then, Eddie would have to call Mr. Periphanitides . No, no point in that. Not yet. He's got to have some kind of plan. So that means, he'll…

Someone jumps out unexpectedly from the first door, far above him on the front porch, slams it, vaults down the outside stairs. Landing on both feet, the person leaps up, turns completely around and a surprised mouth and pair of eyes comes face to face with Eddie. They stare at each other for a few seconds. He's a small wiry guy, black hair, dark pools for eyes. Long lashes. Twisted smile. A leer really. The guy nods. Eddie nods. The guy smiles even wider. Eddie smiles back. He moves closer. Eddie backs away.

Now Eddie's smiling bigger. The stranger-guy moves forward, his smiling threatening to break his face wide open. Eddie backs into the evergreen, then into the wall and then throws his arms out behind him, and balances against the side of the staircase. He's in a kind of corner. They're both behind one of the plants. The guy advances and braces his hands on either side of Eddies face and leans in. Then he leans in some more. His face gets closer and closer. Eddie thinks "this never happens to me when I'm not bleeding and freezing and about to be fired and jailed" and then he hears one of the windows slam open just above his head.

"Hey, Tony. Isn't Marty waiting for you South of Market? Yeah, I'm talking to you, Tony. Hey Tony?" The guy looks up, Eddie can feel his every breath as a pressure on Eddie's own lips, and the guy says "You're right. You're always right." The window closes. Their noses brush as the guy (Tony apparently) looks back down. Tony looks Eddie straight in Eddie's eye. For some reason it's not uncomfortable. Eddie could stay here all day, or even all night. Eddie looks up, away, feeling Tony's breath at his throat. The sky is so close. He could reach out and touch it. The fog hangs like a ceiling just above their heads. It's made their corner into a small private room, and he and Tony... then the window opens up again with a creak and a crash.

"I'm going, I'm going, already. For fuck's sake." says Tony, and raises his eyebrows as if to say "What can you do?" and Eddie can feel the hairs on one of Tony's eyebrows deal a glancing blow to his wounded forehead. The guy waits a second, dives in for a long open-mouthed kiss, lip-locks Eddie for what feels like five minutes, but had to be for only a two or three, max, pulls back, smiles, shrugs, then whips a skate board out of nowhere, and throws it on the ground with a four-wheeled bang that causes Eddie to bash his head backwards against the wall.

Tony retreats quickly downhill, clacking loudly over every ridge and indentation in the sidewalk, hurtling into the night. It's the sound a machine gun makes in a battle scene from a WWII movie. Eddie can't help but think that a skateboarder's life expectancy in San Francisco can't be all that high. Traffic. Hills. Treacherous cracks. He hopes Tony knows what he's doing. He sighs, but he's smiling now. Smiling a little bit more than he was capable of a few minutes ago, and there's nothing wrong with that.

Eddie breathes and thinks. Breathes and thinks. More people drift by, laughing. They don't see Eddie by the bush. He sinks into the shadows and looks up, hands in his pockets again. Pondering.

He can't go up. He can't leave. What can he do? He can't think. He's cold. He's in pain.

He starts humming and clapping to himself, moving his head around to the beat. Just to stay warm. Give him something to do. He claps against the wall in a rhythm to the tune "I Got Nobody and Nobody Cares for me" and gets into it, clapping, bouncing his head around, moving his shoulders, until his head wagging bashes the side of his head against the staircase.

He stops. More people walk by. They're arguing. No one notices Eddie. No one ever notices Eddie. Except skateboarders. But they never ever notice him except when he's trying to staunch the bleeding on his lacerated body. Or when he's in the middle of a mid-life crisis, re-thinking his entire life. Or when he's trying save a boy who's now a man, who's running amok and drowning in his own foolishness. Is that a mixed metaphor? Probably. And where in the hell is Eddie going to get a coat?

Eddie thinks of Tony and the expression on his face as he kissed him and smiles to himself again. Then he thinks about Tony some more.

Life is strange. While he's rubbing the side of his head and looking at his hand to see if there's more blood there than there was maybe a few moments ago, Eddie hears footsteps booming on the wooden stairs above his head. A kettle-drum-like thunder. At least two people. Maybe three. The booming is inside the flat, and it's hurrying down the stairs towards the porch and the street. The middle door unlocks with a metallic clank. He pulls himself deeper into the nearby prickly, pine-scented spirals and crouches down next to the pots and waits.

CHAPTER 8
(Saturday Night 10:18 P.M.,
Eddie by Some Garbage in the Castro)

The fog is getting worse. Eddie hears a guy's voice, and a girl's voice pass his bush and turn uphill towards the Castro. They are moving very slowly. Which is odd. And suspicious. Eddie's suspicious all the time now. It's tiring how suspicious Eddie is.

Eddie tiptoes behind them, ducking into corners, doorways and miscellaneous shrubbery at frequent intervals. It's Ace. Great. And Ace has a pained, earnest tone to his voice. Eddie knows from experience that can only mean trouble. Trouble and heartbreak. Usually for Eddie.

"Look, Charley," says Ace, "you know how I am. You know how it is with me. So give me a break. Just this once. A break. It's all I'm asking."

Eddie can hardly hear them, the fog and mist muffle everything. It's almost suffocating. It might be a little more bearable if Eddie were a lot less bloody and a lot more warm. Ace says something else and Eddie shuffles closer, squeezing past a drain spout, crouching behind weeds and a scraggly bushy thing that's covered in bristly leaves that smells like a shelf in a kitchen cupboard that's all broken bottles and spilled spice. It smells a lot like dinner.

Eddie's stomach rumbles. He's hungry. He breaks of a twig — it's a stand of thyme. And underneath that is a weedy patch of ground being taken over by pushy sprigs of mint. Bored, Eddie munches on a mint leaf. Then he sticks the piece of thyme in his mouth and chews. It just makes him hungrier. They've stopped on a corner. Ace is talking again. Eddie chews.

"I always tell you everything, Charley, everything that's going on in my life. No, Charley, I do. Everything, I tell you everything. So what's with all the negative energy here? Why the hate, Charley? What's up with all the dissing? You've never dissed me, never. Never looked down on me, before. Never made comments about me. Never talked about me, right to my face, like I was an idiot or something. Never. Until now."

Ace sighs, a very melancholy sound. Someone else sighs right back.

"Did I say any of that, Ace? You know Ace, you're a big boy, now. You can figure things out for yourself."

There's more whispering, Eddie munches thoughtfully on another twig. The whispering goes on, Eddie can't hear any of it. It sounds like both of them are talking at once.

"No, Ace, we're not going there. Who says I never speak my mind? Boy, if you ask my opinion, you'd better be ready to hear what I have to say, or don't ask. No, and you know that's not true. You asked, you got an answer. Look, Ace, I told you how crazy you were to get mixed up with that last guy, Dakota, didn't I? And what about all the other guys? Monty and Jonah and Tyson? Huh? And Ruben? And Quint? And what about Pieroraffaelo, or whatever his name was? Yeah, that's the guy. Didn't I tell you there was something funny about him, then he went off and got married to that Senator's what's-his-name's daughter. Don't you remember any of that? Am I just talking to the air, Ace?"

Ace is silent. Or at least Eddie thinks he is. Maybe they're just talking softly. Eddie tries to get in closer. He spits out the thyme. What was he thinking? His mouth burns and itches and he must have bit his lip sometime tonight, because his lip lower lip stings like hell. That probably wasn't thyme. Eddie's probably poisoned himself. He starts scraping off his tongue with his front teeth, and coughs and spits out the chewed up leaves into the bush he's hiding next to. He's making the noises a sick dog would make after eating a mothball. It's not the most civilized sound.

"You can make your own decisions, Ace. I just don't see why it's such a big thing. You tell me. Why is it such a big thing, Ace? Why?"

"Charley, you know people hate me. People envy me. I can't help it. I can't help it if I have my shit together and they don't. Charley, don't be that way…"

Ace pauses. Charley says something else. Ace responds. They're moving off down a side street, walking downhill towards 18th Street. Eddie pushes away from the bush. He smells himself, the aroma of roasted chicken. Charley sounds louder, maybe upset? Eddie jogs around the corner trying to catch up.

"I'm listening, Ace. Look at me. I'm listening."

"Is that all you can do, Charley? Listen? I need someone to *do* something for me. Someone to *help* me."

"No, Ace, I can do a lot more than listen. I can get my freezing butt back inside my warm flat and talk with people who have a civil tongue in their head. That's what I can do, Ace."

Eddie barely has time to throw himself into an alley, as a body strides quickly towards him through the curtains of mist and wet. The alley however, turns out to be the entrance to a basement garage and for the second time tonight Eddie finds himself tumbling downhill on concrete. He manages to land without hitting the garage door too hard and holds his breath while he holds his bruised head with both hands. He hears footsteps walking by, then slowing down, then stopping. Someone runs up the street towards them.

"Charley, Charley, don't. Just don't. Come on, Charley. Charley? Hey! Heh, now, I'm sorry. There I said it. I'm sorry and I mean it. I'm just stressing about this boy here in jail in L.A.. I'm stressing about my dad. I'm stressing about my fucked up life."

Eddie can almost hear someone shaking their head in Ace's direction.

"And, uh… well, Charley… Charley, I'm stressing about you. You too. You know I need you. You're my best friend in the whole wide world. Charley, c'mon…"

Eddie's landed beside a garbage can. He peeks out from behind it, still rubbing his head with one hand and sees Ace's back and his square shoulders outlined by a streetlight in front of him. He can see someone else standing to one side. Suddenly Ace throws his arms out, and Eddie heaves himself backwards into the shadows.

"It's just you and me, Charley. Just you and me. You and me against the world." Ace apparently starts to sing — it might be a tune, but for the life of him Eddie can't figure out if it really is Ace making melodic sounds or a very sick animal crying out grievously with some sort of terminal medical condition. Eddie settles on the serious-animal-medical-condition scenario just as the sound stops and Eddie hears laughter and then hears what sounds like someone's chest being punched and pounded by two feminine fists.

"Dammit, Ace, why do you do it? No! How do you do it? How do you get me so mad, and so happy, and so confused, all at the same time? How?"

"Luck? Talent? Animal magnetism?"

"Stop it, stop it. You're wasting all that on me. Save it for the next lucky boy you'll meet in an hour or two. Probably down in the Police Substation in the Mission. In jail. About to go up before the judge on bail."

"Now that was a low blow, Charley."

"But true, Acer, true. That seems to be where you're finding your boyfriends these days, Ace."

"Nah, It's for real this time. Charley, This one's the one. The guy I bailed out. I mean the guy in L.A., BJ — I just call him Jay. Well, Mr. L.A. and I, whenever we get together, it's like gasoline and an open flame. Boom! Watch out. Explosions everywhere. And I mean explosions. Detonations. Blasts. Blowups and eruptions."

Eddie can hear Charley laughing, saying "stop, stop, way too much information" and Eddie looks around the edge of the big plastic garbage can he's fallen in back of, and he can see Charley's back and she's shaking her head and holding onto one of Ace's muscle-bound arms. Ace is dancing around her, trying to get her to move.

"He's the one. Charley. I know it. I can feel it. He's the one I've been waiting for. I feel it. I feel the power." Ace is starting to sing again. It's a little hard to understand him, because he's going in circles around Charley, running his hands along her shoulders, then around her waist. "Can you feel it? Do you feel - the power - Charley? Can you feel it?"

Ace has got Charley dancing around the sidewalk now, Ace humming tunelessly under his breath, twisting and turning gracefully over the sidewalk and out onto the street, arms around Charley, and Charley laughing. They're doing some kind of samba thing. Finally he hears them quiet down, slow down, shuffle, then stop, a few feet away from him, but he can't hear their voices anymore.

He creeps up to the top of the driveway. Eddie wrinkles his nose. Now his hands smell like thyme and trash. What was that leaking out of the bottom of the garbage bin? And he's covered in scabs and blood, and his clothes are ripped up. He's just a hop, skip, and a jump away from being the poster boy for homelessness at this rate. And if Mr. P. finds out what he's done and fires him, he'll be all the way there. He hunches down beside the retaining wall of the driveway, and tries not to smell himself.

"Whew! Ace. I'm sure you can feel it, Ace, you always do. You feel. You always feel it. You do realize, don't you, Ace? You do realize that I've heard all this before. Feeling it. The Power. Maybe once or twice. Or thirty times."

"Maybe, Charley, maybe. But not like this you haven't."

Eddie peeks around the wall. Ace starts humming again, and tries to wrap his arms around Charley. Charley pushes him away.

"So. I say, let's just cut to the chase, Ace."

"O.K." says Ace carefully, slowing to a stop, standing in front of her, he leaves his hands on her shoulders.

"So, Ace, what is it, exactly, that you need me to do? Why did you ask me out here into the cold and wet? Not just to dance with me. You can do that anytime."

"Ah, there you go again. Don't be that person, Charley. Don't be that way…" Ace stuffs both his hands into his pockets and turns away.

"And what way is that Ace?"

"Charley. That way. You know."

Ace waits, hunching his shoulders over, trying to look pitiful, but Charley isn't responding. Ace looks over his shoulder at her. He bites his lip, pulls his hands out of his pockets and turns around, placing both hands on Charley's shoulders again.

"Look, Charley all I need is some money"

"You need money."

"Charley, Charley, just for a few days, only for a few days, Charley. I promise. Charley, look, I'm crossing my heart and hope to die. Just like back in Porter, Porter Elementary School. You remember, Charley." Eddie can see Ace helpfully makes a crossing sign in front of his chest, then holds up one hand with crossed fingers in front of him. He's waiting for Charley to say something.

"Money, huh?"

Ace drops his hands. "Look, I'll get it right back to you. Didn't your dad leave you and your sisters some decent cash so you three could go to school? It's just for a day or two. I promise. Just a day or two. Please, Charley, please. I wouldn't ask if it wasn't important, Charley." Ace tries to put his hands back on Charley's shoulders, but she turns, swings her body away, hides her face. She faces right at Eddie.

Eddie has to duck down quick. He's not sure he made it in time. He's managed to put his hand down in something pulpy and slimy. He wipes it off on the side of the garbage bin, scowling.

Eddie also lifts one ear up to the edge of the wall he's hiding against. He hears someone breathing hard and walking away again. Which is just great, just great for him. More opportunities for foggy skulking for Eddie, the garbage bin spy. He listens carefully and hears two people walking away. Then he hears one of them stop. It must be Ace. Or is it Charley? Ace is talking pretty loudly. Charley's not saying anything. Really, Eddie can't hear anything behind these two garbage cans here. Not a thing. A cat slinks between his legs as Eddie crouches and Eddie almost hops into one of the bins.

"Charley? Those two muscle guys with the blank expressions? We aren't going to be doing a three-way tonight. Charley, they're serious. It's serious this time. Charley."

Ace stops, but Charley doesn't say anything.

"Charley. Charley, you know how I am, you know how I just don't think. I borrowed from people I shouldn't have. Those two guys are twin fucking World War Threes about to explode all up in my face if and when I don't pay a certain party twenty, no wait, it's forty by the end of the weekend. Charley, that's tomorrow. Tomorrow."

Eddie can hear the footsteps leaving again. Eddie jumps up to follow and nearly runs into Ace's calves. He pulls back spastically and presses his chest against the wet cement again. The cat has to move quickly or get crushed as Eddie rolls towards it. It complains, loudly. Eddie tries to hold it and shush it. It claws him. Then it casually tiptoes to the top of the alley and looks back at him. Eddie tries to scare it away. It sits, licks it paws, which are lighter colored than the rest of it, and stares at him. Then it meows loudly It sounds bored. But maybe that's how cats always sound. Eddie doesn't know much about cats really.

Eddie hears the footsteps coming back, quickly.

"No, I am not doing this again. You are not doing this to me again, Ace. You hear me Ace? You hear me? We are not doing this." They sound like heels. They sound like they mean business.

The steps approach Ace, but don't stop. Eddie can hear Ace shuffling a few steps backwards, then a few more, then a few more.

"Forty, Ace? I know you don't mean forty dollars. So, are we talking forty thousand dollars, Ace? Ace! Answer me! Forty? Are you crazy, boy? Ace, are you listening to me? Hearing my voice? Forty?"

"Now, Charley, you know…"

"Don't even start, Ace, don't even start with it. You know me and Francine and Darlene, the only money we three sisters have in the whole world is that Trust Fund, Ace, now that mama is dead. That's it. We don't get control of those Trust Funds until we're twenty nine. That's a long six years from now. I'm in debt up to my eyeballs. No. No. No. You listen to me, William Ace Periphanitides. I said no. I've been listening to you this whole time, now it's your turn. You listen to me. Stop. Listen.

Eddie throws a small wad of something wet and incredibly gross at the cat, whispering "shoo" as loud as he dares. He misses. The cat begins the elaborate process of cleaning another paw and peers at Eddie as if he's trying to memorize Eddie's face. Maybe to identify Eddie later in Criminal Cat Court for Assault and Battery of an Innocent Feline.

"Ace, I've known you since you were eight years old, and you stole my heart, and we've been all over this a hundred times. There's nothing I wouldn't do for you Ace. You know I love you. You know that. But…

The cat stops preening. It starts calling out. Looking at Eddie, then calling out. Eddie jiggles the garbage bin, and pushes it at the cat. The cat bats at the moving bin with its paw. Eddie stops. The cat stops batting. It looks unhappy. It gives one more pitiful bat at the bin then resumes an even more unhappy expression. Not the most difficult expression for a cat to make. It starts calling out again. Now it sound righteously indignant *and* bored.

"But. Ace. There are other people in the world with problems who aren't named Ace Periphanitides. There are, Ace. There are."

Ace keeps quiet. Wisely, that's what Eddie thinks. Eddie pokes his head up again, over the top of the wall. They're right on top of him. He ducks down, the cat follows, Eddie scurries behind the trash bin again, the cat squeezes in back of him. Eddie sticks his hands into something gelatinous by the side of the bin, he tries to wipe his hands off on some dead leaves piled next to the garage door. It doesn't help much. Eddie misses more than a few sentences. The cat watches him, absorbed by Eddie's every action, a few feet away.

"Ace, my head's barely above water as it is. Forty thousand? What were you thinking? If I thought you had any money, Ace I'd be asking *you* for a loan. Ah, I should have known, if I had any sense... of course, you wouldn't just happen to stop by my flat on a Saturday night. Of course. You'd think I'd be smarter by now. But no..."

Eddie hears footsteps, a lot of them. Coming right towards the three of them. And some voices. Many voices. But he can't tell from where. Someone's calling out "Here Mittens, here Mittens. Where is that damn cat? Jeremy's going to be livid. Mittens?"

A man with an open can of cat food is walking down the street, peering under parked cars, poking around with a broken broom handle. Eddie looks down. The little cat with white paws looks back up at him. She meows. Loudly. Wiping his hand again, on the side of the bin, he pushes himself up to peek out over wall by the driveway. He grabs the cat with the other. Perversely the cat is purring. The voices in the street start multiplying.

"Johnny, it's too early for dancing. What about sushi? You used to love sushi, Johnny. I'm hungry. I know a little place..."

"Mittens! Mittens!"

"You always want to eat. You know I can't dance on a full stomach. I'll throw up."

"Mittens! Damn you. Why do you always do this to me?"

"Let go, Ace. Let me go."

It's Charley, she's trying to pull away from Ace, who is holding her arm and shaking his head.

"Charley! Charley! Wait. Please. Don't run off. Shit. Fuck. I didn't know. Charley! Of course, when I'm flush again, which will be very, very soon, you can have as much as you want. You know you can."

People pass right by Eddie. The cat, most probably the damned Mittens, starts squirming in Eddie's hand.

"O.K. No sushi. What about spaghetti?"

A ways away, someone is calling "Mittens, Mittens. When I find you…"

Charley pulls free, Eddie can hear her running, but can't tell where she's going. Ace calls out to her in the fog.

"Charley, as much as you need. You know I will. Charley! Charley! Fuck. Wait!"

Eddie goes out of his driveway hideaway to follow them, just in time to get his teeth almost kicked out by Charley's fast-retreating high heels. He has to let go of Mittens suddenly, in mid air. The little cat explodes in a ball of bristling fur and claws and sails out into the fog. Mittens is not comfortable with that. Mittens meows loudly and repeatedly and runs off. Probably to get reinforcements and mount a counterattack.

Eddie rolls patiently back against and into the garage door, to get out of the way, but ends up giving himself a vicious bump on the side of his head in the process. But, at this point in his Saturday night, really, what's one more bump? He grits his teeth anyway, and squints his eyes and bites his hand to stop thinking about his aching skull. His headache returns. His numerous scrapes burn and itch. Eddie rolls backwards to get off of the one ankle that's giving him trouble and bounces again against the garbage bin, this time forcefully – it's a manful bump. The garbage bin starts to tip, then to roll, then to tip and roll at the same time, and it rolls on top of him and spills out onto the driveway.

Eddie sits in back of it and shakes his newly-bleeding head. He brushes away the trash. Peels off the bag of orange rinds spewing out onto his hair. He gets up on his knees and finds he's been sitting on a half-eaten hamburger. It just gets better and better. The footsteps stop again.

"Who is that? Ace? Ace, is that you?"

"Yeah, Charley, I'm here. Who else would it be?"

"No Ace, I heard a noise. A peculiar noise. A cry. It's over by those trash cans by the alley."

"Probably some damn cat, Charley. I'm here. Look back over here. Yeah."

"Sure was a big cat, that's all I have to say. Ace? You listening to me Ace?"

"Ace?"

"Charley? You know what I was just thinking?"

"I can imagine. Ace, aren't you going to check on that cat? What if it's not a cat, huh? Ace?"

"What else could it be, Charley? An antelope? Look, Charley, what about Eddie, my dad's Personal Assistant? You know how Eddie is. He usually knows what to do. He's good at that. Doing things. Getting things done. That's Eddie all over."

Eddie can hear them getting closer. He backs up. He hits the bin. The bin wheels move and crunch over bits of chicken bones and cardboard.

"And if Eddie doesn't know what to do, well, Charley, then we're all fucked. Dad'll disown me for good. Dad'll never talk to me again. But wait, I'll be dead before my dad never talks to me again. The Russians will see to that. Hmmm. I didn't think that one through. No problem there."

"That was no cat, Ace."

"I'll have a big funeral, and my pop will be mobbed by paparazzi, and Eddie will be ice-fishing and thinking about all those years he spent with the Periphanitides…" Somebody kicks a stone which ricochets off the side of Eddie's bin.

Eddie bumps his head backwards with a jerk, crosses his eyes in pain, and erupts with an involuntary groan. The sound bubbles up out of the wet shadows by the garage door. He clamps a scarred hand over his mouth. But he clamps too late.

"If you're not going to check, Ace, then I am."

"Nah, they always make that sound. Cats are strange. You know Eddie reminds me of a cat. Always creeping around, listening in on other people's conversations. You know what I'm going to do? I'm going to call him – can I borrow your cell? I had to hock mine in L.A. "

Eddie hears someone shuffling closer to his driveway. Then some beeping. He holds his head. He's going to get a lump there for sure. Suddenly he realizes what the beeping really means, but he is too late again. Beethoven's Ninth Symphony rings out of his pants pocket. He sighs "Fuck me" to himself, wipes his hand again on some leaves, sees it does no good, and crawls up the steep incline of the driveway to the alley. He wrenches himself to his feet as he limps around the corner.

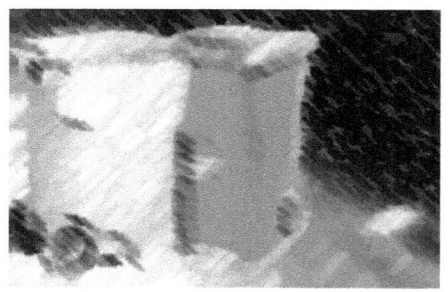

CHAPTER 9
(Saturday Night 10:46 P.M.,
Eddie on a Street in the Castro)

A tall woman crouching behind a big-chested guy with a board in his hand stops Eddie cold. The guy makes a swipe at him, one handed. He's holding a phone to his ear with the other.

"Who the hell are you?" Ace swings again, then talks into his cell "Eddie? Eddie? I can hear you answered your phone, but I can't hear you. Eddie? You there, bro? I'm being attacked by a crazy bleeding homeless person. Hello? Eddie? Eddie?"

"It's me, Eddie. Listening. Again." Ace takes another swing with his board. Eddie jumps backwards. The nerve-wrenching squeal of feedback screeching out of two cell phones begins to fill the alley. Eddie holds up his cell and waits for the metaphorical light bulb to go off above Ace's non-metaphorical head.

Ace looks at the cell he's holding, looks at Eddie, at Eddie's cell, and back at Eddie, then at his phone again. "Eddie, is that you?"

"Why does everyone ask me that question tonight? Who else would I be?"

"Hi Eddie", Charley pipes up from behind Ace's broad back. "You look terrible."

"Thanks, Charley. Well, I may as well say it – welcome back,

Ace. You look good. In fact, you look great. You been going to the gym, maybe bench pressing lately?"

"A little yeah. You can tell, huh?"

"Lucky guess. But, yeah, looking good. Ace, you've got a crazed look in your eye. Why are you swinging at me with a broken piece of two by four?"

A voice floats up over Ace's wide shoulders

"Mental patients often look normal, outwardly. To the untrained eye." The comment is followed up by a crazy giggle. Charley was going to be a social worker before she changed her major to physics, then went off to art school. Ace ignores her.

"Dude, I'm majorly bummed."

"I can see you're fluent in L.A.-speak."

"Well, duh, that's where I've been for the last 2 months. As you well know. But there's been some complications in my life since then. You see, Eddie, there is this guy, Jay, in L.A., and..."

"Ace, wait, before you go on, I have to inform you of something. Yeah, I know, I'll hear you out, just wait a second. Ace, I bailed out that guy, Dakota - Dak - you pointed out to me at the Palace of Justice. I did it two weeks ago. Here in San Francisco. Dak. You know... The guy you kept on sending me emails about? I know you know who I'm talking about, Ace. I got emails every day. For weeks. And I have to tell you, Ace, it cost a lot of money. A lot. Ace? Ace? You heard what I just said, didn't you Ace? Ace?"

A voice erupts from behind Ace's back again "You told me the boy you were in love with, the one you needed forty thousand dollars for was in L.A., not San Francisco, you slime ball. I can't believe it. I am such a fool. I can't believe I fell for one of your lines again."

Ace turns half-way around to say something, stops, breathes, closes his eyes, opens them again, turns towards Eddie. Ace continues with a little edge to his voice "He *is* in L.A., Charley. And he was in jail. In L.A. Or at least he was. No, listen, Charley. There's two boys. The first one, in San Francisco, the second one in L. A. Quit laughing Charley, I'm serious. I *am*.

Ace points his head directly at Eddie.

"Well, Eddie, no easy way to break it to you. All your efforts were for nothing." Ace sighs and looks down, Eddie can see how sad Ace is when the universe makes his life so complicated. And it's not Ace's fault. He tries. He really does.

Eddie breaks in on Ace's thoughts. "Ace, you're not listening. It didn't cost nothing. It didn't cost a little. It cost a lot. It was very expensive. Have I mentioned how expensive it was? Ace, you're not listening to me, again."

"No, Eddie, you're not listening." Ace is still looking down. "I have no interest in that guy up here in San Francisco now. Dagwood, Darnell, Dartagnan - whatever his name is. He's history. I'm done with him. Yes, I know Dagwood's not his real name, I'm sure I can't even remember what his real name is now. And I don't want to. No, don't tell me. I don't want to know. Stop! O.K., O.K., Dakota, Dak, whatever.

"Anyways, Eddie, I don't love this Dak guy anymore. I've thought about it and I don't. Maybe I did, once, for awhile. But not anymore. I love Mr. L.A., my BJ, my Jay-kins. He's the only man I want to grow old with. Buy matching rocking chairs. Rub smelly ointments into each other's arthritic joints, as we watch the sun set in the purple Pacific. Yeah, the whole nine yards. He's got me spouting poetry. He's got me dancing in the streets. He's got me, Eddie. He's got me. And I've got him."

Ace pauses for a second to get his breath. Charley peers out from behind Ace again, glares at Ace, smiles at Eddie, talks to him in a motherly, concerned kind of voice, one that Charley is good at.

"You really need to get yourself looked at, Eddie. You look like hell. You're a mess. Really. My flat's just around the corner. Do you need to go see a doctor?"

Ace looks over at Charley with a pained expression. "Hey, guys, Eddie, Charley, I'm in a lot of trouble here. How about a little help?"

Eddie gives a significant look at Charley - a Charley, who is making a come-closer motion with her pointing finger at Eddie and shaking her head at Ace. Eddie looks back up at Ace who's looking mournfully down at him from the lofty altitude of a six foot seven something tall man.

"I don't know what to say" says Eddie, and nods towards Charley, mouthing "in a second, in a second."

Charley pipes up, still motioning at Eddie. "Well, I know what you should say Eddie. You should say yes. You should say yes, to me, and follow me back to my flat. As soon as possible."

Ace puts one hand on Eddie's shoulder "I'm sorry, Eddie. I was wrong to write those emails to you."

Eddie looks off to one side and allows himself the smallest of smiles. That's actually a first. Ace apologizing to Eddie. Maybe little Acer is growing up.

"Well. Good. Fine. Now that that's taken care of - I'm feeling so much better. Thank you Ace. Thanks. I forgive you.

Ace bows his head, accepting Eddie's forgiveness. Charley stands to one side, hands on her hips waiting.

"Now, Ace. How exactly do I get that money back that I spent to bail out the guy, heretofore known as Dakota, that guy that I saved from jail here in San Francisco two weeks ago. How, Ace? How exactly, do I get that money back? Huh?"

"Eddie, Eddie, Eddie. Calm yourself. Calm. Remember your yoga. Breathe. In and out. In and out. All your conflicts will be resolved. This man," and at this, Ace points grandly to his own bulging chest with the board he's still holding, "this man loves only one man now – the man in L.A. - Jay. So there will be no more late-night trips to the police station, no more raising of bail money, no more bailing at all if I have my way. I'm done. I give you my word. My solemn word."

Ace stops as if he's waiting for applause. Eddie maintains an obstinate silence. Charley looks off to the side, biting her lip to keep from saying something. Eddie knows Ace. This is not Eddie's first time around the old Ace-block. This is not the first time Eddie's been on the receiving end of a significant Ace-bamboozling effort. This is all old hat to Eddie. Just a part of the job description. Handling Ace's disasters. Eddie's been doing this a long, long time..

In fact, Eddie's been doing this since Ace hit puberty. He's good at it. Unfortunately. It's just too bad Eddie loves Ace like he were his son and wants Ace's life to be as disaster-free as possible. That's too bad. For Eddie.

He wants Ace to be happy. Loving Ace just makes Eddie work all the harder at saving him. Over and over again. And Ace knows it. And Eddie knows Ace knows it. And vice versa, back and forth, ad infinitum. They've been here many, many, many times before. They know the game. They could do it blindfolded, arms tied behind their backs, hopping on one foot.

So, Eddie doesn't say anything. On top of it, Eddie's got a raging headache, and besides he's too tired to do an excessive amount of scheming, at this moment in time just too tired. These

Periphanitides. Never satisfied. Never out of trouble. Eddie smiles up at Ace, sees Charley looking over at him, then at Ace, still partially behind Ace's back. She's half-frowning, half-smiling and shaking her head.

It's nice seeing Charley again, though. He wishes he had more friends in his life. Like Charley. More friends period. He works too much. These Periphanitides. He should hang around decent people, people like Charley. That would be nice. He's always liked Charley. Charley's great. Eddie realizes he's drifting. His eyes are open. But he's falling asleep on his feet. It feels good.

Ace waits. Patiently. Eddie knows Ace will wait for hours if necessary. He's done it before. Ace always wins. Eddie sighs. Someone clears their throat behind Ace's back.

Ace sees no one is going to congratulate him, no one's even going to react to him. He sighs piteously and draws in a deep breath and continues talking.

"Look. Eddie. Eddie, my man, It's simple. I have to get my hands on forty thousand dollars by Sunday night, or all hell breaks loose. Most of it on my head, some of it, I'm thinking on your head. Or vice versa. Probably more vice than versa. I always forget which is what. Anyways, Eddie… a lot of breaking is involved in the near future. And remember the part about your head being involved. Remember it."

Ace pauses, looks down at Eddie. Eddie nods at Ace, signifying assent. He'll remember.

"But, if I know you, and I do know you by now, you were eavesdropping, like you always do. Right? Man! I knew I was right! And you heard my whole story already, right? Right again! Charley, am I good or am I good? Yes, I'm good. So I can shut up now and you can tell me the whole, intricate, involved, ingenious plan to save my sorry ass in twenty-four hours. Whew! I can hardly wait. Go ahead, Eddie. Let 'er rip."

Eddie's a little woozy. Eddie feels like slapping his own face, just to wake himself up a little bit. And Eddie feels like slapping Ace's face, for that threat about Eddie's head being broken. But Eddie's not going to do either. Eddie's calm, responsible, an adult. He doesn't slap in public. He waits a second. Ace puts on a sad puppy face. Charley slaps Ace on the shoulder. Eddie approves. Then he speaks up.

"Fine, Ace. Just fine. O.K. All right, already. I'll do it. I'll do it.

I'll help you. I will. So. So, where exactly do you want me to get the money from? What bank? I'll head over there first thing tomorrow, get the banker out of bed, etc., etc., I think we can manage it, once they hear your last name is Periphanitides, at the very least we can get a cashier's check, or... something, I don't know. So, just tell me which of your father's banks do you want me to use?"

"Bank? How the hell should I know, Eddie? Doing is your department. Deciding it needs to get done – hey, that's my department. I'm a get-it-decided kind of guy."

Someone snickers behind Ace's back, but Ace ignores her. Then Ace leans back over his shoulder and talks out of one side of his mouth "I think ahead. I make decisions. Sometimes. I do. I think. I could come up with 10 or 20 examples of my thinking, right off the top of my head. Just like that. I could." Eddie hears more snickering.

Eddie's lost in thought for a moment - there's someone he's heard about recently, someone who could help. But who? While he thinks he tries to keep Ace occupied so Ace can't get himself (and Eddie) into any more trouble than he's already gotten himself into. Eddie says the first thing that pops into his head.

"Well, Ace, that's all very easy for you to say."

"Yes, it is."

"And what about the guy here in San Francisco?"

"What about him? The guy? Dimitri? Yeah, O.K., Eddie, Dak, whatever. You do what you need to do, Eddie, with that guy. Dak, yeah, Eddie, I get it already, I get it. So... great. I trust you. Take care of it. Handle it. You have brains, good brains. I've always said so. Haven't I, Charley?"

Eddie can't hear what Charley answers, but he thinks it sounds affirming and encouraging. Eddie decides again that he likes Charley. This must be the fourth or fifth time he's decided that tonight. Eddie smiles at Charley. She mouths the words "You look like shit. Come home. Now." Eddie nods, smiling, or trying to, through his cracked and bleeding face. Then, Eddie has a thought.

He doesn't want to have a thought. In fact, he won't have a thought. It's not going to happen. He's going to get cleaned up then head for bed. No time for a thought. Not now. No thoughts tonight. This night is over. No. No. Eddie refuses.

But Eddie knows it's hopeless. Once the engine starts revving, up there, above his cerebellum, he's off and running. He can feel ideas beginning to flow freely in the humming gray matter between his ears. It feels good. It reminds Eddie of something. Eddie used to watch the river back home as it broke up in the Spring – ice cracking, thundering, splitting apart, ice restless to start moving, ice relentlessly pushing forward to someplace else. He can feel a breaking up in his head. He can feel a general movement to someplace else. It's starting.

But it doesn't mean Eddie's happy. It's all up there - the crazy ideas - in his head, and Eddie's helpless and being carried downstream again and it's all because of these fucking Periphanitides. It's always because of them. Always. But it's starting. The craziness is starting.

CHAPTER 10
(Saturday Night 11:15 P.M.,
Eddie Still on a Street in the Castro)

Eddie throws his head back and forth, a dog shaking off water, and tries to wake up. He takes a breath, exhales, organizes his mind just a little bit, and starts talking to Ace. It irritates him to no end that Ace is smiling his self-satisfied-see-I-got-you-to-save-me-again smile in his direction.

The smile is an Ace-special-on-high-beams smile. He saves them up for occasions like this. He always looks that way as Eddie begins to pull Ace's irons out of the fire, yet again. And it always works on Eddie, it always works. And Ace knows it.

"You know what, Ace?" Ace doesn't say anything back, he just continues beaming that smile. Ace knows, that all Ace has to do at this point is listen and basically, Ace is home free. It's all downhill for Ace, from here on in. The hard part is done. So Ace is smiling.

Well. Eddie sighs. Eddie briefly wishes he had someone like himself in his life. Someone to pull Eddie's own irons out of Eddie's own fires for him. Someone Eddie could lean on unconditionally. Someone else to do all the work. Why doesn't he have someone like himself in his life? Why? What would be so wrong about that? It would be nice. At the very least, it would be extraordinarily unusual.

But, Eddie reminds himself, these are the kind of thoughts that get you nowhere – and they'll get you there fast. Better just to nip all these Ace-crises in the bud. Bite the bullet. Do it. While there's still time. And do it quickly, before the madnesses multiply.

There'll be time enough for Eddie's own mid-life crisis later. After the princess is saved, after the dragons are killed, after the curse is broken. Later, Eddie. Much later.

Eddie sighs again. Eddie will be seventy at the youngest when all the Periphanitides are finally safe and home and happy. That will be the only time when Eddie can start concentrating on his, on Eddie's problems. Eddie's certain of this.

Eddie sighs yet again. He's been doing a lot of that tonight. Deep, emotional sighing. Sometimes it helps. He looks up and Ace is smiling expectantly down upon him. Charley is still standing with her hands on her hips, watching the two of them. Eddie pulls himself together, returns to the matter at hand.

"Ace, there's a rich old fart up on Pacific Heights - actually he's a cut-throat New York investment banker, a mostly-retired pirate captain type – if that means anything. But anyways, this pirate captain guy was fit to be tied when he saw you falling all over yourself about the guy here in San Francisco. Turns out he was in love with him too. Yes, we're talking about Dak here. Dak, the name of your San Francisco boyfriend, the guy you formerly couldn't live without. The guy I bailed out. The very expensive Dak."

Eddie expects Ace to be rolling his eyes at Eddie. Get mad. React. But all Ace can do right now is smile. Actually, Eddie's gotten to know Dak in the last couple of weeks. He kind of likes him. He's been trying to make Dak feel at home, get him comfortable, since Eddie's the one that got him out of jail. Dak's O.K. in Eddie's book. So Eddie tries a little harder with Dak.

"So, anyways, Ace, maybe I can convince the pirate captain that *Dak* is still sitting in jail and is in need of some bailing out, and I can get the pirate captain to hand over forty thousand, which I will then hand over to you, and immediately hand Dak over to the pirate captain.

Ace nods.

"I don't think Dak would mind. Dak hasn't exactly been overjoyed with you lately. You haven't communicated with him in weeks. Not a call, not an email, not a text. Zip-all. And he's kind of lonely. Not that you're all that interested in Dak's whereabouts, his home-life, his future, his emotional state.

Ace looks at Eddie with a blank expression. Charley hits him again.

"I can see your not. Anyways, I know where Dak is. I put him there. He's safe. So. All that means, Ace, in a nutshell is that neither you nor I will have to go through all the vice-versa-ing you were going on about. It moves Dak out of exile and into a place where someone appreciates him. And it leaves the field clear for you and what's his name from L.A. to live happily ever after. Or at least until you find your next boyfriend. How's that sound for a plan, Ace?"

Ace nods and smiles, nods and smiles. He won't even react to Eddie's sarcasm. And of course Ace is happy. He's getting his money back and getting Jay and losing Dak, all at the same time.

There's no hint of doubt in Ace's eyes. Ace believes, no Ace *knows* Eddie will be successful. Ace has no idea how much trouble Eddie's about to get into. So, Ace is all smiles. It drives Eddie crazy.

"But, Ace, I have to mention, this plan still leaves me out all the money I used for Dak's bail. I'm still fucked. I'm still a thief, bankrupt, a liar, and a bad friend to almost everyone I know. That is, if anyone's keeping count. I mean, don't worry about me, but, well, *are* you worrying about me. Ace?"

"Whatever it takes, Eddie. Whatever it takes, bud. You're the man."

The voice from behind Ace rises and floats over their little gathering in the fog- in a weary tone which makes it clear that this is the last time it will thus arise.

"You guys done here? Look, I'm chilled to the bone. One of us "guys" out here is only wearing a thin dress, nylons and high-heels. And it's not Ace for once. So I vote, boys, we adjourn and continue this discussion back at my place. And you, Eddie can clean up some. I've got iodine and band-aids back there. And hot water. And a shower. And lots of fluffy towels. And maybe even some spare clothes."

Charley pauses here. Ace and Eddie turn to face her.

"And it's fifteen degrees hotter up there than here. And I've got some Tequila I haven't opened yet. And we can also go to the

Emergency Room – if we have to – using Ace's car once we see what's under all that gore, Eddie."

Ace nods, Eddie winks. If he nods too much he might start bleeding again. So no energetic head movements. Not for now. Charley continues. She's the mission leader for tonight's search and rescue mission, obviously. She brooks no disobedience.

"Give me your coat Ace. You can spare it. You're hot-blooded. You and I both know you are."

Ace takes off his leather coat and Charley disappears in yards and yards of beautifully stitched, artfully creased, black calf-skin. It goes down below her knees. From deep inside the coat, Eddie can hear her whispering "And Ace, if you haven't noticed already, your two special friends have just arrived, with a buddy."

Eddie notices for the first time that two bulky silhouettes flank Eddie, one on his left, one on his right. It's like standing between two Sequoias in Muir Woods. Thad emerges from beside one of them.

"Hey, bud" says Ace, seeing Thad. When they get within handshake range, they do some complicated hand movement of welcome that involves something on the order of ten or twelve American Sign Language sentences, and some boxing and wrestling moves. When they're done, Thad smiles. He gives Charley a hug. He looks over at Eddie.

"Edward, why do you smell like coffee grounds and a cheap Italian spice cabinet and vomit rolled together? Huh? And, I have to say, man!, you are looking worse and worse as the evening wears on. You're like that oil painting that decays and decays – what was it? The Picture of Dorian Something or Other. Except instead of the picture getting worse it's you." Charley smacks Thad in the back of the head.

"What? What did I say?" Thad looks back at her with a hurt, innocent expression. Thad, of course, looks fabulous – skin, hair, spotless and perfect and a new trendy outfit on, that shows off his big chest and bulging arms, his spiky black hair and his dark, mysterious eyes. Eddie thinks it's like he threw himself bodily into a One Hour Dry Cleaner's and just stepped out.

Charley puts one arm in Eddie's, avoiding the blood, another arm in Ace's and follows Thad and the lumpy hit men (or whatever they are) up the sidewalk towards 17th Street. Eddie leans over in front of Charley to whisper at Ace.

"Ace, keep yourself scarce, during all this. O.K.?" The two human aircraft carriers sailing up in front of them lean back for a second as if they're trying to overhear. Which is probably not true, Eddie thinks, since Eddie knows they don't seem to speak English very well. But Eddie shuts up anyways. Charley pats him gingerly on the arm. Ace casts a significant look over in Eddie's direction.

"You don't have to say that twice, bro" says Ace, muttering as he saunters, one arm around Charley's back now.

They come to the end of the block, turn down the next block, and the two big guys with Thad watch Ace to make sure Ace turns the same way they do. Ace is not getting away again. But Ace does. Turn that is. And not try and get away. Charley is singing something to herself, something low and sweet, and encouraging.

Ace is alternately adjusting and re-adjusting his coat onto Charley's shoulders. He smiles at Charley, scowls at the two men in short-sleeved shirts walking ahead, raises his eyebrows at Eddie, and whistles off key, trying to match the tune Charley's singing. All the while he's meditatively rubbing the handsome dimple he sports in his very masculine Periphanitides chin.

Eddie rubs his head, with his one free hand, freezing and blood-caked, and when he does, he feels Charley pulling him closer to her with the other, bringing him into the warmth under the leather tent that is Ace's coat. Eddie hopes he's not leaving bloody blotches all over her dress.

And I, thought Eddie, am right back in the manure pile. As usual.

"Hey Alice."

"Now who can this be? I know it can't be Ed Stone, because today's his birthday and he'd be over in my living room, like he agreed to, with the rest of us, getting ready to go out. So who are you?"

"Alice, please. I'm not in the mood."

"Oh. so it's turning out to be that kind of night?"

"Alice, yeah, it's just that..."

"Don't tell me, Eddie. You just got hit with a hefty dose of Ace."

"Yeah, How'd you know? Wait, don't tell me, Alice. It'd be too depressing. So here's the whole shebang. You know the money I stole from Mr. Periphanitides? It was to bail out a boyfriend of Ace's in jail in the Palace of Justice in The City. Dak, his name is Dak. So, Dak is living with Mr. Periphanitides. I put Dak there. Why? He's there because I got the money out of Mr. P. by lying to him. I told Mr. P. that Dak is his long-lost son.

"Of course not, Alice, it's not true, Dak is not Mr. P.'s son. But Mr. P. bought it hook, line and sinker, and I got the money out of him, and Ace used it. Yeah, but that's not why I'm so down. Alice, I've been a fool. No wait, don't say anything yet.

"I paid his money, and paid out my own money – you know all about that – my own money for the mobile home and the land down payment, your money too, all of it. And it's gone. It's all gone. O.K., so go ahead and say it. Say it now, Alice."

"Yes, Eddie, you have been a fool."

"It gets better, Alice. Ace doesn't even want to be with this Dak, the guy I bailed out. He doesn't even remember Dak's name. He barely remembers I spent the money - his dad's and mine – to save Dak. Alice, I think I lost it all. I mean, really lost it this time. At least, I'm not going to get it back from Ace. And you know what, Alice? Now he says he needs more."

"More? More what?"

"Stop it Alice. You know more what. More money."

"You are not going to give Ace any more money, Eddie. Listen. Are you listening, Eddie? You just hop in a taxi and head over to the Mission and my flat. We'll be waiting for you. We can talk about it then. All right? We in agreement, Eddie?"

"Yeah. Yeah. You're right. I'll be over there as soon as I can. The thing of it is, I've got to get more money out of Ace's dad somehow. And it's got to be tonight. I don't have any money left to help Ace get out of this one. Not this time. I'm broke. And this time Ace got himself mixed up with organized crime. At least I think it's organized. It seems a little disorganized, actually. A little unprofessional. Which might be a good thing. I don't know. But still, since I kind of helped Ace get himself into this fix, well, I figure, I kind of need to help Ace get himself back out of it. Besides, he's just a kid. He's a baby, Alice."

"Yeah, Eddie, a baby cyclone. Look Ace is responsible for Ace, Eddie. You can't save everyone."

"Eddie?"

"Eddie? You still there, Eddie?"

"I'm here."

"Come over here. We'll wait for a little while. I don't know how long I can keep this gang happy, just hanging around my place, though. Deb's doing tequila shots off of some of the girls cleavage. She's calling it shooting the rapids in the Grand Canyon. She's pretending to be Hoover dam. It's quite a sight. You're missing out, Eddie. Get your ass over here, pronto."

"I'll get back to you, Alice. Thanks Alice."

"You be careful, Eddie. And call me if you need anything, you hear? You got friends too. Friends to help you out of fixes. You need to start relying on 'em. Call me."

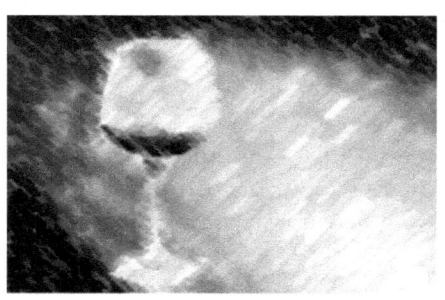

CHAPTER 11
(Saturday Night 11:45 P.M.,
Albert at Paul's New House on Twin Peaks)

Fifteen blocks and five hills away from where Eddie is cleaning up at Charley's, a pyramid of steel and glass with a porch running around the front of it rises on a steep slope. It's a large house. A man with a scraggly, dirty gray beard, deeply etched lines of worry, leather elbow patches, and an un-kept, generally eroded, but mostly presentable air about him – this man walks from room to room in this large house as if looking for something.

He is not. Looking for something that is. His name is Albert. He follows a second man. Albert is doggedly pursuing him, shuffling and perspiring (Albert's a little overweight, well, maybe a lot overweight), trailing behind this second man. The second man resembles Albert in none of those particulars, in fact, he's Albert's opposite in many ways. The second man talks and points with animation at various things in the house. The second man walks with a confident, determined stride, and doesn't often wait for Albert to catch up with him, he's tall and appears to be in excellent physical condition, and so, as a result, Albert often falls far behind him. With frequency. Albert doesn't seem very happy with the situation.

This second man, who is sometimes grandly called Paul Grigor Oinomaos Periphanitides, but mostly answers to Paul, Mr. Periphanitides, Mr. P., or just plain "sir", could double as a senior citizen Captain America - tall, tan, obviously rich, clean-shaven, trim, topped by a flowing mane of deftly gelled salt and pepper hair and overall, as neat and shiny as a newly-minted penny.

Albert hates him. Albert loves him. Mostly they're comfortable with each other. They should be, they've been friends for over forty years. And Albert's a little too old, and it's a little too late in the game now for Albert to be indulging in ferocious, feet-kicking fits of jealousy and resentment towards Paul Periphanitides. Albert mostly rolls with the Paul-punches these days. He gets punched a lot. By life. By Paul. Metaphorically. But he doesn't have to like it, does he? No. He does not. But he can do something about it. Albert can roll.

Right now, Albert is rolling through Paul's house, and for the record, yes, he's not liking it. It's a big place. It's a lot of walking. So maybe Albert's sometimes falling behind on purpose. Maybe he falls behind Paul most of the time.

Albert pulls out his handkerchief and wipes his forehead down. He realizes there's no chair, not even a bench in this part of the house that could support his weight without folding into some kind of aluminum origami. He grimaces. Takes a deep breath. Closes his eyes. Smiles bravely and shuffles forward over gleaming, spotless, nearly frictionless flooring. He closes his eyes more tightly. Albert is, as they say, beat.

He echo-locates, not opening his eyes, following the sound of the second man's voice - we'll just call him Paul, so it's Paul's voice he totters towards - and bruises his shin on a sharp, decorative something, stopping abruptly and hissing between his teeth. Ye Gods, that hurt!

He's not actually listening to him, to this other man, his friend, Paul. He knows that he and Paul are by themselves tonight. They are back from a San Francisco Pops Orchestra concert. Not their best, in Albert's opinion. Middling. A lot of Broadway medleys. Diffident Tchaikovsky. On the whole, not exactly Albert's cup of tea. But Paul had seemed so desperate to get out of this house. Very unlike him. How could Albert refuse? It was a double date. A not very successful one. Albert might add. The women went home early. And now Paul wants to talk, and show him his house. And walk. Well, Albert was here, wasn't he? That's what friends did, wasn't it?

So. It's just the two of them in this five-level, post-modern, glass and cement monstrosity of a townhouse. A house perched on the very edge of one side, a very vertiginous side Albert might add, of the pointy hills overlooking the city called Twin Peaks.

Albert supposes it's safe. But in case of unforeseen earthquakes or sinkholes or what have you, he keeps a constant lookout for the location of the front door. He doesn't want to surf on bamboo flooring and glass and steel rubble down hundreds of feet of hillside into Noe Valley. Not at his age. He's too old for all that. And too dignified to surf. Albert wonders, how far up are they actually? Is it really hundreds of feet? Hundreds? He looks around for the wall of windows he'd seen as they came in.

But perhaps because he's not listening, that's why Albert is so surprised - when he opens his eyes and looks around, and also fitfully rubs what will surely be a sizeable bruise on his right thigh from that metal whatever it was – well, Albert is surprised, but more than that, Albert is dumbfounded when he finds that he is alone. He looks around and Paul is nowhere in sight. He's nipped off. Vanished. Gone. Paul is elsewhere.

Did Paul tell him goodnight? Did Paul leave the house? Should Albert leave now too? Really, Albert was hoping for more wine. It's all devilishly and annoyingly confusing. This coming. This going. This walking. And now this non-talking.

Albert holds a wine glass. It's been empty for some time now, but he can't set it down. Albert has been consistently unable to find a single horizontal surface that isn't upholstered or already supporting a sculpture or some kind of brushed-metal electronic appliance. There's certainly no coasters anywhere in sight.

Indeed, there's hardly any furniture. Just acres of blond, blindingly polished wood. Or is it bamboo, perhaps, after all? Albert peers more closely at it. He stumbles against a wispy small ceramic table. A piece of it snaps off and falls to the floor. It makes a large noise. Albert stares at it in astonishment.

It's just his luck. He bends over with difficulty, breathing hard, almost gasping, and snatches up the offending sliver of furniture on his first try (he smiles to himself – he still has it, as nimble as a Freshman in college) and balances the dismembered piece of table carefully in the place from which it had broken. Albert pats it a few times, to push it securely back into place. There. Good as new.

"You could run a bleeding scrimmage in this space" Albert mutters to himself in a bad imitation of a Manchester accent. He is thinking of his own cramped, dark, and much cheaper quarters miles away in Colma, an apartment that overlooks most of the dozen or so cemeteries taking up the vast majority of land in that town. Albert tells people he has very quiet neighbors. He says they won't even have to move Albert out when Albert goes. Nobody ever seems to get his jokes.

This is the first time Albert's been to Paul's new digs. Paul's been a-building ever since his wife Veronica died nearly two years ago. And now it's done. Albert looks around. He's a little concerned about Paul. Every so often there's a wild uncertainty in Paul's eyes. And then it's gone. Odd, that. He seems... hollower somehow. Yes, that's it. Hollower. An old oak in the forest, standing upright, but just barely. Albert's not sure how to be friends with a hollow Paul. But he'll try, he supposes.

God knows Paul's been there for him. After his own Jillian passed away. That was 15 years ago now, wasn't it? Fifteen years if it was a day. Incredible. Incredible that it has been that long. Jillian's going had certainly been unexpected. Much like Veronica's quick departure.

Paul's seemingly had a difficult time of it. Even though Paul never talks about it. Silent as the Sphinx, that's Paul. Not much of a talker. Albert's actually appreciated that about Paul. A certain reticence, you know. Until recently, they'd shared many happy hours of silence together. But if the whole living-by-yourself situation, if it had been half as bad for Paul after Veronica as it had been for Albert after Jillian, well, then, yes, in that case, Albert could see that...

But where the deuce is Paul? It seems Albert is quite alone. Well then. That changes things. Albert's nearly convinced himself that he will be forced to set his delicately wrought and bone-dry wine glass directly upon this ice-rink of a floor somewhere, soon. He has to set it down sometime. He has to get rid of it. It may as well be right now. It may as well be right here.

Yes, he's decided, that's exactly what he'll do. Albert bends over, and begins to scan the area around his feet, looking for a likely spot, when, just at that moment, Paul, comes tripping up the transparent, acrylic spiral staircase, and waves both his hands at

Albert, smiling. He has something in his hands. He looks jolly. But it doesn't convince Albert, no it doesn't fool Albert. Hollow. That's what he seems. Hollow.

Albert won't use the see-through staircase, it gives him motion sickness. Albert used the other staircase, in the back, when Paul gave him the tour of the place earlier. But Albert does not comment on Paul's use of this dangerous staircase at present. Albert's eyes widen and then widen again - wonder of wonders - Paul is coming up from downstairs with a full or nearly full (actually Albert can't tell) wine bottle in his hand. Albert snaps upright to attention and nearly loses his grip on his empty wine glass in his excitement. Behold, Thy Salvation, he hymns to himself, Is At Hand.

He composes his face into a simulacrum of beaming expectancy. He also braces for another monologue-assault from Paul. Paul's been talking non-stop tonight. But Paul abruptly makes a sharp left and quickly disappears into another room (the kitchen?), leaving Albert standing there, holding the cursed glass, alone in this enormous, empty living room. A fading joy withers on his weary face.

But Albert is hopeful. Either Paul will pour Albert more wine, or Paul will at least put his own empty wine glass down. Paul will have to put his glass down somewhere and Albert will note the location and will be able follow Paul's example with awe-inspiring alacrity. Albert smiles. He will be soon rid of this wretched glass.

"If Thou art willing, O Lord, let this cup pass from me..." he whispers in a sing-song voice to himself, peering myopically out of the stunning floor-to-ceiling windows at the multicolored, twinkling lights of the madness of a weekend in the city of San Francisco, far below. Albert takes a step back from the wall of windows. Then another step. Then another. It is so, far, far, *far* below him.

Where *do* all these people come from? Albert peers over the edge at all the busy blinking lights, at all the cars rushing here, speeding there. Where do they come from, and *where* do they think they are all going? This city is a kind of madness. It *is* a madness.

Albert, in another life, was a college Classics professor (Dept. chair, noted authority, etc. etc.) - Latin and Greek, his dissertation treating the maddeningly intricate and varying uses of the Greek Middle Voice, Aorist tense in the Medieval Byzantine historian

Michael Psellos.

A delicate matter. A fruitful area of inquiry. The implications were enormous. He'd very much enjoyed it. No one had written as much about Psellos as him. Before or after his academic career. Psellos hadn't quite made the splash he'd anticipated, but then again, what did splash nowadays? Next to nothing, really – when you thought about it. And it was probably all worth it. All those years with Michael Psellos. One could live without a great deal of splashing if one set one's mind to it. And Michael had been a good companion. A little bit of a gossip, and a little stuck on himself. Some of Psellos' Greek was impenetrable. But, on the whole, good company. Albert couldn't complain.

Albert, after graduating with top honors from Merton College, Oxford, had taught at various Universities in the States for what felt like centuries. Now he lives (barely) on a sarcastically small set of annuities, his retirement pension from the U.K., and the occasional check from his favorite nephew the surgeon.

Paul always calls him Albert's nephew the sturgeon. Paul must know that it drives Albert to distraction. But Albert says nothing. Albert is not in the habit of referring to the blood relatives of a friend (say Paul) in the piscine sense. But he is resigned to the fact that others do not share his same civilized delicacy of manners.

Albert met Paul at Merton. Paul flunked out. Now, apparently, half the iron filings used in industry worldwide (what possible use could the world have for so much iron filings? - Albert is boggled by it all), well, they all come in boxes marked Periphanitides.

So…Albert boggles at the world and starves in his spare time, yet remains politely silent. Paul, on the other hand, twirls the world on his palm as one would a toy, builds billion dollar houses and complains continuously. If there is any justice in this sublunar world, Albert maintains, he is damned if he can see it.

But, of course, a great deal of all that has changed, hasn't it? In the last 2 years or so. It has become, regretfully, harder and harder for Albert to think harshly of Paul. In fact, in the recent past, a new, odd and disquieting wrinkle in their relationship has developed. Albert doesn't quite know what to make of it all yet. Paul seems to *need* Albert now. It gratifies and frightens Albert, all at the same time. It's not the most pleasant of sensations.

Paul re-appears, looking a little discombobulated, sans bottle, sans glass. Albert gapes. He'll be holding this cursed empty glass for the rest of his natural life.

Paul smiles wanly, wearily. Yes. Hollowly. Albert tentatively smiles back.

Paul launches into another long, rococo explanation about a huge complication in his life currently. All this Paul-talking takes some getting used to. Albert labors to follow his points. Albert unconsciously moves his hand to adjust his eyeglasses somewhat and manages to unbalance the wine glass pinched in the fingers of his other hand. Slowly it slips loose. Sliding down. Farther and farther. He can't grab at it without making a theatrical production out of it.

Paul drones on and on. The glass slips and slips. Albert knows it's gone when he hears the merry sound of crystal shattering and re-shattering on the hard, polished, woody plane at his feet.

Paul doesn't seem to notice. He's holding one hand to the handsome cleft in his perfectly dimpled chin, pointer finger extended, in a graceful attitude of earnest concern, while with the other he clasps something mysterious and small behind his back. He's going on and on about somebody's mother. Or is he talking about his own son? Paul tends to wander so if not reined in. Albert's going to have to leap into the explanation soon and slash his way free out of this conversational jungle. Albert mentally sharpens his interlocutory machete.

While he waits for Paul to take a breath, Albert discreetly shoves the splintered glass with his toe under an oddly shaped octagonal ceramic table – a spider-web-thingy – the table that he's been standing next to by the floor-to-ceiling windows, the whole while he's been listening to Paul for these last 97 hours. He hopes he doesn't disturb the broken bit of the table he replaced on it earlier. He hopes it doesn't plummet to the floor again and famously smash into even smaller bits, adding to his mountain of broken Paul- property. He shoves gently, gently, back and away.

Every time Paul looks off to one side, Albert augments his puny, growing pile of shards under the table with another tiny push of his shoe. He looks at Paul and smiles benignly and twitches his foot, back and forth. He's so intent on cleaning up, he doesn't realize Paul has stopped talking, perhaps for 10 or 20 seconds.

Paul is looking at him, forlornly really. That sad, puppy dog look. It's in his eyes. You'd only see it if you knew him well. He'd looked like that when Veronica and he separated, when their son

William was still an infant, and Paul was starting up that Los Angeles subsidiary. What was it again? Damned if he knew. Then they'd gotten back together. And the company, whatever it was, in Los Angeles had closed. Now what made Albert think of that? Is Paul talking about that again? Albert hadn't thought about Paul and Veronica's troubles in years.

Paul is still watching Albert, Paul slowly starts explaining again. Albert realizes he has to seize this chance at interruption - tries to assemble his thoughts, tries to remember what Paul has been babbling on about for the last God-knows-how-long, tries to weave it into some coherent whole. His old lecturing instincts and skills creak back into a semblance of rusty motion. It actually hurts his head to do it. Oh, what we do for friendship!

"Ahem, harrumph, oh, excuse me, Paul. Please, let me try and get this clear."

Paul slowly rumbles to a complete halt again. He stares in silence with a kind of oppressed expression at Albert. Albert lets him rest a moment.

"You say you had a wild youthful romance with a woman named Filipa. This was soon after William, that is Ace was born but many, many years after you were married to Veronica. This was after Oxford, but before the iron filings really took off."

"Correct so far, Al." Albert winces, he despises nicknames, especially grunting monosyllables, but nobly perseveres. He is, after all, a concerned friend.

"Now, unbeknownst to you, Filipa ended up giving birth to a son Benjamin, nickname of Benjy."

"No, he refuses to call himself Benjy. He calls himself Dak now. And Albert, I did know he was born. I knew. I knew very well. In fact, I visited the baby at first. Edward, later, visited more often than I did, until the baby was three or four years old. Then I sort of lost track of it all. But he likes to be called Dak."

"Dak? Dak?" Albert can't imagine why someone would voluntarily choose a name that sounded like a cat coughing up a hairball. Americans were beyond him.

Years ago, Albert had given up trying to figure out Americans – and how their minds worked. It was simply inexplicable. He had learned the hard way, through long bitter years of struggle, there was no reason for their actions. They didn't know themselves why they did what they did. Probing lines of inquiry, subtle logical arguments - all were lost on them. And questioning their judgment was a thankless task. Thankless. They never noticed. Indeed, they never even knew they were being questioned. Albert looks up. Paul is watching him.

"Ahem, so it's Dak? Or Dak-Benjy rather?""Dak-Benjy?"

"So far, so good, my friend."

Albert sighs. Dak-Benjy – the name resembled that of a Babylonian fertility god. Something you'd find in the Epic of Gilgamesh. The massy brass image of the Great God Dak-Benjy gazed down in baleful wroth... Albert sighs again.

"So. Dak-Benjy had a childhood. Dak-Benjy had an adolescence. Dak-Benjy grew up and was incarcerated. Or at least he was arrested. And was being held pending trial, when you, Paul, through the good offices of your assistant Edward, discovered said Dak-Benjy. You posted bail. And you paid off various other debts of his. So far, so good.

Thus you saved - oh I can't continue this way Paul, please let's you and I simply settle for one name, Dak, perhaps. Shall we? Very good then. Thus, you saved your long-lost son, Dak, because of Eddie's serendipitous discovery and quick thinking. So Dak, your son, is not in jail."

"Thankfully. All too true."

"And now, Filipa is back in your life, in the person of Dak. You feel you want to marry Filipa, to make everything right between you, but you don't think it's fair to Ace (William Paul Periphanitides), your only child by Veronica, to marry again."

"Yes."

"And, just to make it interesting, you haven't actually *met* Filipa in eighteen odd years, since baby Dak was four years old."

"Yes. And I have no idea how to find her. Dak doesn't seem to know either."

"Hmmm. Odd that. So you hesitate. Understandable. And meanwhile, you have Dak-Benjy, I mean Dak upstairs, in this very house."

"Yes."

"But I thought that we were alone tonight."

"No." Paul hesitates and looks thoughtful. "No, we aren't alone."

"We are three?"

"Yes, I believe you've got it."

"I do?"

Paul looks towards the ceiling, nodding. Albert takes this opportunity to aim a few last backwards kicks at the splinters still lying out in the open, under the window. It irks him to know he resembles a large tweed-covered tabby pawing away with its hind legs in the litter box after doing its business. They fly obediently into the little pile of glass under the web table. Albert smiles.

Albert moves his hand upwards to sip more wine, and notices irritably his hand is now empty. He feels odd. His head spins the merest bit, and he notices, out of the sides of his eyes, that the fog's rolled in, rapidly, obliterating all the lights of the city. There is nothing now outside of the window. It is uniformly a gray opacity. The house seems to be hanging now in a dimensionless void outside of space and time. It is as if Albert has disappeared. Albert no longer exists. Albert forgets to breathe for a moment or two. Then three. He feels like he's falling. Falling. Falling.

"Veronica. Filipa" says Paul forlornly, staring at the plank patterning in the ceiling, high above them. "Dak. Dak-Benjy."

Albert hears a loud ringing in his ears and thinks he might be going mad. It rings and rings, more and more insistently. Albert stops breathing again. The fog seems to be coming right through the window glass. Right at him. It's reaching for him.

Then Albert notices. He notes that the shrill sound of ringing is coming from behind Paul's back somewhere. Paul seems confused by the sound also. Then the sound stops. Paul looks around as if to find it. Ah! So Paul hears it too. Albert whispers to himself. "Good, good." Albert feels like laughing, laughing out loud. He is not going mad. The fog is not reaching out to get him. He feels, unexpectedly, very alive. He is alive. And he is here. He remembers to inhale.

Perhaps, thinks Albert, perhaps no more wine tonight.

Albert wipes his forehead again with his handkerchief. He steps away from the window.

Is this what a stroke feels like? How could he tell for sure? Albert feels his pulse in his wrist and is not happy. Not happy at all.

Albert backs away from the ontological nightmare billowing about outside the window and shakes his head and closes his eyes to erase all memory of it. As he closes them, he sees Paul looking elsewhere, looking at something in his hand, so Albert kicks backwards once or twice more, just to be thorough in the broken wine glass department. After this last effort, Albert decides to give it all a rest. Enough is enough. He must have cleared away all the pieces of glass by now, surely. He must have. Paul seems oblivious.

Albert steps backwards, one more time, and a delicious breaking sound echoes in the living room. It sounds like Albert's stepped lengthwise on most of a wine glass stem and half the base. Paul looks up from his hands and over at Albert in an odd, Albert might almost say, discourteous way.

Albert clears his throat loudly and extensively, does it again, and subsequently bursts into speech, jumping feet-first into the awkward silence after the sound of that miniature crystal explosion.

"Well. Look, Paul. This is ridiculous. Filipa's a decent person. You're a decent person. Veronica's gone, and it *has* been almost two years, after all, hasn't it?. Why couldn't you marry Filipa? If you found her?"

"Still…"

"Paul, I can't honestly remember a day when you and Veronica weren't fighting. For thirty years. No armistices. No cease-fires. A great deal of Cold War espionage, hand-to-hand guerrilla fighting and years and years of trench warfare if I recall correctly."

"Well, about that… Veronica, well… You see…

"But wasn't it Veronica's uncle who coughed up the initial capital which made possible the great firm of Periphanitides in the first place?"

"It was a kind of wedding present."

"What a present."

"Yes, and it came with Veronica."

"Well. Paul. I know. She's gone. But still, all those years, that must have been something of a trial…"

"No, Albert. That's not it. That was the best part of it. Veronica. She was the best part of me, Albert. The best part. And now she's gone. And now I'm only half a man."

Albert doesn't know what to say.

"And I want to get married again? What business do I have doing that? Why did I have to find Dak again? What am I going to do, Albert? I don't know what to do. I have to do the right thing. But what is it? What is the right thing? I just don't know anymore, Albert. I don't know. I've always known what to do before. Known it instantly. Now everything's hazy. It's all a blur. Help me, Albert, help me."

Albert stares at Paul. He would not have been more surprised if Australia had shaken itself loose from the South Pacific and attached itself bodily to the San Francisco peninsula this evening between the hours of 11 and midnight. Albert closes his mouth, which had been standing open, and awkwardly places a hand on Paul's shoulder. He has to reach up. Paul is a good head and a half taller than him.

"Certainly, Paul, certainly. I shall do everything I can, surely. We'll think of something. Never you mind. We'll come up with some kind of a plan. You'll see. There. There. It will all come out right in the end. You'll see. There. There."

Albert's going to need at least one, possibly two, probably three more glasses of wine. This looks to be a long night.

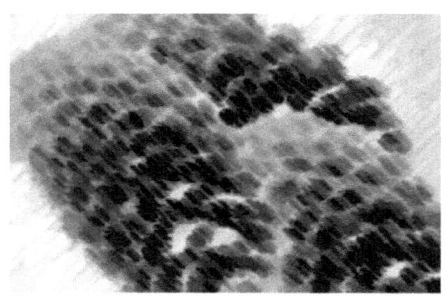

CHAPTER 12
(Saturday Night/Sunday Morning 12:15 A.M.,
Eddie Under a Tree on Twin Peaks)

At some point, maybe a quarter of an hour later, in their island universe, surrounded by the enigmatic, all-devouring fog, Albert and Paul hear the phone ringing again, echoing throughout the Periphanitides residence.

It's Eddie calling. Eddie waits shivering outside, a little ways away, on a corner at the bottom of a steeply-sloped block, braced behind an enormous pine tree. It's solid murk as far as his eye can see, tonight. Which isn't very far, honestly.

The fog is mixing it up now with occasional spitting volleys of wretched drizzle, just to keep everyone on their toes. It's amazing to Eddie how very quickly you can get very, very wet. He had just gotten himself dry. Now look at him. He is agog at how his luck keeps on going from not-so-good, to bad, to he-doesn't-want-to-know-where-his-luck-is-headed-to-next. Eddie tries at least to wring out his sleeves. He's not very successful.

He looks at his phone, hits the number again, jams it next to his ear to hear the ringing starting up.

This is ridiculous. He's ridiculous. He's soaked. He's wearing a once-fluffy white woman's sweater-coat. He is sitting on a moist pile of absurdly large pine cones — they look like something a dinosaur would have stumbled over during a dark, wet night in the Cretaceous. His backbone is tightly wedged against some deeply fissured redwood bark. His lower back hurts because he is squatting painfully, holding his trembling knees with one dripping arm, and twisting sideways to stay upright. He still manages to fall over with embarrassing consistency.

Which he promptly does, once again, right now. Eddie rolls back upright, searches for his phone, which had skipped off into the pine cones, and braces himself against the tree.

He is trying to press himself as closely as he can to the downwind side of the tree — hoping to stave off the rapid loss of what little remains of his body heat. But it's not really working. Water is everywhere. As it turns out, being under a tree is an enormously drip-filled place to be. It must be better, though, than being out in the open, Eddie supposes. It must. Still, the tree and Eddie are very wet.

His cell phone rings and rings and rings and it gets wetter and wetter.

He's bandaged now, bandaged in multiple places, and he supposes he resembles an Egyptian mummy, maybe from the poorer side of town, a corpse from the wrong side of the Egyptian tracks. To top it all off, he's wearing pink tennis shoes, and purple-trimmed athletic socks, and a checkered knit ski cap.

He takes off the cap. It's sopping, and resembles a black and white sponge. The tree drips industriously directly on his scalp. He snaps his phone shut, and leans in another direction, trying to get away from the constant dripping, and falls over again. He picks himself up. Finds his phone. Braces himself. He has to think. He has to think.

He owes these few pieces of clean, once dry clothing/etc. entirely to the charity of Charley. For maybe the fifteenth time tonight, he decides he likes Charley. Charley's great. If Charley were a man, Eddie would be down, right now, on one knee in front of her, proposing, well - proposing something. He likes Charley. That Charley is a keeper.

Then there's Thad. Thad doesn't exactly try to please Eddie. At least, he didn't used to. Lately, Eddie doesn't know what to think about Thad. He's been getting strange, mixed signals from Thad - more mixed than the usual come-over-here, get-away-from-me signals Eddie's been used to getting from him. Sometimes it almost seems like Thad likes him, like Thad's paying attention to Eddie. But then again, when you get right down to it., Thad really only pays constant, devoted attention to Thad.

Eddie's not complaining about the attention. Thad's gorgeous, if a little unpredictable. At any rate, tonight, for whatever twisted, devious reasons Thad has, Thad is helping Eddie out. And being halfway polite. And Eddie is grateful.

Thad drove Eddie over to the block of houses containing the new Periphanitides manse, up on Twin Peaks. Granted, Thad did practically push him out of the car with a mumbled "good luck", or maybe it was "out you fuck", and drove off into the night. But, hey, at least Thad was making the effort. You could call the thing that Thad was doing, "help". You could.

Eddie was squeezing his eyes shut in Thad's car, tightly shut, blocking out the trendy orange-ish light of the dashboard, humming quietly to himself, breathing slowly, trying to shake something loose, trying to pry some insanely clever scheme out of his subconscious. Anything. Some plan. Some course of action. But nothing tumbled out. Nothing. Eddie's frightened. Eddie has no idea what in the hell he is going to do now. He doesn't like this feeling. He does not know what comes next in the Adventures of Eddie.

Except maybe dying of exposure in the rain.

But Eddie doesn't want to think about all that right now. So… When in doubt, Eddie says to himself, you know what to do. Do a nose-dive into the middle of the problem, and let it explode all around you. And improvise. Something will fall out. Something always does. Eddie wishes he felt as confident as he sounds.

So. That means… That means… Eddie's going to meet Mr. Periphanitides, Mr. P., on his home turf. At least he thinks he is. If he can get anyone to answer the phone up there tonight.

He is holding his cell phone up to his ear again. He is balancing again, crouching against the tree. The phone is ringing again. Both the phone and his ear are freezing. He scouted out Mr. Periphanitides' house earlier, jogging, well, limping past it in the cold and wet. He saw Albert's car, parked in front of the giant glass pyramid on stilts roosting on the very top of the hill. It's a big place. He knows it like the back of his hand. He's been overseeing its construction for a long time now.

But Eddie saw only one light on, just one smallish glowing blur in a larger blur of cloudy mist. He's not even sure it wasn't only the porch light. It is kinda foggy out tonight, after all. He'd tried calling in front of the house, but Mr. P.'s cell had rang, then it had sounded like someone answered, then it had gone dead all of a sudden. After that it didn't even ring at all, no matter how many times he'd called. And he was still calling. This is the umpteenth time.

His teeth are chattering. He's humming it's so cold. So Albert's there. So Albert Barnard, Mr. P.'s best friend is visiting him. Possibly alone. "Well," "he stutters to himself in the clinging mist, "here's an opportunity and no two ways about it." Whenever he's around Albert, he finds himself talking like a half-remembered character in a Dickens novel. Or a bad 70's sitcom from the BBC. He can't help himself. It was aggravating. And not just to him.

Well. Hmmm. More teeth chattering, more humming. He gets dripped on some more. He hangs up the phone. He hits redial. Ring. Ring. Ring. He's never told anyone, but he decided long ago, if he ever did start wrestling again (like he did in college), it would be in the Mexican Lucha Libre circuit, and he'd call himself "El Cerebro" or maybe "El Cerebro de la Muerte" – the Brain of Death. Yeah. You had to like it. He smiles again, takes in a long breath, and lets it out. Steam billows out in every direction. Hangs up the phone. Dials again. Ring. Ring. He starts humming and humming, beating his arms and shoulders to stay warm. He falls over. The phone stops ringing when it hits pinecones, must have hung itself up. He hits redial for the millionth time.

Bam! Click! *Eureka!* Someone picks up almost before it rings.

Or perhaps not. Like millions of other poor schmucks dealing with a smart phone, Mr. P. has answered his cell without realizing he's really answered it. He is still talking to Albert. Eddie is hearing Albert and Mr. P. casually conversing in the glass basketball court Mr. P. calls his living room.

Their booming voices resonate like Norse gods, holding deep converse in the gilded wooden halls of Valhalla. Eddie listens in, holding his breath, balancing on one foot, pinning the phone with his free hand to his head, clasping onto the tree with the other hand, concentrating with monomaniacal attention, dodging drops and minor waterfalls that drench the interior of the tree from time to time. The two voices talk into the night.

"No, I'm fine for now. I don't want any wine, Albert. No not thirsty at all. Yes, I know Ace likes wine Albert, but that's not really the point is it? O.K. Albert. O.K. Yes, Albert, what I mean to say. Well, hell, it's all fine and good that Ace likes guys. Hey, this is the 21st century! I say, live and let live. That's my motto. God knows I did. Yes, I know, I know, you were there. But, hell, Al, hell. What can I say? All I want is grandkids. Is that so much? Grandkids? Let him get married first, do his duty, then get divorced like everyone else. His mother would've wanted that." Eddie hears a miniature version of Albert's voice cut in.

"Yes, makes sense, makes perfect sense, Paul. Really, aren't you thirsty? Paul? Thirsty at all?" Eddie thinks he can hear sounds like someone's walking on potato chips – a kind of loud crackling, crunching sound. Or maybe it's glass.

"There's that damned sound again, Al. Where *is* that coming from? Stand still. You'll hear it."

Mr. P. starts whispering "There's more to this story. I've been told he's *involved* already. Some local guy. No, I have no idea who. Wait, quiet, don't move, I just heard that strange noise again."

There's silence for a few moments. Then Eddie hears another potato chip being squashed. Immediately he hears a lot of them, like a potato chip slaughter. Then, almost at the same time, Albert's voice.

"Is your phone on, Paul? Look at it. I swear it just made a sound. Maybe that's the sound we're hearing. Look. Look at it, Paul." Suddenly it sounds like someone's put a microphone on a baseball as it comes into contact with a bat. Eddie's not sure, but he thinks he's deaf in his left ear.

"Damn. I dropped it. Albert" Now the voices sound like they're underwater. "Albert, there was a name flashing at me on the screen, for a second. At least I think there was. You know about this stuff. Hell, you're a college professor. I don't have my glasses on. But I don't hear anybody saying anything. Here look at it. What…" Then Mr. P. and Albert both start talking at once, and Eddie whisks his fingers across his cell screen, cuts the call and slams his phone deep into the front pocket of his fuzzy bedraggled coat.

The pocket has a bunny rabbit with long whiskers stitched across it in off-white on white. The whiskers are three-dimensional and they tickle his hand, especially on the scabs forming on the back of his hand, and it feels odd and he can't tell if he's feeling pain or pleasure anymore.

This is my life, thinks Eddie. Lost somewhere in the great betwixt and in-between. One foot on the boat, one foot on the dock. Neither fish nor fowl. Neither pain nor pleasure. He could go on for days.

When, thinks Eddie, instead of being two or three things at once, will Eddie get to be just one thing? When? He'd settle for warm right now. Well, warm and dry. That's two things, Eddie. Eddie sighs and starts the long, painful trek back up the hill to Mr. P.'s house. Walking feels good, but his chest feels tight.

He gets rained on some more. He trudges on.

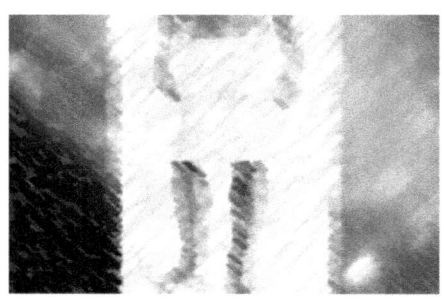

CHAPTER 13
(Saturday Night/Sunday Morning 12:34 A.M., Eddie at Mr. P.'s House on Twin Peaks)

Many minutes later, Eddie rings Mr. P.'s doorbell. He does it again. Then he sits back and waits. It's all taking quite a while. But then again, it is a big house. Eddie knows it well. Maybe he should check the back door. Or the garage side door. Does he remember the entry code? But first Eddie checks his voicemail, not really expecting to get a message from Mr. P., but you never could tell, and picks up a message from his friends Adam and Alice, who sound like they're at a noisy bar and inviting, no demanding that Eddie "get his ass out in the rain and down here pronto, brainy-boy." That was Alice's voice.

Adam cuts in. "Quick translation Eddie: we have a conundrum, O great brain."

Then it sounds like there's a struggle for the phone, and Alice comes back on "Conundrum my ample behind. Don't listen to a word... "

A silence, then Alice once more, "Hey, I know you're not sneaking off with my beer again, Deb... Did you just try and knock this phone out of my hands, girl?"

There's a lot of thumping going on then, Adam comes on one last time "If you're not down here soon, you'll be bailing a bunch of us out of City jail – but then, that's one of your many talents, huh, Eddie? Just come…"

Then it sounds like the phone is flying through the air. Then the message ends. He smiles. He notices he has six more messages, wait, the next screen is full of them too, there must be dozens, all in the last thirty minutes, and they are all from Ace, and each one seems to be desperately requesting a status update on Eddie's plans. He's listening to the last one when the door creaks open and querulous voice calls out "Who is it?"

It's Albert. He stands, peering out, trouble knitting his brows, a frown buried in his uncombed beard, looking from Eddie's cell phone to another phone in his hands and then out the front door again.

"Did you just ring the doorbell? Or did you just ring us up on the phone?" Eddie has to bite his lip, he loves Albert's British accent so much.

Eddie swipes his phone off and slides it into his wet front pocket again in one swift move. "Both, actually, Mr. Barnard. Would you be so good as to allow me to enter?" Albert steps aside, pointing with one arm towards the inside of the house, but looks at him in a mildly irritated way, as if he's just remembering something vague but unpleasant - something he'd managed to forget and now it's all coming back to him and it involves this Eddie person standing in front of him.

Eddie smiles weakly and sidles past. Eddie has got to stop. He has got to stop. It's the Dickens thing. Eddie's going to get in trouble. He sounds like a bad Merchant Ivory film. But Albert sounds so adorable. He's got to stop. He's just got to stop. Eddie looks up and over at Albert, who is standing motionless with his arm in the air. Eddie realizes he's been talking to himself out loud. He tries smiling again. Albert blinks twice, then lowers his arm and closes the door. Eddie thinks he can hear him say "Adorable!" and "Americans!" under his breath.

Albert's looking Eddie up and down and shaking his head.

"Good. Well then, my boy. Don't let's stand here waiting on ceremony. Come on up. Paul's just on the next level. Interesting costume, by the way. What are you supposed to be?" All Eddie can think to do is smile again. Albert grunts "Yes. Well. Up you go."

and he points directly ahead of them at some spiral stairs, seemingly made from irregular chunks of clear glass, held together with globs of library paste. Albert makes a beeline down a tastefully decorated hallway to the right, scurries off, and abruptly vanishes. It gets very quiet. Eddie waits. Nothing happens. He makes his way towards the disturbing staircase. He places one foot on it, then another. It's surprisingly solid. When he gets near to the top, Albert is peering down at him, tapping his foot. There's a large and very full glass of red wine in his hands. He's smiling.

"Back stairs. Kitchen. I loathe that transparent monstrosity. Thirsty?" Albert whips another full, red glass from behind his back, hands it to Eddie with a proud smile not unmixed with victory, and they both, the two of them slide, while Albert sips, across a large flawless floor of white wood towards an impressively muscular back with flowing white hair. It turns around, and Eddie comes face to face with Mr. P.

Albert is smiling from ear to ear. Mr. P. is distracted. He has that look he gets sometimes when he's been arguing with somebody. Bloodthirsty. And Albert looks like he wants to torture someone, anyone. These two. Worse than teenage sisters. One minute they're fighting the whole planet, backs against the wall, just these two against the world. The next minute they've got knives in their hands and are dueling each other to the death.

Eddie's sure not jumping into the middle of that. Eddie steps back to give them both a little more brawling room.

"I say, Paul, *you* didn't want any wine, did you?"

"Wine, Albert?"

"Yes. Wine. Want any, Paul?"

"Well, let me see…"

"It's red, Paul."

"Oh, well…wine, red wine? hmmm?"

"Yes, Paul, because, you see, if you *had* wanted some, I'm sorry to tell you, there's none left."

"Really? None? Are you sure about that, Al?"

"Well, Paul, Let me put it this way…"

"Yes, tell me Albert…"

Eddie forces his way into the conversation, just to get it moving someplace – somewhere - anywhere.

"Here, have my glass, sir, I haven't had any yet. I'm fine, really. Thanks." Albert frowns at Eddie. Mr. P. smiles and takes the glass.

Eddie makes sure not to notice Albert, but nods at Mr. P. who nods back. Eddie nods again. Puzzled, Mr. P. nods, starts to comment on the wine. Albert starts to make a wine comment of his own. Eddie cautiously forges ahead, politely interrupting what looks like the opening moves of a violent and ferocious verbal game of chess.

"But, sir, did you know that your son Ace, I mean William returned from Los Angeles? Just arrived back tonight."

That stops them both in their tracks, in mid comment. Albert's busy smiling and quaffing, observing Paul. Paul's is rotating his body slowly in mid-sentence and turning his gaze on Eddie. Eddie feels like a small primitive mammal that has just acquired the full attention of a T-Rex. Eddie starts to break out in a sweat.

"Ace is back? Are you sure? Absolutely sure Edward? I haven't heard a word from him. Are you dripping all over my floor?"

"Uh, Yes, sir. And, yes sir. He's back here in The City. I just saw him."

"Just now? Could they have settled that damned lawsuit so quickly? Look, Edward, we can't have you warping the substrate. I'd have to pull up half the floor to resurface this living room. Check the hall linen closet, and grab a towel and do whatever you have to do to get dry. Thank you, Edward. I appreciate it Edward. We'll wait on you, don't' worry. Take your time. Take your time, Edward. No, don't mention it. Thanks. We'll be waiting. Thanks."

Eddie hustles off down the hall, hearing Mr. P.'s gratitude getting fainter and fainter. And as he's hanging his clothes (well, Charley's clothes) out to dry in the bathroom, and folding multiple towels, and then a blanket towel around his white, wet, and wrinkled body, Eddie's tries to figure out what he's doing here tonight.

What's he going to do? He hears Mr. P. and Albert arguing about something, then laughing. It's not a happy laugh. What? What will Eddie do? They're arguing again. Then another laugh. This is getting him nowhere. He can't stay in this bathroom until morning. He's got to do something.

So he calls Alice.

"So, why aren't you here, Eddie, why? I keep on asking myself that question." Eddie hears someone in the background yelling "Give 'em hell, Alice".

"Alice, I can't stop now. I've got to see this thing through. I'm at Mr. Periphanitides house, right now. And I'm soaked to the skin. And I need to trick, well, let's be honest, steal more money from old man Periphanitides. And that's not going to be easy. And I need a plan. And I don't have a plan. And I'm fucked, Alice, I'm fucked."

"It's dry where we are, Eddie-boy. Water-wise. Alcohol-wise is another story. You know, Eddie, you've got me thinking. It's too bad you couldn't get Mr. P. interested in some girl, like Ace got interested in those boys. Like father, like son. Get him hooked up with a young girl that would want to spend a lot of his money, and if you could siphon some of that money off, before she got her hands on it, you'd have it made, buddy boy."

Eddie hears someone calling out, down the hall "Edward? Are you all right, Edward?"

"Just a moment, Mr. Periphanitides."

"It's Albert, Edward, not Paul. Are you sure you're all right? My there's a lot of water in this hallway, isn't there? Edward?"

"Wait, Alice, who was that young guy, the one that wrecked that banker's car you guys fixed at the garage, the one that moved back to Florida, or wherever he was from? What was his name, again?"

"Oh, I know who you mean. Was his name Fulk?"

"Edward? Are you there?"

"Yeah, what I need is a guy, not a girl. A guy who's not there."

"Edward?"

"Alice, I gotta go."

"Well, birthday boy, you're not making a lot of sense, but you're sounding like you think you're making sense. Which is progress. I guess. Keep me posted. And get down here and get drunk and that's an order. You hear?"

"Edward? Edward? I was sure you were in the bathroom."

"I'll talk to you later, Alice. Thanks again, Alice. Bye."

Eddie arranges his towels about his body. He resembles a walking pile of laundry. So… Maybe Fulk would help. Maybe Fulk could be Ace's new boyfriend, and somehow, Mr. P. would pay for him to leave the city. Maybe. Maybe not. A very shaky and tenuous scheme. A scheme that everyone will see through, in a matter of seconds. One that could, possibly, get him in a lot more trouble. One that's sure to fail. Eddie likes it immediately.

He takes a deep breath. He'll have to start slowly, and build carefully. The important thing is never to show fear. Mr. P. can smell a hint of fear in a conversation as accurately as a shark smells a single drop of blood dissolving in the middle of the Pacific. Mr. P. lives with, for, by, and on fear.

Eddie carefully assumes a blank, helpful expression and a blank, helpful attitude in his mind. "I am calm. I am insignificant. I am harmless. No use paying attention to me." He tries to breathe in and out and slow himself down, but his lungs are bunching up – they're as tight as a drum. He puffs himself with his inhaler and stands waiting for it to take effect. The bathroom door cracks open. A face peers tentatively in. It's Albert. Eddie motions with his inhaler at his chest and doesn't say a word.

"Oh, Edward, I'm sorry. I hope you feel better. Is there anything I can do?"

Well, yes, thinks Eddie, yes I think there *is* something you can do. He hopes he didn't say it out loud this time.

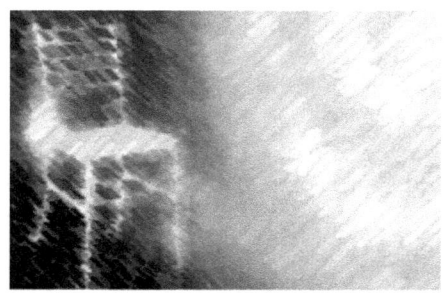

CHAPTER 14
(Saturday Night/Sunday Morning 12:48 A.M.,
Eddie at Mr. P.'s House on Twin Peaks)

Brandishing his three towels, and his blanket towel Eddie enters the living room, speaking. Albert comes padding in after him.

"Sir? I've been thinking. About Ace that is. Well, I don't know sir, I don't know if they've finished the lawsuit yet down in Los Angeles. I only saw him for a moment this evening. Just for a second. But he was looking good. Very good."

Mr. P. smiles at Eddie, and then smiles at Albert, who looks at the two of them with the merest hint of confusion starting to rise in his eyes. Maybe a little panic. Albert looks miffed. Eddie can tell. Albert can see something's afoot, and he, Albert, will probably become involved. Involvement and trouble – that's Albert's future. Eddie can see him working all this out.

Eddie watches Albert, who is sneaking a look down at Eddie's bare feet. Naked men are obviously not the usual for Albert after a concert. Albert moodily slurps his wine and watches. Eddie can see him squinting his eyes and mentally bracing himself.

Eddie lowers his voice a bit, as if it's possible he's betraying a confidence and leans forward. Paul leans in. Albert reluctantly leans in, and forgets to sip. Eddie continues in a whisper

"Ace looked like he had a lot of money. Dripping in an expensive diamond watch the size of a small plate on his right wrist, a huge stud earring in his left ear, matching emerald gold rings, lion rings if I'm not mistaken, on the middle finger of each hand. Some kind of gold necklace thing too, maybe not. I didn't see him for very long. Oh and, I thought I saw the new car, also. I'd assumed you'd given him all that." Mr. P. stops leaning. He looks dazed. He talks to Eddie, but looks at Albert. As if he's looking for support.

"No, no, the car was traded. Temporarily. Another subsidiary of mine. Ace had the title, but you know about all that – it's the Tesla – got to return that this next week. And get back the town car. We should make a little money on that transaction. Make a note of that, Edward. But I'm sure you already have. As for the rest…"

"Uh, well, sir, uh, Ace was uh, getting a lot of attention in the Castro. Guys were uh, crawling all over him."

"Really." Mr. P. is silent for a moment, then opens his mouth to speak, then closes it again. He opens his mouth to finally say something to Albert, and Eddie knows that he's beginning to lose Mr. P. It's all going to fall apart. Right here. Right now. Think. He has got to find some way of cranking up the heat. Bring it to a full boil. Make things start to happen. Do it, Eddie, do it.

He jumps forward, between Mr. P. and Albert, trying to catch Mr. P.'s eye. Albert almost jumps out the window. Albert spills half his wine on himself. He daubs at it with his handkerchief. Muttering something about nudity and American abruptness.

"Excuse me, Mr. Barnard. Sorry Mr. Barnard. Yes, sir. Lots of people out tonight." Albert glares at Eddie, and works his handkerchief and whispers to himself.

"Why, sir, as I was walking from the Muni stop at the Castro, I saw him waiting there, all of them and that guy. Just waiting. That guy. And all of them. Right there. Waiting. He and all of them."

"I'm sorry, Edward." Mr. P. turns slowly away from Albert. "What are you talking about? He and all of whom?"

"The new guy's friends. His gang. And the new guy himself. The new guy Ace has fallen for here in San Francisco. The guy he wants to pamper and coddle with what's left of his inheritance. That guy. That Fulk guy. Fulk, uh, Fulk Faulkner."

Albert looks enthralled, but Eddie notices he has the good

manners to pretend to sip the tiny amount of liquid left in his glass and peer out at the windows at the fog. He's stuffing his red-stained handkerchief into his vest pocket. Strangely, Albert, after he looks out the windows for a few moments, seems to grow pale, his face turns a greenish color and he looks like he's more than a little dizzy.

Paul paces silently in front of Albert, as Albert sways a little from side to side. Paul looks deflated. Albert tips his glass back, finds nothing and flies across the living room, skips down the hallway to the right, hell bent for leather. Eddie hears him flying down the back stairs. Mr. P. watches astonished.

Eddie watches Mr. P. closely. Mr. P. is silent for quite awhile. Then he looks up, with a sad, questioning look on his face.

"Ah. I knew it. I knew it. I could tell Ace was up to something. I just didn't know what."

Mr. P. falls silent again. Eddie lets him stew.

Eddie hears someone coming up behind him down the hallway to the right. Mr. P. looks up. Eddie figures he'd better take the employer-bull by the horns, so to speak. And wrestle him to the floor. Eddie likes that image. Eddie calls out to Mr. P. just as Albert reappears.

"Sir. The guy, this Fulk guy, he looked great too – dressed like a million bucks."

"Well, at least Fulk's making a good impression" says Albert taking a long swig of wine. Albert doesn't notice a murderous scowl winging in his direction from Mr. P.

Mr. P. turns from Albert and sighs in an anxious, overwrought way which was not like him, not at all. Eddie senses a win in his future.

"What was this Fulk person dressed in? Did it look... costly?" Eddie waits, counting to five, before he answers.

"Well, sir, I couldn't tell exactly. He, Fulk that is, and his posse moved around so much, and they were all wearing such great clothes. I don't know - maybe some Moji Kamamoto, some Van Der Vriess, Van Oskar too, definitely some Jean Pierre Daumier. I thought one shirt was Alex Arnaud, but I couldn't be sure. No, it was Batanstok. Of course, some Saint Cristoffe and Devish Aschar. A pair of pants was David Karol. You know, sir. Stuff like that. You'll be glad to know they all made quite the impression. All of them. I don't know how much things like that cost, but even if only some of the money that paid for it came from you, well from Ace that is, then you should be proud. Proud, Mr. Periphanitides.

"Proud…" echoes Mr. P., not sounding proud at all.

"But I'm sure you paid for all of it, sir. That stuff is incredibly expensive. Like buying cars. Mind boggling prices. Like I said, you should be proud."

"Well, well, well" says Albert. He's clearly enjoying himself, rocking back and forth on his heels as he drinks in small, civilized gulps from his newly-filled glass.

"Then, sir, I heard two guys, dressed I might say, in much cheaper clothes, obviously off the rack, probably from Gent's Dress for Less, you know, well, they were all talking under a streetlight, over by where Ace's car was double-parked. I couldn't quite hear everything they said… but…"

"Edward, tell me what you heard."

"Well, I knew they were talking about Ace, and…"

"And… don't leave out any details, Edward. Please. Don't' spare my feelings. Don't. Go on, Edward, go on…"

"Well, sir, one leaned back and the first one whispered into the ear of the second one…"

"What? What?" says Albert, who is obviously forgetting again, to pretend to sip at anything at all. This evening is turning out to be quite the success for Albert. Albert's looking happier and happier he came over. Eddie can see Albert scowling briefly at his nude feet from time to time, but clearly, Albert is eager to hear the rest of Eddie's story. Albert speaks in a series of gasps.

"Don't stop now, boy, not now. What?"

"Patience. Patience. I'll tell you. They were whispering, we were in heavy traffic, and I was yards away. It wasn't easy to overhear, you can be sure of that."

"I'm sure it wasn't Edward, and we won't interrupt you anymore", says Mr. P. with a cautionary glance towards Albert, "go on."

Albert harrumphs into his glass and sprays himself with wine. They all wait in awkward silence for a few minutes as Paul and Albert make their way down to the kitchen to get a wet towel to clean Albert up. Eddie watches out the window, trying to think of something to say next.

They return. As Albert rubs and scrapes away at his tweed jacket with one hand, balancing his re-filled wine glass in the other,

Eddie waits politely. It's difficult for Eddie to tell which stains are new, which are old and what the original pattern in the tweed may have been before all the staining occurred – but Eddie supposes Albert knows what he's doing. About that time, Albert looks up in consternation and Eddie realizes he's talked out loud again. This time Eddie smiles and blushes. Albert glares. Eddie looks over at Mr. P., whose expression is patently neutral, but who may be hiding a discreet smile under that patrician set of facial features.

Albert finishes his wiping, Mr. P. nods at Eddie in an encouraging way and Eddie takes a deep breath and continues.

"The first one said to the second one something like this. - you probably know already, that guy over there, Fulk, he's luckier than shit, he's going to marry a rich fucker' - excuse the expression Mr. P. I'm just repeating what I heard – then the second one said – 'who are you talking about? Which guy?.' Then the first one said – 'William Ace Periphanitides, the multi-millionaire's son, that's who!' So, what do you think Mr. P.?"

"I'm ruined, Edward. That's what I think. I'm sunk. I'm done for. I'm finished. Why does everyone know all there is to know about my family but me? Why am I always the last to know? First I gain a new son. Then I lose my first son. When does it stop? When does it all stop?"

"Wait, there's more."

"There is?" says Mr. P. weakly.

"Then, the second one said – 'how do you know all this?' The first one said – 'I have a friend who's got a friend who's married to a lawyer, Ace has to pay for a settlement in a divorce first for that Fulk guy, the guy in the Kamamoto suit over there. After that, Ace can get married. It's going to cost him a fortune to do it! He must really love that guy. It's all legal. Documents an inch thick." That's what the first one said. Word for word.

"Is that all?" breathes out Mr. P. in what is for all practical purposes one long sighing exhalation.

"Well, just that the first one said the document looked pretty official. And the dollar amounts mentioned were pretty large."

Mr. P. moans. He looks at Albert. He groans. He leans against a porcelain table that looks like a white spider web and crunches down on something. As the crunching sound ricochets in the tall, barn-like living room, Albert almost spills all his wine again. Albert drops his rag on the floor, puts his glass next to it and rushes over to Mr. P. Mr. P. droops. Albert lightly patting him, in kind of a nervous syncopation on the shoulder tries to encourage him somewhat. Mr. P. moans softly to himself. He sways a bit.

"Here, here, we'll think of something Paul. But we'd better do it with all due dispatch. That means rapidly, Paul." Paul glares at Albert momentarily, then starts swaying again.

"Daumier. Clothes by Daumier."

Albert looks worried. Mr. P. is looking more than just a little discomforted. He's looking ill. "Paul? Paul? Remember, Ace, that is William is sure to show up here tomorrow, Sunday, if he's already here. And Sunday started an hour ago now. Whatever you're going to do, you'd better do it right away." Mr. P. is opening one eye, then the other, then closing both and squeezing them shut. Albert is looking alarmed. He motions towards the center of the room.

"Perhaps a chair, Paul? Would that be in order?"

"And a Batanstok, Albert? What in the hell is a Batanstok? Tell me Albert. A Batanstok. What is it, Albert? What is it? What? What? Oh, Albert."

Eddie clears his throat. Albert looks aghast. Mr. P. seems to have lost his center of gravity. His oscillations are becoming greater and greater. Albert follows him around the room, prodding him towards the vertical when he can. Mr. P.'s voice is barely a whisper now.

"Albert, we've got to buy back the Kamamoto. Or sell it. I don't know what the hell it is, but we've got to find it and get it back and sell it and as God is my witness…. Oh, it's all going to cost me, Albert. I know it will. As usual. But this time it will break me. Cost. Break. Break. Cost. Help me Albert."

Mr. P.'s mouth is moving, but no sound is coming out. He starts to wobble, then to sag, preparatory to a total collapse onto the hard, pale parquet-like flooring. Albert, seeing no chair in sight, obviously watching in consternation, jumps in behind him at the last minute, almost stepping on the mostly full wine glass he left on the floor, and props him up, grunting and breathing heavily.

Then Albert too succumbs. He's looking more and more exasperated, and starts to sink beneath their combined weight. The floor grows nearer and nearer. Eddie clears his throat again, louder this time. Both Mr. P. and Albert look around, hesitantly, panting and puffing, apparently hardly seeing Eddie standing there in front of the two of them, wrapped in his complicated layers of towels

"I might be of some help, possibly, sir."

Albert holding Mr. P. up by his armpits motions with his head for Eddie to come closer. Albert rolls his eyes at Eddie to grab an arm. He lets go of one side, as Eddie throws Mr. P.'s other arm over Eddie's toweled shoulder. Mr. P. drapes himself gracefully between the two of them like a cable of the Golden Gate Bridge hanging between two support towers.

He is stable. Albert however, honking and gasping with every breath, glaring alternately at Eddie and Mr. P., Albert wobbles and quivers. His knees are shaking. The three of them stand that way for a minute or so. Mr. P., seems to be resting easily, and actually appears to be recovering. Albert's face is getting redder and redder.

Things are looking up for Eddie. Eddie figures this is the time to start the conversational ball rolling again.

"But first, tell me what you think we ought to do, each of you. I'll listen. I'm sure you both must already have a plan. If I had my phone with me, I'd take notes. Wait, I'll get it. I'll just be a second. It's in the bathroom. I won't be long, I promise. After you're done, telling me your thoughts, I'll summarize for you, add any thoughts of my own, and then, well, we can go ahead and make a plan. Back in a moment."

"No, no, wait. Please, Edward. Please, be my guest. You speak first. No need to get your phone" says Albert, huffing and puffing as he supports Mr. P. and looks in vain for any nearby piece of furniture designed for sitting. Albert doesn't look like he's breathing at all anymore. Eddie hears him muttering "Surely a sofa exists in this place. Surely at least a chair. But no."

"You'll laugh" says Eddie, starting to pace in a small circle, making tiny revolutions around the two of them. Albert is trying to follow Eddie with his eyes. He's not doing too well. Mr. P.'s eyes are closed, but Eddie can tell he's listening.

Eddie flings his one blanket towel over his shoulder like a toga and re-adjusts his many remaining towels. He walks confidently back and forth, back and forth. He appears to be deep in thought. And the truth is, Eddie is. Once again he has no idea what he's going to say next. Well, that's not quite true, he has *some* idea. Albert wheezes in Eddie' direction. He coughs. He tries to get Eddie's attention.

"No, Eddie, I won't. I won't laugh. I can promise you that." Albert is searching efficiently and desperately with his eyes over the entire room. Eddie sees his eyes go wide when he finally spies a tiny chair hiding behind a table over by the wall of windows.

"Help me <huff> maneuver <puff> towards <huff> <puff>chair, Eddie."

Eddie pulls the two men forward, attempting to hold onto his numerous towels, which he is starting to shed, as both Mr. P. and Albert grab at him for support.

"No, really, Mr. Barnard, Mr. Periphanitides, sir, one of you go first. I'd like to hear what you're thinking"

"Go <huff> on <puff>. Oh my! Have you gained weight Paul?" Albert can barely talk.

Mr. P. makes no answer. He's obviously in misery. He wants them to know about it. His eyes are still closed. The three of them struggle, and bump and bash their way through the living room. They nearly tip over the chair. It's an ingenious chrome and steel single-seat artistic reconstruction of the new Bay Bridge, cables and wires everywhere surrounding a small basket-like perch. Eddie thinks you'd need an instruction booklet just to operate it.

When they get there, Albert can't seem to help himself, he collapses into it. It sways and groans, musically, as wires tense and supporting structures bend. Mr. P. opens his eyes. Albert is seated, wiping his forehead with a large limp handkerchief. He's smiling up at Mr. P. Mr. P. is not smiling back. Eddie watches them both, pondering furiously.

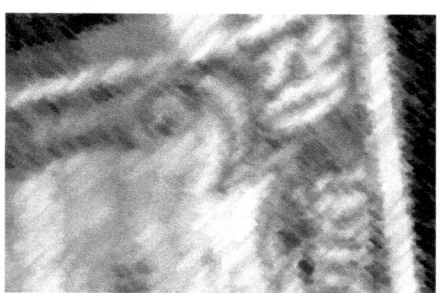

CHAPTER 15
(Saturday Night/Sunday Morning 1:09 A.M.,
Eddie at Mr. P.'s House on Twin Peaks)

Mr. P.'s rueful look seems to force Albert to struggle to his feet again. Mr. P. sits down in the now empty chair. Albert sways in front of him. Eddie begins pacing once more.

Paul watches Eddie, and stands up again. He looks over-wrought and agitated and seems to have forgotten completely about the chair. Albert looks yearningly from chair to Mr. P. to Eddie to the chair. Gradually the look becomes mournful. Eddie walks and walks.

Abruptly Eddie stops directly in front of Mr. P. and Albert. A halt so dramatic, it startles the swaying Albert and he falls backward and almost lands on the chair. It's a near miss. Albert squarely hits the floor. Mr. P. waits, frowning, eyebrows drawn low over his eyes.

Albert watches from the floor. As he struggles to get up Eddie can hear Albert whispering to himself again, but it doesn't sound like Albert. It sounds like he's spiritually channeling someone else. Someone who works in a dockyard. "Don't mind bleeding Albert. He's fine, he is. Don't mind him." Eddie looks at Mr. P.

Mr. P nods at Eddie to start talking, as Mr. P. helps Albert up.

And Eddie nods back, slowly. Eddie can feel himself stalling. He's just fooling himself. Why did he think this was going to work? What was he thinking? Mr. P. watches Eddie. He's beginning to look suspicious. There's a hint of impatience, a suggestion of disgruntlement forming on his face. Eddie takes a deep breath, as deep as he can manage under the circumstances, and jumps in before it's too late.

"It's simple, sir – marry Ace off to some other guy. Leave Mr. Fancy Clothes Fulk hanging high and dry."

There's an awkward and prolonged silence. Mr. P. looks over at Eddie then turns to look at Albert (who's not quite up all the way yet), offering Albert both his hands. Eddie can tell, Mr. P. is cogitating. He looks pained. He shakes his head, looking beseechingly at Albert.

"Grandkids?" blurts out Mr. P pathetically.

"Adoption" says Albert with the firm but gentle voice of a teacher. He straightens up, adjusts his jacket, runs his hand through his beard, then seems to drift off in thought. Mr. P. looks over at Eddie, questioning, but not convinced.

Eddie nods once in wise agreement. Then he nods a couple of times more - for extra measure, and to provide positive behavioral reinforcement. But Mr. P. does not seem bowled over. Mr. P. tries to look severe. He tries to glare at Eddie.

But he just can't do it. Mr. P. sags. He seems oddly uncommunicative. And pale. Albert's starting to look green and unwell generally also.

"All right. All right. I'm ready to do anything at this point" says Mr. P. wilting even more noticeably.

"Well, I'm sure Ace will be showing up tomorrow, so we'd have to move fast." says Eddie.

"How do you know?" says Albert, falling back into the chair. Albert squirms a little bit, the chair squeaks. The chair's obviously not the most comfortable place to rest. But Albert's apparently discovering it's better than the floor.

"Someone told me."

"Who?" says Albert, leaning backward and briefly opening his eyes wide. Then Albert rests his head against the tiny metal headrest cantilevered off the back of the seat, and half-closes his eyes. Eddie doesn't answer, hoping everyone will forget the question.

Mr. P. stares pointedly at Albert. Albert catches the look-of-death this time from Mr. P., but doesn't seem to have the energy left to react properly. Albert drifts off to sleep. He seems not to hear the chair's wild keening cry as Albert's weight shifts slowly from right to left. Metal makes a sobbing sound as if it's being wrenched in two.

"Then what can I do?" says Mr. P., looking at Eddie, giving up on Albert. Eddie thinks "And here we go…"

"Well, if I were you, I'd pretend to be in love with this new guy Fulk Faulkner myself. I'd give him an extravagant gift - one that couldn't be mistaken for anything other than the wildest form of infatuation. I think Mr. Faulkner has some kind of legal problems. You could help Fulk, in a very significant way monetarily, you could be doing something like that. I think. A gesture. A gesture like that." Eddie ends on what he hopes is a hopeful, upbeat note. Mr. P.'s face is unreadable.

"Extravagant gifts? A gesture? To a young man?"

"You'd be doing it for Ace. And for yourself. I'd do it, if I were you, Mr. P."

"You would, would you? Well. Edward. It's just a good thing you aren't me, Edward. A good thing. That's completely unacceptable. Completely. Don't bring it up again."

"A… good… thing…" says Albert, nodding off, falling to one side. Cables and plates cry out as the center of gravity shifts now to the right. The chair's left legs begin to leave the floor.

"I think, sir, this is the only way – the quickest way to redirect your son's affections. He won't compete with you, sir. I know that."

Albert's head falls forward onto his chest. The chair touches down on the floor again with a bang. Albert looks up startled. Everyone is staring at him.

"Well, Eddie, maybe so, maybe so" says Albert quickly. He looks confused. Then he looks asleep.

"Maybe… maybe…" says Albert, his head dropping forward again, this time to the right. There's more metallic squealing, more chair legs leaping off the ground as if they were taking flight.

Mr. P. quickly and gently pushes Albert, so that all four legs are safely resting once again on blond hardwood. He shakes his head, smiling a lopsided smile.

"You know, Eddie, Albert's a good egg. He may be difficult at times, but then again, who isn't? It's hard to believe we met in college. So long ago. Albert was there the first time I went out with Veronica."

Mr. P. leaves his hand on Albert's shoulder, and watches Albert falling asleep.

Eddie leans forward "Sir?"

"The only way, Edward? You think so?" Mr. P. holds his hand on Albert's back, but the chair still bounces up and down on its suspension cables every few seconds, in rhythm to Albert's slow, sonorous breathing. Suddenly Albert chokes, snores, and snorts for a second, then comes to. He sees everyone is looking at him again.

"Well, what should I say? What can I say?" Albert says, looking hopefully from Eddie's face to Paul's and back again. "Hmmm?"

Eddie continues. "Then, Ace will forget all about him, and you can get Ace hitched to whichever or whoever person you want, sir."

"Whomever you want" says Albert, blinking and rubbing his eyes.

"Oh, all right, Edward. All right. What a life-saver you are, Edward, what a jewel! How would I get on without you?" Mr. P. is watching Albert, who looks like he may be falling head over heels out of the chair entirely.

"Just one more thing, sir. You don't have to actually give the money yourself, in person." Mr. P. looks up sharply from Albert towards Eddie.

"Oh. I don't, do I?"

"No, you don't. In fact you won't."

"I won't?"

"You're a trifle confusing, you know that, don't you Edward?" says Albert, rocking gently in his chair. His eyes start to close.

"You'll see…" says Eddie, then he pauses. "So… what we want is to make sure the person giving the gift is something of a mystery. Fulk can't think it's Ace giving him the money. Or someone related to Ace. He's got to forget all about Ace. The key is, this new boyfriend Fulk Faulkner can't know he's being tricked. Mr. Faulkner's got to think someone else is interested in him. Someone who's not a Periphanitides. We'll fool him, and we'll bring Fulk back to your new house. No one will know your Ace's father. But we have to find someone who's not a Periphanitides to bring him over here."

"Not a Periphanitides? Why?" says Mr. P.

"Well. This is the great part of my plan, sir. It's because, I know of a banker, a kind of pirate captain of the banking industry type, who is crazy about this Fulk Faulkner guy. And, if we're careful sir, I can get the banker to give me money to help out Fulk, say I bailed Fulk out of jail and need to be reimbursed. Then, I'll just give all of the banker's money to you, and you, sir, will be reimbursed for your extravagant outlay, your expensive gesture. The banker won't know.

"But that leaves me with the boy. And won't the banker want to be reunited with him? Won't he? Go on, Edward, go on."

"Well, sir, we'll arrange a chance meeting here at the house. After I get the money from the banker, you'll hand Fulk over. Fulk is gone."

Mr. P. looks like he's considering it. Eddie plunges forward.

"So, sir, that way, you maneuver your son Ace away from this guy Fulk, but it costs you nothing out of pocket. You get it for free. You give me or someone the money, then a few days later, I get all the money back, except from someone else. Then Fulk disappears. You're happy. Ace is happy. The banker is happy. Even this young guy Fulk is happy. Everyone's happy."

"Happy, happy, happy" says Albert to himself.

"Perfect, Eddie. You amaze me. You delight me. I'm going to have to give you a raise, a substantial one."

"Why thank you sir."

"There's just one catch, Edwards. Where can I find someone to deliver these extravagant gifts and pick up that that silly young man, Fulk Faulkner is it? Yes, Fulk. Where can I find someone I can trust with so much money? Someone who won't gossip and blab about our little problem here? You can't pick him up, Edward. You work for me. He'd know you. He knows Ace. It can't be you."

"Well." Eddie has to think quickly now. How is he going to get his hands on the money if he's not actually carrying the money? So that he can get it to Ace in time. Where can he find someone in the next couple of hours? Where? Who? Albert kicks and sways in his chair as he snores.

Eddie blurts out "Why, Albert, of course. Albert can pick up Fulk. He can take the money."

Albert struggles, wiggles upright, struggles some more and opens one eye. "What? What was that?"

"Couldn't have found a better choice" says Mr. P., smacking Albert on his back. Albert falls out of the chair, but manages to scramble to his feet. The chair, the entire cable suspension system singing, snaps violently upwards and the chair hops three feet to one side colliding with a spider-webbish end table. A horrible grating and cracking sound, punctuated by sitar-like twanging fills the room. Mr. P. looks down. There's a pile of glass under the end table. It looks like the remains of a wine glass. The table itself has a piece broken off. It's lying off to the side by the little crystalline mound of shards.

"Oh, drat, Albert. It looks like I've broken a glass. And I've nicked my table."

"Yes, yes I believe you have" says Albert, crossing his hands happily across his ample stomach and rocking back and forth on the heels of his feet. Suddenly Albert doesn't look tired at all.

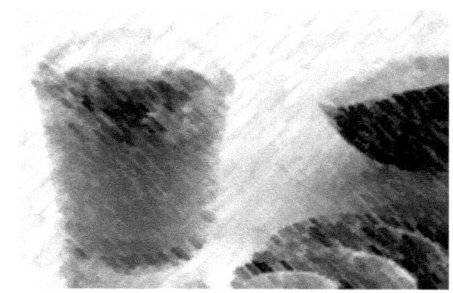

CHAPTER 16
(Saturday Night/Sunday Morning 1:37 A.M.,
Eddie Walking Down From Twin Peaks)

A half hour later, wearing some old (dry) clothes Mr. P. lent him, which hang on Eddie like expensive, preppy curtains, Eddie walks down a steep hill, and ponders. The fog is still there. The rain is not. The streets are wet and glowing. Eddie hails a taxi, gets inside, heads for the office where he left his Vespa on Friday. Friday feels like a thousand years ago now.

What to do next? He has no idea. As usual.

His cell rings. Eddie doesn't want to answer it. But he does.

"Alice."

"Dead Meat. How are you?"

The conversation goes on in this vein for a few minutes. Alice is not happy about being stood up. Country Western music throbs in the background. Once Alice is satisfied that Eddie has been appropriately cudgeled and bludgeoned into remorse, Eddie explains about finding a fake boyfriend and getting yet more money out of Mr. P.

"Boy, this bullshit just gets more and more interesting, Eddie. So where are you going to find this fake?"

"His name is Fulk, you know, the guy that moved to Florida a week or so ago. Fulk. And I gave him a last name of Faulkner. Fulk Faulkner the fake. Yeah, yeah, I know, lame. I'm sorry, I had to think quick, on my feet. Alice, is Adam there? If *he's* still speaking to me, I wanted to ask Adam something – does he have any friends that want to make some money tomorrow? Tomorrow, meaning today, Sunday?"

Eddie hears bar stools being pushed, bodies being roughhoused. After some grunting, he hears someone being pushed towards the phone "C'mon, git over here. Git!" and then a breathless and slightly inebriated Adam coughs then laughs then coughs some more. "Alice, that last shot of Tequila went down like sand." Then more laughter. Eddie waits.

"Hey Eddie, Happy Birthday! Or was that yesterday? Is this Eddie? Where the hell are you?"

"Adam, how are you?"

"I'm good. Things are moving right along. They're moving really fast now. Faster and faster. Deb stop it. I'm talking on the phone for fuck's sake. So. Alice says you need some help. I'm free tomorrow, although I don't know what kind of shape I'll be in exactly. Just don't make it 6 A.M."

"Great. I'll call you later on."

"Well, I'm going to see you later, anyways, right? After all, it is your birthday, Eddie. This is your party. You're still coming out tonight with us, right? Eddie?"

"Right." Eddie hears someone pawing at the phone. It's Alice.

"Don't make me come out and start searching for you, O.K.? Eddie? We're moving on. I'll give you a ring when we settle down someplace new. Ah, hell. Forget it. They're calling last call. What Deb? Of course we will. Look, Eddie if you're still interested, we're heading back to my place in the Mission. Deb, get us a cab, will you honey? Nah, just one. We'll be chummy. Be talking to you, Eddie. Or should I say Dead Meat?"

Eddie doesn't have a chance to respond. The line goes dead.

He has to get his bike, and get back to Albert's place in Colma, way the hell down the peninsula, since Albert's on his way home. Mr. P. had someone drive Albert back in Albert's car. Anyways, it's a long trip. Well, it seems that way to a San Franciscan from The City. It's probably only 8 miles away. Eddie's mind is wandering. Still. Eddie has to pick up the money from Albert, after convincing Albert to give it up, and then Eddie has to find Ace. And then maybe find some sleep. And then... Eddie can't think. His brain cells are shutting down, whole sections of them falling silent, vast curtains of darkness closing fast on various portions of his cerebrum.

Eddie's worn out. He's toast. Eddie's way too old to be doing this kind of Jedi-saving-the-empire shit anymore. Eddie's cab passes an all night Donut and Chinese Food shop and Eddie has the driver wait while he jumps inside to get two cups of coffee, some cream-filled long johns and sweet and sour sukiyaki to go

At least eleven couples try to steal his cab as it sits, motor idling, waiting for Eddie to wait his turn in the long line at the counter. Yup, thinks Eddie, must be last call. No wonder he's Dead Meat now.

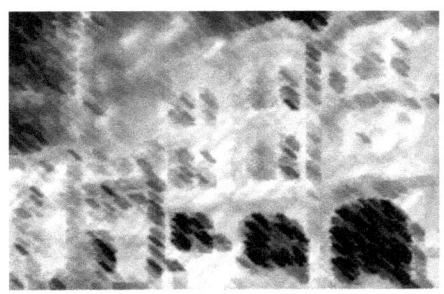

CHAPTER 17
(Saturday Night 11:45 P.M.,
Thad, Ace & Charley at Charley's Flat)

Two hours earlier, Thad is bored. He checks out his reflection in the front window (flexes his pecs beneath his new blue silk shirt - nice!) and imagines all the guys roaming the streets right now who would beg to spend time with someone who looks like that and wonders why he's still inside, listening to stale house music from last summer and answering Charley's boring questions.

Is it so wrong to want some action? He pulls his hands into a fist, flashes a secret smile and pulls his shoulders back. He watches himself again. The shirt makes him look like he's a fucking walking brick wall. A whole house. Looking good Thad-monster, in this blue shirt he looks like he's naked. It's time, Thadster, time to try out this new secret weapon on some unsuspecting hunk.

Thad looks at his tight pants, his shirt, it's a good thing Ace brought their luggage from the airport. Otherwise Thad couldn't have changed clothes and Thad could have been very, very uncomfortable. And you don't want Thad uncomfortable. Thad looks at his reflection, remembers how Eddie was copping a feel the whole way down the street, while Thad helped him out with that sore ankle. It felt O.K. In fact it felt good. That old guy Ed, he was a joke. A real card. Although, there was something about him. Yeah, he stared at Thad constantly. Who didn't? But he was cute, in his way. And word was on the street Ed had money. Word was that Eddie-boy was hung like a horse. Maybe he should give that little horsey a ride. Sometime. Not tonight though. Tonight he was looking to hook up. At least three guys. He had a lot of excess energy to work off. Thad had had a tough day. A fuckin' rough one. He has some kinks to work out. Thad smiles. His reflection smiles back. What a stud. Even Thad's impressed with himself, and Thad's hard to please. He needs to get out of here. Meet some guys. Make it happen.

"So, what are you studying now, Thaddeus? What classes?" Charley asks him from the other room.

At least she's calling him by his given name. He opens his mouth to say something, decides to take a slug of his tequila instead, and sees the time flashing on his own cell phone sitting on the sill of the window. Fuckin' A! It's almost midnight. He's been a prisoner here for a couple of hours, watching Ace from the front bay window, *not* having a conversation with Charley.

"What'd you say, Thaddeus? I didn't hear."

Maybe you didn't fucking hear because I didn't fucking say thinks Thad, but he doesn't say it out loud. He doesn't answer either. He has class. Thad just doesn't do what he doesn't want to do. Learned that from Ace. Watching Ace. Like Thad's watching now.

"Thaddeus! You still here?"

Ace can't get good reception for his cell phone in Charley's flat, so he goes outside every ten minutes and stands hunched over all sad like, totally tensed lats and bunched biceps, leaning motionless against one of the columns on the porch, punching and calling and punching and calling on his cell. Always saying the same thing, always leaving the same message. Thad stopped going down with him the fourth time. Now he just watches.

Thad wants to do something this evening besides sit at some girl's house and watch his friend self-destruct. Boring. Been there. Done that. Ace already self-destructed in L.A. with that Jay kid he flipped over. Hasn't been the same since. Love is sure embarrassing to watch.

Thad hears someone clomping across the back porch in loud shoes. "Thaddeus, you just better not be here, or I'm going to clobber you. Thad slips quickly into the hall, down the stairs, four at a time, and barely gets the front door unlocked and open before he hears Charley hit the hallway. Thad hears her stomping back across warped kitchen floorboards, back to the back porch. Thad's not sure what she's doing back there. He's not sure he really cares. He leans on the molding, leaving the door open, kicking the doorframe, watching Ace. He hears Charley clomping back up to the front of the house. She must have been checking the bathroom.

"Thaddeus! Thaddeus! Where are you? Ace, are you still here? Am I crazy? Am I just talking to myself?"

Even Charley's beginning to lose her patience. Ace is out there as usual. This time he's standing next to two girls in long coats and funky shoes who are out smoking on the front steps, giggling, looking back at Ace, swapping one-liners, and giggling again. Ace is ignoring them. He's used to all this attention, constantly, from both sexes. Thad can see his ears are icy red. They look frost-bit. His cheeks are flushed. His nose is red. Like a cartoon reindeer. His feet look numb – he keeps kicking on the steps, kicking his feet, over and over. One two kick. One two kick. Boring.

Thad closes the front door, and starts to head up the stairs, Charley's waiting for him at the top.

Thad can hear Ace even through the front door "My life is shit. It's turning to shit."

Thad pushes past Charley without saying anything and resumes his post by the window. He picks up his glass again, sips some more. He watches Ace. The girls watch Ace. Ace is watching his phone.

Abruptly Ace stuffs the beanie cap he's wearing in his back pocket and ruffles his short blond hair over and over again, jabbing at it, apparently trying to get circulation going in his scalp. He keeps on doing it the whole time he's dialing the phone again, the whole time he's listening on the phone. He does it while he's leaving the millionth message in Eddie's voice mail. He's probably sent a million texts too.

Thad notices, no matter what Ace does to himself, Ace looks gorgeous, he always looks like a million bucks. Of course, having a million bucks helps, but still. Ace looks great. And Thad's not sure what he thinks about that. Ace always makes Thad feel lesser, smaller somehow. Like now. He looks great, but he's not even trying. That's the part that Thad doesn't get - why doesn't Ace try?

Thad's trying all the time, 24-7. If he didn't try, try all the time, hey, Thad would be ordinary. Very ordinary. If Thad can do it, Why can't Ace do it? Ace just never has to work at it. Ace has never ever had to work at anything. Ace just gets stuff. Thad doesn't know what to think of that.

The girls smoking on the porch keep sneaking peeks at Ace. They start staring more blatantly when it looks like Ace is trying to beat himself up. Ace's voice starts to echo, in a funny muffled way, up and down the foggy street. Like his dad, everything he has is super-sized. He has a bullhorn amplifier instead of normal human vocal cords. Thad shakes his head. But Ace has no idea what kind of impression he makes. It's like he's blind that way or something.

Charley strides up to Thad and pulls the glass right out of his hands. Charley is ready to throw Thad out the window, no problemo. Just bam! and he'd be flying through the air.

"Didn't you hear me calling Thaddeus? Or didn't you want to hear?" Charley and Thad both remain silent for a moment as Ace yells at his phone again downstairs.

"Eddie, it's Ace. Call me, as soon as you get this. I've called like ten times man. No, twenty times at least, man. Where *are* you? Call me. Just call me." Thad sees Ace almost pitch the phone out in a long arc, a real throw from centerfield to home, but Ace stops as he notices the girls watching him wide-eyed. Thad hears giggling as Ace trudges back up the middle staircase to Charley's rented room.

Thad carefully pulls the glass from Charley's hand as Ace enters the room. Charley closes one eye, squints at him, nods to herself, says "Um hum", then turns her back, puts both hands on her hips and blocks Ace's path into the room. Ace walks around her.

"I can't take much more of this shit" Ace says as he throws himself into a well-worn, sofa-bed, whose springs complain as his solid, six-foot-plus frame hits them. He bounces back and forth aggressively, making them complain louder and louder. Charley gives him a look. A very plain and clear look. She's about to go thermonuclear on him. She's firing a warning shot across his bow. Thad puts down his glass.

Ace ignores her. "Nothing's working. Nothing. Zip. Zilch. Nada. Its' all shit. All of it." Charley doesn't even look like she heard him. Charley hasn't in fact.

"Look, "says Thad, "Eddie isn't your only option, bud. You know, I wouldn't rely on that little fucker to keep my boat afloat.

I'd have a plan A, B, C, *and* D, man." Ace keeps on bobbing back and forth. He pulls out a stick of gum and starts chewing. Ace says, between mouthfuls "It's all shit man. Shit." Charley is staring at Ace.

"Hey, easy on the furniture, Ace, that's where I'm sleeping tonight."

Ace looks up at her, chewing conspicuously and carefully, but doesn't say anything. He slows down the bouncing, but he doesn't stop.

"I mean it Ace. Stop it." Charley takes a step towards Ace, and Thad steps in between them.

"Awright. Forget the other plans. Forget Eddie. Hey, c'mon. I know what you need. It's only midnight, we can still get out and go dancing – plenty of guys out on a Saturday night. No use just sitting around here. C'mon Ace, let's get wasted someplace. Whaddyasay?"

Charley takes another step towards him and adds in a warning voice "Ace..." Ace stops chewing, spits his gum out into his hand. He stares at it as he mutters loudly.

"What great friends. What great friends I have. Always thinking of other people. Never of themselves." Ace looks up. "Thad, really, do I *look* like I want to go out tonight? How about you coming up with a plan B, C, or even D, huh? How about you doing something useful for once, huh? Big guy?" Ace looks out the window. Thad watches him, cautiously. Ace looks back at his hand with the gum in it. "Nothing. I didn't think so." He stares out the window, pulls out his phone, checks to see it's on, starts to ricochet off the sofa like it's a trampoline.

"That's it, Ace. Get off the couch. Off." Ace stops bouncing, gets up, and starts walking up and down the front hall.

Charley stands and talks at his retreating back. She's talking softly, but you can hear her, she sounds as if she's underlining every word three times with a red pencil.

"It always comes down to this, doesn't it, Ace? Me wanting... You walking... It's never going to change is it, Ace? It's never going to change. Unless I do something." Ace yells back over his shoulder.

"And you Charley, have I ever asked you for money before?" He's pacing. They can hear his voice down the hall, by the kitchen, seconds later he resurfaces at the door to the living room/bedroom again.

"You're a mean son of a bitch, tonight Ace." Charley looks over at Thad as she says this.

"Both of you, worthless." Ace's voice disappears again into the darkness.

Thad looks at Ace, as Ace walks away again down the hall, then looks at Charley and shrugs. He figures he better make things up a little with Charley. Besides he's been an asshole too, and he doesn't feel like getting into a fight. Not now. Not tonight. Thad does not want to fight. Thad wants to get laid. Multiple times. Thad just has to figure out how. First, he has to get out of this dump.

Thad gets up and follows Ace out, saying over his shoulder, "You know how he is, when he gets like this, Charley."

"I know, but I don't have to like it."

"Yeah, sorry for bringing him over. Maybe we should get out of here. Maybe I should get out of here, before he picks a fight with me too. Getting drunk is seeming like less and less of a good idea ."

"Is that so?" Charley starts picking up glasses, she turns off the music. She heads back with her hands full to the kitchen. She doesn't look like she wants to talk much anymore.

Charley's back at the same space Ace always gets her to – a room full of pain. Charley's looking at the clock, wondering how quickly she can get rid of the two of them and get some sleep. If she can get to sleep at all tonight, her hands are shaking she's so wound up.

Charley has an oil painting due Monday first thing, in class. She's going to have to work all day Sunday to get it in any shape whatsoever to show. She turns on the faucet in the sink and starts slamming dishes and glasses around. She stops herself after she breaks a saucer. Then a glass. Then two glasses. Damn that Ace. And damn that punk Thad while she's at it.

She walks back into the hallway to see what they're up to. They're too quiet. It feels like someone's taking a cheese grater to her nerves. She's either going to burst into tears, or throw someone down the stairs. Or both. Both sounds like a good idea.

Thad intercepts Ace as he turns around in the hallway, and links his arm in his.

"Hey, Ace, why don't we try my phone out on the front porch? See if I can get a hold of old Eddie."

Ace cocks his head at a funny angle, looks back up at Charley as they walk past the kitchen and Charley's back and head down the stairs. Something crashes in the kitchen sink. Then a couple of more things. A second later Charley flies out and watches them heading towards the stairs.

Ace starts to drop his gum on the floor. Charley almost backslaps him. Thad stops. Charley has a hand out, practically sticking Ace in the eye. Thad sees now the hand has a Kleenex on it. "Drop it.. Here." Ace does.

And then Thad and Ace are descending the stairs again, clomping on the hollow hardwood in a weird syncopated rhythm together, and Charley's not even waving goodbye, which really is no surprise, Thad doesn't think he's going to be invited back, which probably wasn't the smartest move Thad has ever made, and the both of them find themselves back out on the front porch. In the cold. The girls are gone, no, Thad can see them walking up the street, turning the corner, but the porch still stinks of their cigarettes.

Thad coughs, Ace hunches. Then Ace turns his back on Thad.

"Look man…" says Thad, with the sound of another question in his voice.

"Just give it a rest, huh? Thad? If you can't help me out, you can't. Just leave it alone. O.K.? Is that so fucking much to ask? Thad? I don't know. You tell me. Do you…"

But Thad's already down the stairs and walking uphill towards Market Street, talking to himself and shaking his head, and kicking at rocks on the sidewalk with vicious side-kicks from his instep, mentally making goal after goal in the World Cup, making all of them, coincidentally, by beaning the goalie viciously on the head with the ball – the bruised and staggering goalie, in Thad's imagination, bearing a striking resemblance to one Ace Periphanitides.

Ace picks up his phone, thinks about throwing it at Thad's head, knows he could hit it even from here, but stops. With his hand raised, Ace looks over at Charley's locked door. Then he looks back out at the street, still standing like the statue of liberty, and he watches Thad's back fade and disappear into Thad's Saturday night, and Ace doesn't move.

In what is a rare event in his young life, Ace restrains himself. He lowers his hand some. He's done enough damage, to everyone, including himself, for one day. Holding back. Fuck, it's an odd feeling. Then he feels an even odder one.

He lowers his hand all the way and looks back, over his shoulder and upwards at Charley's windows, but the drapes are firmly shut and closed. Thad's gone around the corner. No one's watching him. No one's looking. He realizes something. "Shit. Shit. I really am on my own. No one's scrutinizing him. No one's looking out for him. It's only Ace now. Only Ace. Ace is alone."

"It's not my fault. It's not. Why isn't anyone listening to me?"

An enormous blob of ultra-foggy fogginess blows down towards him, on top of him, all around him – it settles in and boils and swirls. Ace can hardly see his hand when he waves it in front of his face. He feels for the banister on the porch. It's like walking through wads of dripping, discarded Kleenex. Ace is soaking wet. He looks up

"I only did what I always do. I'm not doing anything different. I haven't changed."

Somebody turns off the overhead porch light above him. The porch goes black. He is in a vaporous dark, now. He hears the two Russian guys from the corner coming up the porch stairs, slowly, carefully, feeling their way. So they've been out here the whole time. Man, they must have been frozen. Ace has never had a job where he'd have to stand out in the cold and freeze. Really, Ace has never had a job. But what the fuck? What the fuck difference did that make? What did people expect of Ace? What?

"Look, everyone. I haven't changed. It's everybody else who's changed. I'm the same. Everybody else is going strange It's not my fault. It's not."

He can't call his father. Eddie won't talk to him. Charley's bolted the door. Thad's run off. He really is on his own. Alone. Well, not quite. The two muscle guys, now in huge ski parkas (they'd apparently been re-supplied from Slavic Central) step out of a piece of mist and appear four steps below him. They wait. Ace waits. The fog slaps repeatedly at them with fat pillows of moisture. It covers them all. Then it shreds and thins.

Ace stands in a wilderness of shadows. A globe of fuzzy orange-pink floats out over what must be the street. A series of them lead uphill and downhill. Cars slide and hiss by drippingly on wet pavement, pairs of disembodied headlights and taillights floating away on important errands. Everyone else knows who they are. Everyone else has a place to go. Everyone else has somebody.

But not Ace.

Wisps of cold hit his face and hands. He has a sweater knotted around his waist, but he doesn't put it on. His body heat radiates out into a wet night. He kind of hopes he'll get sick. Get pneumonia. Nobody would probably even come to visit his hospital room. They wouldn't even know if he died.

Why does crazy shit like this always happen to him? Why? What did he do wrong? He wonders where Jay is right now. He wonders if Jay is thinking about him. What if Jay needs him?

He looks at his phone, which is still in his left hand. He doesn't have Jay's number. Jay disappeared. Kidnapped by the Russians. Jay's depending on him. And Ace's help is worth shit. Ace thinks he ought to call Eddie again, then he thinks, no, no use man, no use, and puts the cell back into his pocket.

Nobody answers for him, anymore. He's used them all up. There's nobody left. What's the use? What's the fucking use?

He eventually buttons up his shirt, puts on his sweater. He stands there. On Charley's porch. The guys step back down to the street below, stamping and whispering back and forth, in a musical language with a lot of y's and w's in it. But they don't leave. They watch closely as Ace moves to his parked car, slumps into his passenger seat, runs the window down, closes his eyes, feels the rain dripping in on the leather interior and on his freezing face. They move closer and watch him as he falls asleep under his leather jacket.

And that's where they were still standing as Ace's phone rang some time later.

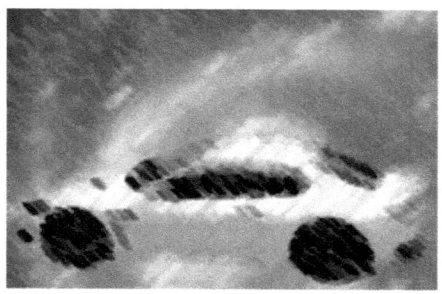

CHAPTER 18
(Saturday Night/Sunday Morning 2:57 A.M.,
Eddie in Front of Charley's Flat)

The light changes in front of him, and Eddie slows his yellow Vespa – the Great Banana - to a stop. Eddie fingers twenty worn, but serviceable bundles of twenty dollar bills, hiding under his shirt, and is amazed once again at the extreme ease with which Mr. P. pulls up these ridiculous amounts of cash out of nowhere - in the middle of the night, consistently. He doesn't want to know how or why Mr., P. can do it. He just does. Eddie has always witnessed it occurring. It never ceases to bedazzle.

Eddie has the money in a bag tied around his neck. It took half an hour to argue it out of Albert's hands back at Albert's place. He has the bag double-tied again around his chest, like a papoose. If it looks like Eddie has a diminutive pair of breasts and a training bra on, well, thinks Eddie, so be it. It's a small price to pay to get this over and done with, even if it does mess with his professional image. Not that he has much of that left tonight.

Damn, it's cold. And slick. Eddie takes it easy on the long uphill grades. Eddie motors even more carefully when he goes downhill, taking it slow and sure on the steep streets in Noe Valley and the

Castro. He lets a couple of cars fly past him, and of course, gets sprayed in the process. He occasionally throws up one hand, trying to keep the currency dry, and motors prudently on into the night, up and down, swerving and braking, hoping he remembered to put gas in his bike last week, not daring to look and see if he had.

After a few minutes, which seem like hours, Eddie stops in front of Charley's house. It looks dark. And empty. Eddie can't see anyone around.

His phone rings.

"It is nearly 3 in the fucking A.M. shithead, how the in the hell do you expect to keep your good friends if you treat them like used dildoes? Answer me that, asshole. "

"Deb, would you please put Alice on? Please? Thanks."

"How the hell you know this isn't that soft-hearted slob? It could be. You think you're a mind reader? The Stupendous Stoneinksi or something? Huh? Ha! You think you're so smart. Why, what if I arranged a meeting between your face and my fist and we…"

Eddie hears someone bodily grab the cell, ripping it through some very noisy music, it sounds like Heavy Metal, with a lot of grunting and groaning. It echoes, like it's a garage. Eddie hears Alice yelling "Deb, just head on over to the pool table, those two young girls desperately need your experience and skills. Go teach 'em something. Something they'll remember." Then Eddie hears a low, growly voice say "Yes, sir. Understood, sir." And Eddie can hear a lot of music and laughing, maybe a fist fight or two, and then quiet and the sound of wheels on wet pavement, like someone just stepped outside.

"Sorry, Eddie, Deb snatched my phone when I went to the ladies. Although, I have to say, I agree with most of what she said."

"Look, Alice, things got more complicated. Is Adam still there? Good. Just tell him to be at the Embarcadero, in front of the Ferry Terminal at 11 A.M. Is that too early?"

"He's nodding. I guess that means he's in agreement. He know what he's in for?"

"Tell him, he's Fulk. Fulk Faulkner. All he has to do is bring a weight belt and a dolly and help Mr. P. move some boxes tomorrow. That's it. Yeah, Fulk. He can spell it any way he likes."

Eddie hears Adam yelling "See ya tomorrow" and Deb yelling "Take it off, take it off" and then Alice says "We need to talk,

Eddie Stone, but right now, I've got to go put out some fires. Take care of yourself. Remember there's more to life than your job, O.K.? Now promise me you'll do something nice for Eddie tonight and then say goodbye, Eddie."

"I promise. And goodbye Eddie."

"Ha ha. I'm holding you to that. You think I'm kidding. Deb, give that girl back her bra. No, not yours. Yeah, didn't think you were wearing one. Look, gotta run, Ed. Bye."

Eddie looks around, but he's still very much alone, and Charley's looks even more deserted, if that's possible. Eddie calls Ace and is surprised to hear a phone ring, just as his cell connects to Ace. He realizes the car, a Maserati Gran Turismo next to him is ringing. The windows are tinted and fogged and one is half down, but he thinks he can see a body inside. He calls again. And again. It sounds like an echo chamber. He lets it go this time and knocks on the window.

As the car engine starts up, the window motor whines and the glass descends all the way down. Eddie can see Ace's unshaven face grimace blearily from next to a leather headrest. Eddie slips the thing from off his neck and tosses bag, money, and knotted rope, all into the car. It bops Ace on the nose. Eddie hears a muffled "Fuck" and the motor whines and the window goes up again. All the way up this time. The car turns off. Eddie waits.

A few seconds later it's all done again, engine, window, grimace, and the bag pops out the window at Eddie this time, empty.

"So how much is this?" says a phlegm-covered voice from deep inside the funky smelling car interior.

"More than the forty, probably, no, knowing your father, exactly forty-four thousand."

"You're probably noticing that I'm not asking why you just mentioned my father."

"Don't bother asking, I'll tell. It's getting easier and easier with your dad. He nearly died of a stroke paying out that slim packet of bills to get Dak bailed out of jail in San Francisco. This time, tonight, he only got desperately sick paying out this great wad of cash to get you uninterested in Fulk. But you're off the hook for Dak, so rest easy."

"Off the hook. Sounds good. Who the hell is Fulk?"

"Tell you in a sec. Sorry Ace, I misspoke. You're not off the hook, not yet. You know, Ace, I still need to get that money back somehow for myself. I've got to. I cheated and borrowed to get that money for Dak.

"What about Jay, man?"

"And as for Jay, I think that's just going to have to be a total write-off. Your dad'll never agree to that. Not after all this."

"Off the hook for Dak. Lost Jay.

"Ace…"

"Just never going to happen. I'll run off with Jay and live on the streets in a cardboard box before I'll let dad take Jay away from me. I love Jay, Eddie, I love him."

"Ace…"

"I stayed out on the streets last night man. I'll do it again."

"Ace, you slept a few hours in a parked, 150 thousand dollar car. I'm not sure that qualifies as living on the streets."

"And I'd do it again. For Jay. I'd box it for Jay, I would, Eddie, I would. I love Jay. Why doesn't anyone listen to me when I say that?"

"I'm listening, I'm listening. Well, maybe you won't have to."

"Have to what? Say it? I'll say it over and over again. Oh, wait. You mean the box? I'll do that too, I swear I'll do it, I swear. You just said…"

"I've been telling your dad about Jay. Kind of. I've been telling him about a guy named Fulk, from around here, a guy your dad thinks is Jay."

"You've told everyone about Jay? And Fuck?"

"Fulk. But Fulk's imaginary. Nobody really knows about Jay. So, Ace you're safe from Dak. And Jay is safe from your dad. So far everyone's happy. Except me. Well, and your dad. But he doesn't know that he's unhappy. Not so far. Your dad's on the point of being Very Unhappy. He's just not there yet."

"Where is this heading, Eddie?"

"This is where it's heading, Ace. Hopefully, if I'm going to stay out of jail, your dad won't find out about all the crazy scheming that's gone on tonight, not ever."

"And…"

"And, I, Eddie, am the only person in this whole scenario that really truly knows he is unhappy, right at this present moment, now. Unhappy. And no way out of it. That's me. Eddie. Unhappy Eddie."

"Wait. Start again. Who's Fuck?"

"That's Fulk, not Fuck. I just made him up. He doesn't exist."

"O.K. but what is the whole thing about Fuck? And why the fuck would you name a make-believe person 'Fuck', Eddie? What a stupid name. No one'll believe that. Fuck? "? Is he Asian? What's his last name "Yu"?"

"It's Fulk, man, Fulk. With an 'L'. Never mind. Now listen up. The reason why you're off the hook for Dak is that if your dad asks the Good Times Bail Bond company about Dak, I've told the Good Times Bail Bond Guys to say that a guy who's nickname is Fulk was sprung. You paid it out. You paid it for Fulk. You were in love with Fulk. That's where the first umpteen thousand in cash went. So our tracks are covered as far as Dak is concerned. It looks like you were in love with Fulk the whole time."

"Nice. So, Eddie to recap: Jay is 'Fulk'ed and Dak is 'Fulk'ed, and I guess the little lambs eat ivy. Ha ha. I threw that last part in for you. Your kind of humor. So. Eddie. I think I got it. But what if dad asks to see Fulk, he won't have fuck to see."

"Oh, very funny, and I'm counting on it. He has to. Albert is waiting to pick Fulk up down by the Ferry Terminal this morning. Eleven A.M. sharp. It's already arranged."

"Albert's mixed up in this? He's waiting for a fictional man to meet him?"

"A situation that many of us find ourselves in. Sorry I couldn't resist."

"Resist what?" Ace clowns it up, makes wide eyes at Eddie as he stares all around the car. Eddie can see him smiling. Somehow that makes everything he's gone through so far tonight worthwhile. Ace smiling. It's good to see, again.

"Eddie, you resisting, you struggling with someone out there?"

"Never mind. Never mind, Ace. I've got a friend Adam who is going to pretend to be Fulk. He'll meet up with Albert. So Albert can tell your dad. And keep you off the hook. Adam thinks he's helping your dad move his office."

"Uhhh... Look, I'm really tired. Really fulked. So, sounds good. I've got someone I need to see this morning. Make a payment. See those two beefy guys in the ski parkas parked on the corner?"

Eddie jumps back and notices the two huge guys for the first time. The guys are looking at him. Not with cordial, good-humored expressions. More like militant mistrust. They look like they're memorizing Eddie's face. They look back and forth, at him, and at

Ace. Eddie squints and stares back at the two of them, and they look away, quickly, clapping their hands, mumbling to each other. When Eddie looks away, he can see the two of them resuming their Eddie-observation.

How could he have missed these guys? They took up most of the sidewalk. He blinks, shakes his head. He must have been sleep-Vespa-ing all the way over here. Lucky he didn't kill himself. He'd better get his ass over to South of Market and fill up the old gas tank too, and get some more coffee, and then,...

"Hey, Eddie. Earth to Eddie? Ace here, over. Yup, I'm still talking. Look, they've been watching me all night. I need to swing by my dad's, shower and take off."

"Just a sec, Ace. Seeing your dad right now isn't' the best idea."

"Well, I'm open to any suggestions, Eddie."

"Ace, just give me a sec."

The car window goes back up. The two guys stamping and coughing into their hands look away when Eddie looks over at them again. How could you miss them? Like missing a couple of billboards standing in your living room. Eddie pokes his cell and makes a call. It picks up after the fourth ring, but goes into voice mail. He calls five more times before someone actually picks up.

"The answer is no, Eddie."

"C'mon Charley. He's in a tight spot. He just needs a place to shower, maybe shave, get in and out. Twenty minutes tops."

"No."

"In and out. You know how stubborn he is – he'd never call you himself. I'm calling and apologizing for him. Whatever he did, he's an idiot. Give him another chance. In and out, Charley."

"No and no."

"Hand me the phone, Eddie" this from the cracked voice from inside the car – the window is back down again. Eddie hands the phone inside.

"Charley, he's right. I am an idiot. But I'm trying to get my life right for once, trying to do the right thing for someone. Jay needs me. I need Jay. Help a guy out, Char. Please?"

"No."

"Pretty please, with low-fat milk and sugar-free sweetener on top?"

<Silence> Ace hands the cell back to Eddie. They wait. They both hear a long sigh from the cell's speaker. Eddie can hear the

stamp, cough, stamp, cough, continuing from the corner. Then he hears footsteps approaching. A pair of walking billboards.

"Eddie, put Ace back on the phone. Tell him to explain to me again how much he is an idiot, and how sorry he is that he is an idiot, and how unfortunate it is that he keeps on opening up his mouth and proving that he is an idiot to all his friends especially his best friends over and over again. Tell him." Eddie opens his eyes wide, and raises his eyebrows, looking at Ace hunched over in the car – he'd put the phone on speaker again. Ace grabs the phone.

"Charley. I was wrong. I'm sorry. I treat my friends badly. I need to change. Even if you don't let me up there this morning, I understand. It's fine. I deserve it. Just help me change in the future. O.K.? Here's Eddie." Ace hands the phone back to Eddie.

"Eddie Stone, did you write that for him to say, like a script or something? That was not Ace."

"I'm as surprised and shocked as you are, Charley." Ace shrugs, shakes his head, makes a face at him, wiggling his fingers. Eddie pokes out his tongue back at him. At least, Ace is still smiling. "Pleasantly surprised and shocked, Charley, actually."

"Look, give me five minutes to get my stuff together. Then come up. If he needs a couch for the night, he's got it."

"Awright, Charley – you won't regret it."

"Too late, Eddie , I already am. See you in five."

The two guys are now standing behind Eddie – this is getting to be a habit with them. The three of them peer into the Maserati. Eddie pushes his phone back down into his pocket, and claps the two guys on their shoulders (which are solid as cemented masonry) as he backs out from between them. Ace has a shit-eating grin on his face.

"Have fun you guys" says Eddie and Eddie's gone.

CHAPTER 19
(Sunday 11:22 A.M.,
Paul and Albert at Paul's House on Twin Peaks)

Paul Periphanitides sniffs and sniffs at the air. He's totally lost his sense of smell. He can't smell worth anything anymore. Getting old was not supposed to be like this. He was supposed to be rich and vital and electric and magnetic all at the same time. Irresistible. Exceptional. Unprecedented. A force of nature.

Instead he's mostly baffled, sometimes worn out, at all the wrong times energetic, and almost always – nowadays - struggling just to keep up with his son's latest lunatic escapade. It's not that Paul's complaining. He's not. At least, not much, that is. It's just, well, this new senior life of his, it's just not what he'd been expecting.

He squints off into the eastern sky, searching for the horizon. The sun is there, he's sure of it, a yellow-white intensity in the foggy haze, no, you can't exactly see it except if you close your eyes and follow the presence of the light as your whole body turns toward it. Like a sunflower. Or a tulip, maybe. Do tulips move? That doesn't seem right, somehow. Why is he thinking about flowers? Albert's the would-be gardener. What could be bringing on all these strange erratic ramblings, this mental vagrancy? Mental vagrancy. That's an Albert phrase if anything is. Paul sighs.

It's going to be that kind of day. Monochrome. Gray, but with the cruel hope of sunlit, blue skies. It's almost as if you can see escaping patches of blue being overwhelmed by vicious wolf-packs of cloud jumping on top of them, all just out of your peripheral vision. But the blue's nowhere. There is only a general grayness. Paul guesses that this, this indistinctness, is what is passing for morning this Sunday. Brighter shadows. Ghostlier sunbeams.

Paul sniffs again and remembers why he is holding his front door open and calling out to someone in the fog-covered street to hurry up. He can just barely make out a green Jaguar by the curb. It looks like his, Paul's. Although he can't see its racing stripe, or the black convertible hood. If he remembered to put the hood up at all on Friday night. Did he? If he didn't, the new upholstery will be ruined. Absolutely ruined. It rained all night. Paul hears a scraping sound and grimaces. It's very close to the Jaguar. Too close.

"Al what's going on?" No one answers. It comes to him that he's holding the door open for Albert. But Albert's taking his sweet time getting from the curb to Paul's front door.

"Is it done? Careful of the car, I just had it waxed. Careful, Albert! Could you see if there isn't a top on my car?"

Albert is pulling a tall someone out of the door of his ancient Corolla and leading this person hesitatingly up the barely-seen steps towards a yellow oblong which Albert apparently fervently hopes is Paul's front door. This person seems to be carrying a great deal of extraneous stuff. Paul wonders what's going on.

"Hurry up, it's freezing out here. That is you, isn't Albert? And you aren't alone?"

"Were you just asking me if someone were topless? Why would we be half-nude at this hour of the morning? You never make any sense anymore, Paul. Well, you're lucky, that's all I can say."

Paul impatiently pushes the front door open even wider, trying to encourage them to move faster. Albert is still explaining.

"Yes, yes, all is, as they say in the vernacular, going according to plan. And, no, Paul, not alone, no. Coming. Coming. Yes, this is it, this is the house. And that's Mr. Periphanitides above us. Waiting, impatiently. Now up the stairs with you. Up. Up."

Paul motions them to come in. Adam and Albert walk, then run up the short sidewalk. Adam's carrying what looks like two baseball mitts, some chains, and a small leather saddle. Who has Albert picked up at the Ferry Building? An unemployed cowboy outfielder? Why two gloves, why not one? Paul shakes his head. Albert seems non-plussed by it all. Paul decides not to notice.

Paul looks up and down the street, peering through his half-open door. He motions brusquely for Adam to come inside and glares at Albert.

"Quick, get him in before anyone sees you and that person. And Albert, for heaven's sake, get that person upstairs and out of sight. Don't let him meet Dak. It wouldn't be right, to have my son Dak seeing me hanging around on weekends, sneaking young men into the house. What if Ace saw him?"

Albert efficiently pushes a young man in and past Paul, mouthing "Ace?" as they stumble inside past the door. Paul looks out again, scanning the streets for motion, holding his long-distance glasses up to his eyes. He's lost his trifocals. These lenses are covered in thumbprints. Damn! He tries to clean them off on his shirt collar, and peers out, frowning at the street.

"Ace?" says a voice in his ear.

"Oh, Ace. Albert, yes, I completely forgot about Ace. What would he think? Me? Stealing his boyfriend? Me, flaunting my power and personal appeal? Oh, this is not good. Not good at all. What was I thinking to bring him here? What? Quick, upstairs Albert. But quietly, please."

Albert disappears and returns in a moment. Paul is still watching the street, anxiously.

"So, Paul, so far so good. You've done well for yourself. You've taken Ace's new beau away from him and safely ensconced him in your own house. And you did it just in time. In some little way, thanks to me, of course."

"What? What do you mean?" Paul closes one eye and holds the glasses to the other, trying to find a clean place in the lens. This is not working. He wills his eyes to pierce the mist and rain in front of the house, looking for a following shadow, or the glint of a camera lens, or some clever espionage animal even. You never can tell.

Albert obviously sees he's going to have to be a little more direct. If he wants any recognition at all from Paul for all his strenuous exertions on Paul's part, and his (very) early morning assignation down by the docks. Not to mention the gas money. Well. Maybe he can go at this from another angle. Maybe a frontal assault is too obvious. Maybe the back door, this time.

"That Eddie is a treasure, a jewel."

"A what? Why are we talking about minerals? What are you babbling about now, Albert. I can never understand you."

"Eddie saw Ace earlier today. You got Ace out of this new boyfriend's clutches just in time."

"Ah. Ace." Paul looks very worried again.

"So, yes, Eddie is a great asset for you. Worth a great deal."

"Yes, ten times his salary, no a hundred."

"And what a jokester he was, when he brought this boy to me. He was telling him, this young man Fulk, that he was needed to do office work for you - lifting, carrying papers, moving furniture. He brought gloves, a weight belt. There's even a mechanical contraption to leverage and transport heavy boxes in my trunk. I think it's called a dilly."

"You don't mean a dolly, do you Albert?" Albert looks thunderstruck all of a sudden. His face is pale. Paul glances at him concerned, puts his arm on his shoulder. Paul doesn't want him fainting again like he did last night.

"You can call it anything you want Albert, it doesn't matter to me. Really. Anything."

"Drat. No, no, Paul. It's not that. It's just damned heavy. I barely got it into my trunk. I should've had him take it inside. Before we made that last dash up the steps. I would have. But I was rushed." Albert stares in what he hopes is a helpless but defiant way at Paul.

"Oh, well, just pop out and snatch it, will you, Albert? And make sure you're not seen."

Albert stares at Paul in disbelief.

"Me? Pop? Snatch? Carry a dilly up all these stairs?"

"Dolly. Quickly now, how heavy could it be?"

Albert squints evilly at Paul.

"Go on now. Go on…"

Albert backs down the stairs carefully. Noisily opens his trunk. Huffs and puffs and pulls on something inside, but can't get it out. This continues for a bit.

"Paul, you're going to have to help, if you want this dally thing."

"Quiet, Albert, quiet. Please. Well, maybe Albert it's not all that necessary."

"Necessary my arse. It came with that Fulk person and it's

leaving with that Fulk person. It's certainly not staying in the boot of my car. Or rather the trunk of my car. Well, it's not staying in my car, Paul, either way. It isn't and it won't."

There is a minute or two of silence. When Albert realizes that Paul is not going to leave his door and come down to help him, he starts opening and slamming the trunk of his car, as loudly as he can.

"Albert, quiet down there! Please!" Paul hisses between his teeth at the dimly seen street in a stage whisper.

Paul scans the block for activity. For any motion at all. An insane metallic flapping sound is coming from the curb. Then a heavy slamming starts again. If anything, this time it's louder.

"Can't seem to close my trunk with this damn thing in it."

Paul is holding his breath, looking up and down the street. Slam. Slam. Slam.

"Damn." The mist parts a little and Paul can see Albert below.

Albert slams the trunk, opens it, curses. Slams it, opens it, curses. All the while he's looking up at Paul, waiting for a reaction. He slams it especially hard and this time gets his sleeve caught in the latch mechanism. A horrible rending sound is heard as Albert jabs at the trunk lock with his key and tries to pull away at the same time.

"Damn it all to hell. Get your derriere out here Periphanitides. Unless you want the whole block by my side and helping me get this fool contraption of yours up into your house."

Paul rolls his eyes, but scurries out, not letting the front door slam behind him. He closes it gently and quietly. The two of them manage, with a great deal of sweat and mutual recrimination to position the dolly on the street, wheel it to the curb, lift it up and over the curb, and bump it slowly up all the steps to the threshold of Paul's firmly closed front door. That's when Paul realizes he's locked himself out.

Paul looks at Albert. Albert glares at Paul, waving his ripped sleeves in Paul's splotched and sweaty face. Then the front door opens. Adam peers out. He's listening to an IPod, but has the earpieces hanging around his neck. It sounds like a miniature nightclub at 3 in the morning is bouncing in the air in front of them.

"So, you gentlemen wouldn't be needing some help, would you?"

Albert looks at Paul and quickly says "Uh, regrets, Paul. I have a brunch I have to get to." And disappears into the new bank of fog that's rolled down on top of them.

Paul yells into the mist "Hurry back." But his voice cracks when he says it, and there is no reply.

A car starts. It rapidly rolls away, and moves quickly and efficiently down the hill and is lost. Adam looks at Paul.

"Let me have a go at that." Adam takes it and heads back inside. Paul doesn't trust himself to speak. He turns to follow Adam back into the warmth and a hand plops down on his right shoulder. Paul doesn't turn around. He won't. Albert will just have to wait for Paul this time. He talks to the air in front of him, ignoring the hand on his shoulder.

"No use apologizing now, Albert. The damage, Albert, is done."

"Who's Albert?" says a very well-dressed, older man with fierce gray sideburns and a stunningly black, short, clipped haircut, and the largest aviator glasses Paul has ever seen – all of which Paul sees at a glance as he looks backwards. He thinks the glasses are a bit much.

The hand, the one on his shoulder, now that he's noticing it, is very nicely and expensively manicured, with a couple of large silver rings with even larger stones. The grip is firm, but the skin of the hand itself is soft. Maybe more so than his own. Supple. Like fine Spanish leather, aniline, top-grain, not corrected. Paul has unfortunately, in the last month or so, become very well-acquainted with leather. Especially for cars. He's forgotten to put the top on his Jag twice in the last three months. Between water damages, Eddie, Ace, and Dak his long-lost son, it's been a very, very expensive three months for Paul.

Paul looks back up from his shoulder to the politely questioning face – a face which he finds is frankly appraising him in a not-unfriendly manner, but a not-unprofessional manner either. Paul feels like a side of beef hanging above the counter of a wholesale meat marketer. He is being valued. An unseemly and uncomfortable feeling of foreboding creeps over him.

Unconsciously, he reaches for his back pocket and his pocketbook, to protect it, somehow, to keep it safe and whole. But it is hopeless. Paul knows it. He knows, in his innermost self, that it's already too late, much too late for Paul. This is going to cost him, like always, and cost him dearly.

CHAPTER 20
(Sunday 11:47 A.M.,
Paul at His House on Twin Peaks)

"Never mind about Albert. An angry guy trying to close his trunk down by the stop sign at the street corner said the glass house at the top of the hill was the Periphanitides' home. I don't know if this is the place or what, but it's imperative I talk to him, that is, Mr. Paul Periphanitides. Immediately. Urgent personal business. Have to find him. Very important matter."

Paul peers sharply toward the corner, putting on his eyeglasses (rather than holding them to his face like a lorgnette) to preserve at least the little bit of dignity he still retains, but can see nothing beyond his lawn. Weepy wisps of fog and vaguely darker spots, that's all there is. Although, now that he looks more closely, could that grayish blob could be a car he sees in the distance, or could it be an overly greasy fingerprint smear? Impossible to tell. He's going to kill Albert. At least make him hurt somehow. He's directed some kind of bill collector right to Paul's house. Right to him. How could he?

He turns back to the well-groomed but overly-inquisitive stranger. His eyes take on a steely determination. What if this man were a criminal? Or an axe murderer? Or worse, a process server?

Paul frowns at him and looks him up and down, trying to discover where the stranger's hidden the Summons he's going to spring on Paul. The stranger looks on, puzzled, handsome, well-groomed, but determined. Paul realizes he's going to have to say something eventually. He takes off the useless glasses, and steps out on the front porch, slowly circling the stranger and observing his clothing closely.

This situation requires subtlety and tact. Maybe evasion. This matter screams for the skills of Paul Periphanitides. Paul assumes his mildest, most amiable, most accommodating voice.

"I'm sure it is. An important matter, that is. And if I could tell you where he lives? What thanks would I get, well? Hmmm"

"Plenty of thanks, let me tell you. I'm a thankful guy. I'm huge in this town. Huge. In fact, I'm a huge benefactor to this city. I am my own line item on the Symphony's revenues budget. I paid for all the new bus stops on Market Street, out of civic pride mind you, my name isn't displayed anywhere – you know, the new wired ones that tell you when the bus is coming, and remind you to keep your feet dry, and sometimes mention a brand of gum you might want to chew. That's mine. That's me. I'm huge. I'm Mr. San Francisco."

"Your last name is San Francisco?" Paul stalls for time, he's trying to revolve back and squeeze into his front door and get through it and behind it and beyond it, so he can slam it. In this huge guy's face.

"That was a metaphor. Actually it was metonymy. A toponym."

"Oh, really? Toponym you say?" Paul could ramble on like this all day. And he would. But Paul is going to escape. Soon Paul will be safe inside where no legal document can ferret him out. And the stranger? The stranger will be rubbing his face exactly on the spot where Paul's steel-reinforced door will hit him. The part that shouldn't have been poking where it wasn't wanted. To be precise - his obnoxious pointy nose. Paul smiles, thinking of flattened and bruised facial features as he steps backward towards the front door.

"Yes. Toponym. And much as I'd like to stand and engage in witty rhetorical flourishes, I have to ask… once again… Do you know a Mr. Periphanitides?" Paul bumps loudly and finally, as he steps backward, into what turns out to be a closed front door. He'd forgotten he'd let it shut. It is, of course, locked.

He thinks briefly of making a dash down the steps and out into the street. The stranger, seeming to recognize Paul's intent, steps back and to one side, effectively blocking off the steps of the porch. Paul wonders who, of the two of them, would win a wrestling match, but shrugs his shoulders, rolls his eyes, and sighs repeatedly instead. Some days you just can't win.

<sigh> "Yes, yes, you have found Mr. Periphanitides. It is I." The stranger grimaces. "Me. I. Whatever. Who, or rather, what the hell are you, anyways? Lieutenant with a Roving Commission, an officer in His Majesty's Grammatical Police Force? You most certainly are not."

The stranger has no response to Paul's question. Paul waits a moment, for dramatic effect, then continues.

"And I have to tell you about huge... Let's talk... huge. Just for a moment. Just a moment. Indulge me. You know all those palm trees down the middle of Dolores street? Yup, my family. Over the years. So, your braggadocio is lost on me. Try it at another house. I think one of my neighbor's should be up by now. Grab an innocent shoulder over there and flourish away to your heart's content."

"No, once a morning is enough. I give you my word." Paul feels the door open up behind him. Adam peers out briefly, then starts to close it again. Paul sticks his foot in the door.

"Then, I say good morning to you."

"And to you."

But as Paul turns to go inside, alarmed now that he can hear Adam clearly dragging the dolly in a long, lingering screech across the expensive and as-yet-unscarred bamboo flooring of his living room, he also hears a loud voice exploding behind his back, and at the same time, a familiar, firm, masculine grip with well-manicured fingernails clamping down on his shoulder blades like a hydraulic vise.

"Wait!"

"Unhand me! You promised you'd stop."

"You really are Paul Periphanitides."

"You're finally realizing to whom you've been speaking. Yes. The head of the Periphanitides family. Iron filings. Palm trees on Dolores. We're well-known."

"You." The stranger's voice goes up an octave, then back down again. "You. You. You."

"I. Uh, I, I what, exactly?" Paul pulls but cannot free himself. The stranger has a maniacal strength. Really, an unnatural strength.

And he seems to have lost his vocabulary. Paul wonders if escaped lunatics would be so spiffed up. Maybe rich lunatics. Rich homicidal lunatics, perhaps, escaped from exclusive, well-appointed private asylums.

Paul redoubles his efforts to get free, he grabs both sides of the door and pulls the two of them inwards. In the distance, he sees two long, undulating lines of black skid marks curve gracefully across the floor and head towards the hallway. It looks like that young man is trying to get the dolly down the acrylic spiral stairs. Unsuccessfully. There's a lot of bumping and ringing going on. Paul hears a voice bellowing in his ear.

"You. You thief. You've stolen away the only man I've ever really loved – Dakota – my Dak. You. You. You and your money. Dazzling the impressionable. I know what your kind are capable of. I've come to get him back, to get Dak back. Whatever the cost. To get back my Dak."

Paul's hand squeezes the frame of the front door so hard, he's surprised he hasn't crumpled it to splinters. He thinks of a crushing rejoinder and turns to crush him with it. When he pauses to deliver it, happily rolling the syllables around in his mouth, staring malevolently at the neatly-trimmed gray sideburns bobbing beside him, he stops, leaving his own mouth hanging open.

Paul understands.

This is the investment banker Eddie was talking about. Eddie called him the pirate captain. The man in love with Fulk. Who for some reason thinks Fulk is named Dak. That stops Paul for a second, but the angry face of the man breathing heavily into his own has a marvelous ability to focus Paul's meandering thoughts.

Let's see. Lets' see if he can figure out the whole Dak-Fulk enigma. So. His son is named Benjy but goes by the name of Dak. This man destroying his floor with his moving machinery is named Dak but goes by the name of Fulk. What is the strange mystery surrounding this tiny one syllable name? And why does every Dak in the city end up living or working in Paul's new house?

Paul's head hurts. Maybe Paul won't try and figure it out. No, maybe not. Another day, perhaps. Paul closes one eye, which is getting breathed on and spit on a little too hard and looks at the man in front of him.

This man choking him is the man who is in love with the person in his house right now carving deep trenches into his expensive wood flooring with a rusty dolly. Ah. But there's more to this. Right now - and this is the best part - this is the point in time where Paul gets back all his money back, well some of it at least. The issue here is that Paul gets money instead of giving money. Get instead of give. Maybe this day isn't going to be an all-day all-Paul-catastrophe. Maybe at some point Paul will begin to win. He closes his mouth and it forms by itself into a broad smile.

"Yes, it's true. I have him. Fulk. I mean, Dak. Yes, Dak, that's who I mean."

"You admit to having Dak?"

"I do."

"Oh. Well. In that case, Mr. Periphanitides, do you mind if I call you Paul? You do? You do. O.K., then Mr. Periphanitides, in that case, I'd like to make you a proposal. A kind of trade, options for shares for money. Or a like-kind exchange. Whatever the cost. Whatever you wish. But a trade. What do you say to that?"

Whatever the cost. Whatever you wish. Paul likes this man. Paul waits a moment to show he is no amateur in the arena of business negotiating. No stranger to the hurly-burly of high finance. No, not Paul. The Captain eyes him anxiously. Paul clears his throat several times. He looks up significantly at the ceiling of his porch. The captain follows Paul's eyes to the coffered surface over their heads, with a haunted, confused expression. Paul smiles to himself. He's got a live one. He can feel it. He clears his throat once more, starts talking before he looks back down again at the Captain.

"Well, let's see. I made a gift to him of forty four thousand dollars. Just so he could pay off some debts, and have some pocket money, you understand, while he was around and about town. I'll convince him to leave with you, if you reimburse me for that. And you can have his dolly, which he brought with him, and his baseball mitts and his chains. You can have the whole bundle for forty four thousand. A bargain, at twice the price.

"Uh, his mitts and chains?"

"A bargain, I tell you."

"A bargain. Well, let me be truthful with you, Periphanitides. I'm a truthful guy. I mean to marry him. I can't live without him."

"You can live any way you want, with or without him. As long as I get paid. But I think we have an understanding, you and I."

"We do? Then it's done?"

"It's done."

"Oh, thank you. Thank you. You have no idea what this means to me. Thank you. Thank you." Paul's shoulder's assaulted again and again by the muscular hands of the Captain. Paul pulls away as soon as good manners and his polite duties as a host allow him to.

At that moment, a small, very small, patch of blue, hardly more than a hole of brilliant turquoise in the eastern sky, shines off to their right. It is followed by more blue breaking out all over the bay. Suddenly, far below them, a single, intense beam of morning Sunday sunlight attacks the waves. More beams follow. The morning sunshine bathes the waters in a frothy glow.

Paul stares in astonishment over the shoulder of the strange pirate-captain cum investment banker standing in front of him. The fog breaks apart and a sunny day pours down upon the two of them - the banker's face limned with rays of sturdy gold shot through with a delicately trailing silver mist. The Captain looks like an icon for the patron saint of Lovers Found.

The Captain turns his face back towards Paul, his eyes shining brightly. The furnace switches on in Paul's house, (the door, after all, has been open for quite some time) and the two of them are enveloped in a blast of warmth and comfort. Somewhere (in his own kitchen? Is that young man cooking something in Paul's kitchen?) Paul smells cinnamon rolls baking. Paul expects a flock of angels chorusing in unearthly harmony to descend upon the two middle-aged men standing in this very doorway. It's all just a tad too sentimental for Paul. The universe is just being a little too obviously pro-Paul, at the moment. The other shoe has got to fall sometime for Paul. Something's going on. Something.

The Captain smiles, shaking his head and weeping. Paul looks away and down. And notices again, the long skid mark stretching off into his living room. It looks like there is smoke spiraling up his spiral staircase. He's going to kill Albert. The hand grabs him again.

"Uh…"

"Many thanks. Many thanks. Many, many thanks, Periphanitides."

"Uh, yes… well… I'd better just go in and get him, shouldn't I?" Paul hopes he can get to the kitchen before this person burns down his house.

"Thanks. Thanks." The Captain makes no signs of letting Paul go.

"Yes, yes. I quite agree. I think I should. Go. That is. Go

immediately." The Captain apparently hasn't heard a word Paul has said. Paul moves towards the inside of the house. The Captain follows, placing one foot in Paul's doorway, one foot still out on the porch. Paul stops, gently removes the Captain's hand from his shoulder and now free, marches off. The smoke is getting thicker.

A few minutes pass, then a few more. Apparently the Captain doesn't notice it, because he is pretty much in the same position, half in, half out of the house when Paul returns - dragging a bemused Adam. Paul is smiling and nodding to himself and trying to hurry Adam up.

"So", says the Captain, "I suppose this man knows where Dak is."

"No." Paul's smile is frozen on his face. "No, this is the man my son was desperately in love with. This is your young man. Your Dakota, Dak as it were." Adam looks from banker to Paul to banker again. He opens his mouth, thinks, then closes it again. The Captain is looking less benevolent by the second. A certain violence re-enters his eyes.

"Well, Periphanitides, I can't speak for your son, but as for this one, I've never seen him before in my life."

"Not possible. He is the one."

"He is not. I don't know what you're playing at, Periphanitides, but it's not going to work." The Captain's voice begins to rise in both volume and pitch.

"He is. He is the one. I know it. I certainly paid a fortune to get him here into this house this morning."

"He is not. And you must be an idiot to have paid so much and not known what you were paying for."

"But... but... but... this is the young man. A friend just brought him here. I have it from a reliable source, an employee of mine, I, uh, that is, well... Look here, this has to be the same man." The Captain says nothing to this. He looks at Paul. He looks at Adam. Then he looks back at Paul. Now he's smiling.

"So you're not playing. Too bad for you. I'd say your employee has taken you for a ride. And much as I'd like to continue exploring the depth, height and breadth of your own incredulous foolishness, I have other leads to follow up on. So, good luck and good bye, Periphanitides. You'll need it."

"I, uh, you... that is... he... I..."

"Not much for farewells, are you? On second thought, let's not make this good bye, just *au revoir*. Which is French for how you'd probably say "later dude." I'll be back this afternoon, just to check and see if you've found out anything new that would be useful or practical. Don't worry. I expect you'll just be bamboozled again, and pay out even more money. But I'll check back anyway. It'll give me some exercise. Keep your eyes peeled, Periphanitides."

"You'll what? I'll what? My what?" The Captain nimbly trots down the steps, two at a time, consulting a Blackberry, hits the sidewalk, turns and bounds downhill. In a flash, he's passed behind some large bushes. He's gone. Paul looks at Adam. Adam cocks his head and looks at Paul.

Paul circles Adam with a frantic look in his eyes. Both of them watch as a low, black car pulls away from the curb across the street and takes off down the hill towards Noe valley and the Castro. More and more sun breaks through the clouds. The fog is almost non-existent. The temperature starts to rise.

"So. So, Fulk. Tell me. Who are you then?"

Adam opens his mouth to answer then, for the second time in the last five minutes thinks better of it.

"Didn't Ace, my son, give you a great deal of money? Didn't he support you in a grand style? Don't you wear Baldacchinos? Or whatever the hell kind of fabulously expensive clothes it is that Eddie says you like to wear?"

"Baldacchinos? I have no idea what you're talking about. I've never heard of this Ace guy before. Never heard of him. I'm here to move some office furniture for an old guy, help with boxing up old files, that sort of thing. Is this the right house, anyways? Oh, and sorry about the rolls man, I'm not used to gas ovens."

"Boxes? Moving? Gas ovens?"

"Yeah, I mean, they were sitting out, and I thought I'd be nice and make 'em for you, since it looked like you were having a rough morning and all. Man, those stairs sure aren't built to make it easy to haul stuff up and down. I hope we're not moving too many boxes between floors. Although, if you need me to, I'm not complaining, you understand…"

"I understand. No. No, I don't understand. Tell me, Fulk, you don't, by the by, happen to know a man named Dak?"

"Dakota? Yeah, sure, I've seen him around."

"Have you seen him recently?"

"Well, since he got bailed out of jail, I don't know for sure. I haven't seen him, like in the last month or so. He used to live with some friends of mine in the Mission. Someone said he was dating some rich guy. Hey! Whaddyaknow! Do you think that was the guy? That Captain guy?"

"I'll pass on that last question. So, Fulk, don't know anything, huh? Do you at least know who bailed him out?"

"A guy named William P-something or other, I think he calls himself Ace. Hey! Ace! Do you think that's the same guy you were talking about a second ago? This is so weird. How do you know so much about all the same people I know so much about?"

Adam waits for Paul to say something else. But Paul isn't talking to Adam anymore. Adam leans closer, because Paul is now whispering furiously to himself, fizzing, hissing, and whistling to himself like he's about to explode into a million pieces. Adam steps back, to give him some room.

"Eddie! Eddie's done it again. What to do? He's bilked me out of tens of thousands of dollars. This time's he's going to pay for it. Eddie! The bastard. Why do I let him keep on making a fool out of me? Eddie! Well, even complete fools know how to hit back. Eddie! Ruin him. That's what I'll do. A criminal action first. Yes. Then, what? A civil action for damages. Good. Then what? Oh, he'll pay, he'll pay, Eddie will pay for this. There's got to be something else I can do to him. Got to be. Do they allow prisoners to be tortured?"

"Are you still talking to me?"

"Get the hell off my property!"

Adam inches past Paul, who's pacing up and down the porch now, then stops. He plants both feet in a direct line in front of Paul, as Paul comes pacing back down the porch, he collides with Adam and rebounds hitting the side of the house.

"Why are you still standing here? Get lost!"

"So, that's how it goes, huh? What about my equipment? What about my belt and my gloves and my dolly – and hey, what about the boxes we brought over? We stacked them by the side of the house."

"Get out before I call the police. No gloves. No belts. No boxes. No dollies for you. Get out." Paul stares crazily at Adam, shakes his head, and begins walking towards the end of the porch again, scheming animatedly under his breath. Adam waits, but Paul seems to have forgotten he's there. Adam starts to walk down the steps but stops on the first one. He turns around.

"Get!" says Paul seeing him staring at him.

"All right. I'm going. I'm going. But expect me back with the police later. You just can't steal a guy's equipment - no matter how many trees your family planted on Dolores."

Paul stomps and mutters and stomps in front of his front door. He follows Adam down to the street to make sure he walks completely away.

Adam moves off, at a calculatedly sullen and slow pace, over the top of the hill. He shuffles down the street towards the corner, looking back every couple of feet. Paul shakes his fist at him. At that, Adam starts laughing. Adam continues to laugh as he turns the corner and a car stops in front of him. It sputters to a halt, backfires a few times then comes to a rest and Paul can hear some angry yelling. Adam walks off. The car begins to move again.

The car drives feebly but quickly away, up the hill. It approaches Paul. Paul watches in disbelief. It goes slower and slower as the hill gets steeper and steeper. It comes to a halt just as the engine dies. It's in front of his house. Unbelievable. The driver's side opens and a woman steps out, her makeup dripping, sobbing to herself. She's obviously lost. And in the wrong neighborhood. She doesn't belong here.

Paul is in no mood. He realizes he's still got his arm in the air and he's still shaking his fist. Paul backs up the stairs and backs onto his porch. He prepares for a siege.

CHAPTER 21
(Sunday 12:16 P.M.,
Paul and Filipa at Paul's House on Twin Peaks)

"There's nothing here for you, here. Move on. Move on."

She's a bit of a blur, since Paul doesn't have his far-seeing glasses on, but she appears to be a feminine blur with a purpose.

Paul barks commands, sweeping his right arm back and forth. He dramatically points at his cell phone, which he didn't know he had in his pocket, but which he has now providentially retrieved and wields, as this crazed woman stumbles around her car and up Paul's short flight of steps – all obviously with the intent of somehow engaging Paul.

Well, if Paul has anything to do with it, and he does, it isn't going to happen. Not today.

"I'm calling the police." Paul starts poking at his phone. He doesn't have his reading glasses on, so he's actually poking at random, but she doesn't need to know that. He motions at his blinking cell, showing it to her, which is flashing a message 'Erase All Contacts?' He picks at the screen again, and the phone chirps as it does its work. The woman hasn't heard a word he's said.

"Excuse me, please. I'm sorry. I have troubles, difficulties. They've taken my son. I do not know where he is. I have no place where I can go and ask for help. I have no one to turn to. Except Los Periphanitides. I am looking for them. Please, would you do me the kindness of helping me? Please, señor?"

Paul keeps on poking at his phone, but with less conviction. A small tinny voice erupts from the speaker "This is 911, please state your emergency."

"Someone just finished saying to me that the house of Los Periphanitides, it is here. At the top. Although they were very angry when they told me where to find it."

Paul is muttering to himself "How the devil does everyone know my name? And where I live? And who is this frantic old woman?"

"Would you, could you perhaps, give me the kindness, señor, and assist me in finding the correct address?"

Paul's phone is still talking to him with an increasingly urgent precision "This is 911. We have your location. What is your situation? Can you talk? Can you move? Hello? Hello?"

Paul is looking down at the grass, thinking, memories flooding through him. The stems sway and bend in the breeze at the top of this hill, sparkling wet in the surprising noon sunlight. In his mind, Paul can see a woman running. He can see cut grass like this, and bare feet. You know, even though her mascara is running, and her hair looks like two cats fought in it, there's something familiar about her. Something odd. It's strange. Suddenly Paul can smell the grass clearly. It smells like warm brown eyes and the soft back of a hand against his cheek.

The woman looks twice, then three times at Paul. She whispers to herself. "I've seen you before." She remembers late nights and moons spilling over window sills and hushed laughter and doors closing and pillows wet from weeping.

Paul jams his phone into his pants just as a small voice says something about dispatching. He stops for a second, thinking he ought to figure out what all that was about, then forgets about it. He forgets because he realizes with a start, that he, Paul Periphanitides knows this woman, this wild form asking favors of him, dragging herself up his front walk. It's the woman from Los Angeles he had that wild three months with, back when he was in college, when he thought he and Veronica were finished. Wait, no, that's not true. This is the other one. Oh. Oh my. That One. The One. The one he fell for when he was starting his company in his early thirties, long married to Veronica, and already raising a little boy, Ace. His great mistake.

Filipa. But maybe it's not too late. Is it? Does he want it to be?

The woman looks carefully at Paul. She's certain. It's the guy that left her with a newborn son, alone in Los Angeles, and took off, although, yes, he did visit for the next couple of years. And yes, his employees visited a great deal more often, at first. Yes, it's him. Her great mistake.

Pablito. But better late than never, no? But really, what is she doing here?

Paul realizes that therefore, the boy Eddie found for Paul, the boy upstairs, Dak, is this woman's son.

Filipa realizes – this must be Paul. Maybe he can help her find her son, yes, certainly he could help her.

Filipa mumbles to herself "It might be him, then it again, it might not. If it *is* him, will he not run away again in the next five minutes? If it *is not* him, then will he not certainly run away in the next five minutes? Oh… Why is everything so complicated for me? No matter what I do, I must do it in five minutes. That's so little time. Just five minutes. It took me weeks to get the courage to look for him. It took me days to get to this city. And five minutes is all I get?" Filipa holds her head and massages her temples with both hands.

"What? What is that you're saying? Speak up woman. What do you have to say for yourself?" Paul tries to sound severe, tries to sound how you're supposed to sound with an unwanted trespasser, but ends up sounding like he's reciting lines poorly in a badly written play, one that's sure to close on its own opening night. Paul doesn't even convince himself.

Meanwhile, Paul talks to himself also "If this is her, I'll have to step carefully, very carefully. She probably wants money. Lots of it. If she doesn't, then I'll have to be even more careful. What could she want, running up and crying here in front of me? Ah, Filipa! God, she looks so much like Filipa, holding her forehead in that way. I used to rub her temples just like that, when she had her headaches. Oh, why did she come back? Do I really want to marry her? She is still very beautiful. I wonder how he her hands feel? The same? Why is she here? What will I do? What will I say?"

"So…" says Filipa thinking to herself "Here we go… I've got to trap him somehow into telling me. Telling me if he is Paul. Telling me what he feels. Before he traps me, and sends me off. I have only five minutes. Then it's good-bye Filipa. Oh dear."

"So…" says Paul, unsure of himself. Damn. He is losing the initiative to her. Paul jumps in and throws out a phrase, eyeing her with what he thinks is crafty observing glances. Filipa thinks he looks the way a boggle-eyed fish would, jerking its head out of the water to examine the fisherman.

"So. I hope you're well, madam. Be well." Paul sits back - watches and waits, eyes peeled, noting her every reaction. It's a little disconcerting to Filipa.

"Well, oh yes. Good wishes. For me and mine. Then, I accept. I accept on behalf of myself, and on behalf of my entire family. Especially on behalf of my son." There. Let's see if the old trout rises to the bait. Filipa steps back one step. Paul advances one. He's not exactly sure what Filipa just said. He's damned sure he doesn't know what she meant by it all.

"Yes. Yes, I see. And anything else? Anything else to add?" says Paul moving closer, closing one eye and peering into her face, trying to figure out where she's lying and where she's telling the truth. Filipa takes another step back.

"Well. There might be." She has to think. What else is there for her to do? She has to add something. But what?

"There's a…health back to you, to you and yours of course. Thank you, sir."

"No" says Paul, "I thank you, madam." Paul stops. He's completely run out of conversation. A sentence pops into his head and it bursts out of his mouth before he has a chance to think about it.

"And do I know you, madam?"

"Should you know me?" Filipa steps back. She knows there's a step back there somewhere. If she could make herself trip, would he catch her? Or just let her fall? Knowing Paul, he'd just let her fall. There's one way to find out. Her five minutes is almost up. He's going to escape any second. She has to make her choice.

"I don't know. Should I?" Paul steps towards her again.

"Why do you press forward so?" says Filipa stepping backwards, at which point, she feels with her heel that there's thin air in back of her. This is the point where she may tip over backwards. So she promptly does just that. She cries out "Paul!"

Paul takes three quick steps forward and pulls her back. He

saves her. Unfortunately, the rest of his body continues moving out into space, and he finds himself throwing Filipa towards his porch while he runs quickly down the steps in front of his house trying to keep his balance. He ends up on the hood of Filipa's car, panting, bent over the front of it, and staring up at her, over his right shoulder.

"Ah, that's better. You do remember, Filipa?"

Filipa yells down from the front porch "Of course I do."

"Los Angeles" says Paul shifting over onto his back and looking up at her, while she's looking down at him

"Downtown" says Filipa

"The lights of the city."

"You and your platform shoes."

"Ah, the platform shoes. And the rain."

Paul is sitting up and breathing more normally by now. He starts to make his way up the stairs.

"There wasn't any rain. We were in the middle of a drought."

Paul isn't listening. "How I was a help to you and your mother."

"What? Leaving me alone, unwed, and with a son? No job. No address for you? You were there for three months and then you were gone. Yes, you came back. But only for a few minutes each time and then you'd leave, once again. I hated you for many years. But that was long ago. I almost do not remember that girl now. I'm sure you do not remember that boy."

Paul still isn't listening. "So here you are." Paul seems to be trying to work something difficult out in his head.

"Give me your hand" says Filipa, "It is good to see you." Paul doesn't answer, walks by her aiming for the door.

"Yes. Yes."

"Take my hand, please."

Paul turns around thinking still. Filipa thrusts her hand into his. Paul looks at her as if for the first time.

"But why are you here, Filipa? Why now?"

"I am lost, Paul, lost. My son has disappeared. My family is dead or far away. I have no one. And I must find him. I must find my son."

"Yes. But why are you here? Why, in particular, are you looking for me? Why now?"

"I've lost him, I've lost our son, Paul. I need your help to find him." Paul looks at her, then starts laughing. Filipa jerks her hand out of his.

"You are an odd man now, Paul."

"No, Filipa. Well, yes, I suppose I am. But no, not for the reasons you're thinking. I had my assistant, Eddie, look out for your son. You remember Eddie? He came for the first 10 years or so, bringing money, presents. Eduardo, Tio Eduardo yes, that's him. Well, Eddie found Dak in jail. Eddie bailed him out, with my money of course, quickly and discreetly, and brought him home to my house. He's upstairs, right now."

"You know, Filipa, you can rely on Eddie for some things, like finding lost children, and closing complicated financing negotiations, but you can't rely on him for other things, apparently, like locating boyfriends accurately."

Filipa is nodding appreciatively. She is remembering now. How it was. Often her biggest job was the nodding. And the hand holding. Both of which she also remembers were very pleasant. She smiles. And nods. And grips Paul's hand just a little tighter.

"Filipa, let me tell you what just happened to me, and then *you* tell *me*, does this sound like the kind of behavior you'd expect from a trusted employee? Well, a month or so ago, Eddie…"

Filipa wakes up to herself like someone threw a bucket of ice down the back of her dress. What did Paul just say? She breaks in on what looks to be an involved story and Paul looks over at her, a surprised but content look in his eyes.

"Excuse me, Paul, no, Pablito. Have you just mentioned my son? Did you say you found my son already? You found him? He's upstairs? Up there?" Filipa points over Paul's shoulder. Paul looks up, just to see if anyone is looking down. No one is.

"Well, yes, now that I think of it. I suppose I have. And yes I did. And yes he is. Or at least he was."

Filipa, who had been looking more and more joyful, begins to cry and Paul lends her some Kleenex he is carrying.

"No, no, Filipa. He's just upstairs. I'm sure of it."

"Well, what are you waiting for, Paul?"

"Nothing, I'm sure of that too. Nothing. I'll just go up and get him."

CHAPTER 22
(Sunday 12:34 P.M.,
Paul and Filipa Still at Paul's House on Twin Peaks)

Paul backs into the house, Filipa watches anxiously. Paul opens the door, which is standing open a little ways, and yells up into the high ceilings and heavily polished woodwork and metal and glass.

"Dak, could you come down here? Right this minute?"

A young man pokes his head out of a side window on the third floor and says "On my way."

Filipa collapses into a swing at the end of the porch after she hears the sound of his voice. She has a puzzled, troubled, pained expression on her face. Paul can't bear to see it. He wants to see her happy again. Well, thankfully, she will be − very, very soon. Paul can see tears in the imminent future. It doesn't take an astrologer to see that. Women cry for the strangest reasons. And often. And with feeling. Paul can't wait to see the new expression on her face. Can't wait.

"Now what did you want, father?"

Paul, filling his chest with pride, nods at Filipa. Dak doesn't move. Odd that. Paul then motions towards Filipa sitting on the porch swing, and goes to stand beside her.

"You see" he says in what he hopes is a whisper in Filipa's

163

direction, "he calls me father."

In a larger voice Paul says, "Come. Come greet your mother, son. Make an old father proud."

"What mother?" says Dak, looking around the porch, smiling sympathetically at Filipa, and marching to the end and looking around the corner, then down both ends of the street. "Where?"

Paul, who was watching Filipa, and is puzzled by her lack of screaming and joyous tears hasn't noticed Dak's reactions. "Go ahead, give your mother a kiss."

"Who?" says Dak.

Filipa stares straight at Paul, her head slightly askew, as if Paul is talking philosophy to a round of cheese, and looking at bystanders for applause. "Why do you want that nice young man to kiss me? Is this some cosmopolitan San Francisco custom?"

"He's your son, Filipa. That's Dak. Don't you know your own son when you see him?"

"Who? Him?"

"Who? Him?" mimics Paul under his breath, shaking his head "Yes, him. Who else is on this porch with us?"

"What, you want me to kiss that man?"

"Don't you kiss sons in Los Angeles?"

"You are crazier than I remember you Paul. And you've grown to like strange customs."

"Alright, I give up. Why not kiss him?"

"Because I've never seen him before in my entire life."

"Maybe it's just his clothes. Or maybe his haircut."

"You really think, Periphanitides, that a mother would not know her own son?"

Paul looks from Dak to Filipa to Dak. He hops on one foot then the other squinting out of one eye. "Oh, Eddie. It's Eddie. Eddie did it to me again." He hops and squints and hops.

Filipa looks sympathetically at Dak. She talks to Dak in a low voice "Has he been like this for long?"

Dak shrugs. "Not long. Just as long as I've known him."

Filipa nods sympathetically. She pats Dak's hand with her own. Dak smiles down at her.

Paul is pacing the front porch again. With energy that reminds Filipa of the younger Paul. She smiles despite her concern for his sanity.

"I fell for it. I fell for it again. I pay. Eddie takes. And strange men come live in my house rent-free. "

Paul turns on Dak. Dak jumps back. Paul explodes at Dak with a single syllable - it contains the force of a Paul-sized pile of TNT detonating.

"What?" Paul sputters, and points at the house then at Dak then at himself. "What?"

"What what?" says Dak innocently.

"What are you doing here? Kissing me every morning, calling me father. What are you doing, just standing there on my porch? What?"

"What do you want me to say?"

Paul points dramatically at Filipa. "What do you say?" He points again. "She says she is not your mother."

"Well, the way I see it, she doesn't have to be if she doesn't want to be. As for me, I'll be my mother's son no matter what she wants. You tell me, father, why should I demand that she declare herself to be my mother? That doesn't sound polite, does it father?"

"Stop calling me that. Wait, why do you keep on calling me that?"

"Calling you what, father?"

"There, you did it again."

"Well, that's your own fault, you know, father. Shouldn't I call you father when you go on and on calling me son? And what about her?" Dak points at Filipa, who sits with a Kleenex at her nose, ready to cry, but too engrossed now by this conversation to remember to do it.

Paul looks at Filipa. Filipa looks up at him, expectantly, reasonably even. Suddenly Paul thinks Filipa might have a rational explanation for everything – today, yesterday, the last three months, maybe even for the last twenty years of his life. Maybe she knows. Maybe she can answer all his questions. Paul holds his breath. Filipa smiles weakly at the two of them. Then she blows her nose, and delicately re-seats herself on the porch swing. She rocks, dabbing at her nose and waits.

Paul stands with his mouth open, painfully disappointed. It looks like Paul will have to do it the hard way, like always. He turns back towards Dak.

Dak continues blithely on, when no one answers him, and the silence grows too long, even for him. All you hear on the front porch is the "creak, creak, creak" of the rusty chain rubbing against the porch swing's hook in the ceiling, and Paul's labored breathing.

"Well, father, if she calls me son, I'll call her mother. If she says I'm no son of hers, then she won't be my mother. Is that so complicated to understand? No, it's not."

Dak looks over at Filipa. Filipa shakes her head, no, shrugging her shoulders, smiles at him. Dak looks over at Paul, just in time to duck, as Paul's fist flies through empty air where Dak's head just was.

"Look, Eddie explained it all to me when he brought me here. It made perfect sense to Eddie and me back then, and up till this very minute it's made perfect sense to everyone I've ever met in this loony house. Now, I admit it. It's making less and less sense. But it all made sense at the beginning. I can guarantee you it did."

Filipa looks like she might be ready to cry again. The conversation is getting less interesting. Paul, who was winding up for another punch, suddenly makes a break for the opposite end of the porch. He's moaning.

"Eddie. Always Eddie. He's ruined me again. Eddie will be my death."

"And I suppose you'll blame me for that too, father?" says Dak.

"Stop" says Paul, turning around, and taking a step towards Dak.

"Saying" Paul continues, raising his voice, taking another step and looking for something solid to pick up, in order to hit Dak.

"That" and Paul finishes in a roar and tries to kick Dak and simultaneously make a jump towards him, both his arms outstretched, reaching for Dak's neck. Paul suddenly seems possessed of an almost supernatural strength and agility. Filipa jumps to her feet, to get out of the way of both male trajectories.

Dak screams, but easily dances out of his way. Filipa helps Paul get back on his feet, untangles his feet from the chains of the swing, sets the tables and chairs upright that Paul's tipped over, finds the rug Paul slipped on, and places it back by the front door.

"You only have to ask me once" says Dak, carefully keeping a column of the porch between him and Paul's hands and feet.

"Ask you once, what?" says Paul, moving towards Dak again.

Filipa looks at Paul speculatively. She calls out to him as Paul runs after Dak again.

"So… Paul… you helped this young man, thinking he was our

son. How did you recognize him?" Paul stops running, looks back at Filipa.

"I didn't"

"You didn't. Well, that explains it all. Well, Paul, then, why did you…"

Both Paul and Dak say "Eddie" at the same time.

Paul lunges for Dak again. Dak jumps off the porch and holds onto it from the outside, hanging on the porch rail over the alley by the side of the porch. Unfortunately, right here he has a twenty foot drop to cracked concrete and broken glass. So instead of jumping off, Dak wraps his arms around the column and swings to get his feet back on the deck. Paul watches, so that he can step on any hands or feet that are giving Dak a foothold. Dak throws a foot up. Paul kicks it off.

"Hey!" says Dak.

"How could you not have known?" says Filipa and collapses into the swing again in a heap of sniffles and sobbing.

"Your own son?" she says weeping. Paul looks between Filipa and Dak, torn between comforting the one, and dismembering the other, and decides with the utmost difficulty, to force himself to turn towards Filipa.

Dak sighs loudly. He throws a foot up again. Paul glares in his direction, but leans over Filipa, he grabs one of her hands and holds it. Dak throws another foot up.

"Why did you think of coming to San Francisco, Filipita?"

"One of my son's friends said that a man from San Francisco had bailed him out of jail and brought him north, back to his city, to here. So I followed. And I looked for you. When I had no more hope."

Paul pats her hand. He is annoyed to find that Filipa has grabbed Dak's hand with her other hand, and that she is holding on to Dak's hand with what Paul would call a maternal ferocity. Paul will never understand women.

"Pablito, I mean Paul, Do I have anything to hope for now? What will I do? What will you do? Oh, Pablito, what will we do? Where is my son, Pablito? Where?"

Paul glares at Dak, but his glares have no effect. Filipa continues to hold on tight, and Dak lets her. Paul bends down to speak to Filipa, rubbing her hand, trying to reassure her with his voice and touch.

"Look. Filipa. It's been an eventful morning. An even more eventful last fifteen minutes. Take this imposter inside with you and keep an eye on him. I'll go out and try and see what I can find out about your, I mean, about our, son.

Dak, by now, is standing beside Filipa. Paul aims a kick at his behind as he passes by, but of course, misses. He ends up stubbing his toe on a table. His toe starts bleeding. Hopping on one foot, he follows the two of them towards the front door.

"I think," says Paul talking out loud, "the best way to do that, is to find Eddie. And quick." Dak helps Filipa in the door and sends a meaningful, supportive look her way as he pats her back, gently and politely. Dak gives Filipa more Kleenex, and Paul notes, while he's doing that, Dak sends a murderous glance back at Paul as if to say look at what a mess you've made of everything and everyone here this morning. Dak and Filipa both go inside. Dak is holding both her hands now. Filipa is leaning her head on his shoulder.

Paul mutters to himself "I can't ever win, can I? Then Paul thinks of Eddie. He starts talking out loud, in a very authoritative voice. "I'm going to be looking for Eddie, for the rest of my life. I'll never rest. You hear that, Eddie? Never. Eddie, you just better hope I don't find you. Hope and pray, Eddie. Hope and pray".

Filipa and Dak both look out of one of the front windows, wondering who he's talking to. Dak just shakes his head. Paul starts wondering how in the hell he's going to get across his living room floor without bleeding all over it.

Yup, Eddie just better hope I don't...

That's the point when the fire engine pulls up and the Emergency Response Team piles out of their ambulance, calling out "911 here", and both efficiently descend upon Paul as he hops fitfully across the porch, trying unsuccessfully to limp away to the front door and to safety inside his new house.

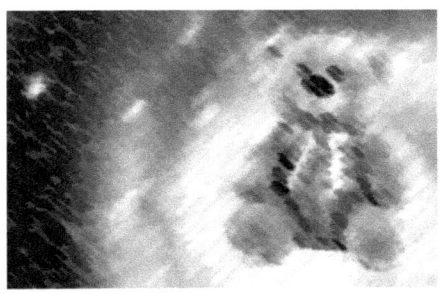

CHAPTER 23
(Sunday 12:00 P.M.,
Ace and Eddie on Market Street in the Castro)

The sun beats down, from clear blue skies, grilling The City up to a toasty summer temperature of 69 degrees. It's noon on a Sunday morning, now almost afternoon. The Castro, being on a hill which is vaguely east facing, always gets lots of morning sunlight and soft, early evening shadows. So, it being noon, and since for the moment the fog is nowhere to be seen, the streets are brightly lit, people are thronging the sidewalks, dense knots of individuals are walking to or from brunches, and the Castro is bathed in clarity and illumination.

Ace jogs out of his gym, Nike's hitting the concrete with satisfying traction, having nailed his workout, right after breakfast, first thing in the morning, after a night on Charley's couch. He's whistling. He's pumped. His endorphins are flowing freely. His car is parked four blocks away at a dry cleaners that won't open till Monday. He's found parking, and he's happy. He's stoked. Life is looking favorably upon Ace. And Ace is looking favorably back at life.

Jay is in Ace's near future. Ace is vibrating, his happy ending is so close he can taste it. He can hardly stand to be himself, he is so satisfied.

Ace steps up the volume on his MP3 player and hums tunelessly, but energetically. It's a little cold here on the shady side of the street. He needs to meet Eddie at the coffee shop on a corner a couple of blocks up, on the sunny side. He's going to pay off his muscle-bound creditors. He's going to propose to Jay. He'll finally be able to stop skulking around and meet his dad face to face.

"Nice" says Ace to himself. He hums louder, looks both ways, jogs across the traffic-filled lanes of Market Street and dances uphill in the sun, making odd moaning sounds to the music periodically.

Eddie punches at his phone, really not expecting anyone to answer. A very sleepy voice picks up.

"Uh, Hello?"

"Hey. Is this a bad time? Wait, is this Alice?"

"Nah, Eddie. This is Janey. Wait, hold on a sec."

"Wait, Janey, wait. Don't get her up. I'm sorry for waking you guys. I can call back later...Janey? Janey?"

"Eddie? It's the crack of dawn. Oh, wait. It's noon. Where did the morning go? Oh, my aching head. You better be all right. Where were you Eddie? Were you out all night? What's going on, cowboy?"

"Alice, I'm in big trouble."

"Go on, talk to me. What's up?"

"Dak called. Adam called. Mr. P. is out to flay me alive. He knows I stole from him to bail out Dak, who was pretending to be his son. He knows I stole from him to pretend to pay off Adam who was pretending to be Fulk. He knows Dak is not his son. He knows Adam is not Fulk. He knows there is no Fulk. God knows what else he knows. What's next?. What am I going to do, Alice?"

"Slow up there!, Whoa! Tell me again, why any of this is your problem? Didn't you spend all that money on his own son, Ace?"

"Well, yeah, but..."

"When are you going to stop taking responsibility for everyone in that berserk Periphanitides clan? Seems to me it's about time they worked all this out for themselves, without putting you in the middle."

"Neither Ace nor his dad have a strong appreciation for reality. His dad is going to blame me. I'm going to go to jail."

"Look, we'll cross that bridge when we come to it. What do you do next?"

"Help Ace pay off his Slavic Mafiosi creditors."

"Then do it. One step at a time, Eddie. Call me if you need me. Goodnight, Eddie."

Eddie says good night, but he's already just talking to his handset – the call's ended and Eddie is alone on Market again.

Eddie, hair mussed, stained clothes half on half off, has obviously been hiding and sneaking all night, watching out for police and now the Periphanitides. He hides on the steps in the entryway to a store. He gazes longingly at the piles of bread and boxes of biscuits stacked in the windows. Fuck, he hadn't even felt hungry a minute ago. Now he is starving. Not time for that now. He hasn't been home yet, he's afraid to go there. Besides the clerk in the store looks like she's coming out to shoo him away. He must be licking the window or something. Eddie shuffles off.

Ace texted him to come and meet him at the coffee shop on Market, at noon. He ducks behind a tiny hatchback, as he closes his phone, leaning against a trash can, popping up now and then to make sure that no green Jaguar with a white racing stripe and a black roof convertible top is slowly cruising up or down Market Street. He closes his eyes tight, and marshals his energies. He eases himself up into a crouching position, knees snapping, and pokes his head over the hood of the car, and again, not seeing any green sports cars, he sprints across the street and heads to the corner, running into Ace, who is adjusting the earphones to his player and texting someone, while he loudly chews gum and sings.

Ace is looking up and down the street with the anxious expression of a dog anticipating a juicy bone. He's making grunting and yammering sounds. Eddie bounces off Ace the way a ping pong ball bounces off a brick wall - the kind of brick wall you'd find in a basement supporting a 40 story building. Ace doesn't even notice Eddie ricocheting off onto the sidewalk.

Eddie (waving his hands in front of Ace) "Hello? Hello?"

Ace realizes someone is tugging on him and looks down, sees Eddie and smiles. "Eddie!" He looks again "Eddie?" Eddie looks off into the distance. "Eddie, you look terrible, what's wrong?"

"I'm going to need a passport and a plane ticket to Brazil to escape your father and Albert. I'm sure they're carrying sawed-off shotguns and hiring hit men even as we speak."

"What are you blabbing on about? Why would my dad want to go to Brazil? Look, Eddie, I'd love to hang with you and hear all about dad's travel plans, but really, we have business to attend to, right now. Important stuff."

"That's all right. Don't worry about me. I'll face death bravely. I'm sure your dad will make it quick and relatively painless. Well, quick at least…"

"Ah, just give it a rest. It can't be that bad. So you're obsessing about dad. And death, I guess. Well, if dad's mad at you I'll help you. You know I will. Don't worry about dad. Just don't you worry about it. I'll take care of everything. You'll see. Everything."

"I've heard that before. By the way, who precisely are we waiting for here? And who are all those people crowding up onto the sidewalk by the corner, looking our way?"

"It's him, isn't it?"

"Him? Who Ace? Him who? Looks to me like an older guy, surrounded by a bunch of body builders, all dressed in black. Well, except for that nervous guy in the middle of the crowd. We better move off the sidewalk, they're bustling towards us. This doesn't look good. Maybe we should go and meet and talk somewhere else."

"It's him. Just look at him."

"Him. Again with the him. Do you mean the nervous guy? The older guy? One of the anatomical miracles walking towards us? Which him should I be looking at?"

"Just gaze upon him, Eddie. Open your eyes. Have you ever seen a more handsome face? Dark, shining eyes. And just look at those eyebrows, just look at them. I mean, really, Eddie, just look at them. Like a Renaissance painting. I could do this all day. All day, man. I wish I could paint man. I'd paint him all day. All day, man."

"Are you talking about somebody *not* walking towards us? What are you going on about, Ace? I'm lacking context here, Ace…

"And I haven't even started describing his chin…"

"I hope Mr. P. and/or Albert aren't hiding behind all those squared off shoulders and broad chests rolling towards us. It's like watching a tsunami approach. Ace? Ace, are you listening to me?"

Ace yells out, making Eddie jump backwards and bounce off a car.

"Hey! Guys! Over here. Well, you took long enough."

An older man separates himself from the crowd, he's dragging a young man with dark eyebrows, and, yes a chin, and a sullen, peevish look. The young man brightens when he sees Ace. Eddie puts a lamp post between him and the growing crowd on the sidewalk and watches.

The older guy points at the younger one "This one, he takes forever to get moving. He didn't want to come. It's too early. Oh, so early. On a Sunday. Hmmph!" Ace hears none of this. He's devouring the nervous guy with the eyebrows with both of his eyes and all of his heart. Ace is busy. Ace starts babbling in a voice you'd use addressing a new-born puppy.

"Well, whatever J-boy wants, J-boy gets. You should have waited and come in the afternoon. How are you doing my little J-kins? They treating you O.K., J, hmmm? Ahhhh. J. My J."

Eddie doesn't know how much more of this he can stand. Apparently the guys in black feel the same way.

"Enough. Enough, already. Well, so much for the small talk – we're not standing here for the improvement of our health. So. There's the boy. Where's the money?"

"All here, counted and ready, as agreed." Ace pulls out a wad of bills. The older guy jumps back, the muscle guys surround them in a protective huddle. The young man with the eyebrows is left standing, outside the group, which is beginning to look like a protective circle of musk oxen, guarding the wad of green at its center from the dangerous brunch crowds of the Castro.

The young guy leans against the lamp post, which ends up meaning he's leaning next to Eddie too. The both of them hear excited voices wafting up and out of the circle of men on the sidewalk in front of them.

"Hey! Careful, tall man! Watch it! Stop with the flashing. Not on the street, not all that cash. Here. Stuff it in the hat. This one. The one I'm handing to you, tall guy. Yeah, its behind my back, just grab it. Good. There. Good. And sliding it back to me. And, good and we're done. Why is that so hard, huh?"

The guys surround Ace and the older guy. The hat is examined and its contents thoroughly and jointly counted.

Eddie leans forward. He can see the boy with the chin in profile now. And he doesn't like what he sees.

"This can't be happening. Your mother isn't named Filipa is she?"

The young man steps quickly backwards and then takes a few steps back more slowly. He studies Eddie with a cool, appraising glance. For a moment or two it looks like he won't even speak. Then he barely opens his lips, eyes still glued on Eddie, and nods his head in Eddie's direction.

"Who's asking?"

"Benjamin, don't you know who I am? It's me, Eddie." Jay just stares. "Jay or whoever you are, look at me. It's Eddie."

Jay or BJ or Benjamin allows his mouth to hang open. It's not a good look for him.

"No… No, I don't know you. Why would I know you? I swear, why are so many people asking me that lately? Do you remember me? No, I don't remember you. But do you remember *me*? No, I don't remember you. It's getting very tiring. Actually."

"Well, I won't ask you that again, Benjamin. But do you remember a certain yellow toy car, a taxi cab, and a whole set of different colored toy cars and trucks you had as a kid? No? Well, what about a teddy bear named Mr. Jenkins?"

Benjamin does not look pleased with Eddie. He's beginning to edge back towards Ace and the huddle counting the cash behind him.

"How do you know about Mr. Jenkins? Who are you? What the hell is going on?"

"Who do you think gave you Mr. Jenkins? Huh? Benjamin? It was me, Benjamin. I did. I gave you that bear. And the toy cars. And a lot of other stuff. Are you remembering it now?" Ace comes out of the massing of muscular men and approaches the two of them. The old guy calls out to him.

"Nice doing business with you, thanks for the tip, and take care of yourself. You need anything, just call. Anything. You name it, Tall Man."

"Yeah, yeah. Nice doing business with you too." Ace comes in on the tail end of the conversation. Jay-Benjamin is holding Eddie by his shoulders and looking into his eyes. Benjamin's eyes are starting to mist up a bit.

"You're Uncle Ed? Tio Eduardo?"

"Yes. I am. Unfortunately. And that's your brother" says Eddie, grabbing one of Jay-Benjamin's arms and pointing with it at the approaching Ace.

"Oh."

"Yes."

"My brother."

"Yes again."

My brother? Tio Eduardo, you're not shitting me? Please tell me you are."

"No Benito, it's true. Same father. Different mothers."

Ace breaks into their conversation with a loud yell.

"Yeehaw! And what are you two talking about so seriously? My little Jay bird? What are you talking about, huh? Mr. Jay? You just come here, come to Acey. I can't wait to get you home. You just come here and show me how happy you are to see me, my little J."

Ace kisses Benjamin and pulls him into a huge bear hug and whirls him around like Benjamin's on a merry-go-round. Round and round. Laughing the whole time. This goes on for awhile.

Benjamin however, looks very serious. Uncharacteristically serious. Eddie would think Ace would be wondering where that look was coming from. Ace is not wondering. Ace is not catching on. Eddie makes eye contact with Benjamin at each revolution and yells over Ace's laughing.

"Yup, brothers. That's no lie." Eddie has to say it a couple of times, nodding his head at Benjamin to be heard. Ace looks at Benjamin's face as he sets Benjamin back down on Terra Firma.

Ace can hardly talk, he's laughing so hard. "So, who's brother are you talking about, Eddie? I know you don't have a brother. Does Jay have a brother I don't know about? Do you, Jay? Am I going to have a new brother-in-law?"

Benjamin looks at Eddie then at Ace, then he holds out his hand out to Ace like he's asking to shake hands.

"Well, Ace, I guess I do have a brother I didn't know about. That brother is you."

Ace frowns, stands stock-still for sixty seconds, then knocks Benjamin's hand down and (of course, thinks Eddie) looks not at Benjamin, but straight at Eddie.

"What the fuck are you up to Eddie? What is that devious little mind scheming up now? Whatever it is, it's for damn sure not funny. You hear me, Eddie? Not fucking funny. None of this makes sense. None of it."

Eddie steps over by Ace. Ace is staring now at Benjamin.

"None of it…"

Eddie steps in front of Benjamin, who looks like he's starting to get mad, and puts one hand on Ace's shoulder, and another on Benjamin's.

"It will and it does, and if you'd just think about it for a second, Ace, things will go a lot smoother. Think about it instead of just jumping into things fist-first, and expecting everyone else to clean up after Ace makes his usual mess of things. What do you say, Ace?"

The three of them stand there for a minute. Ace staring mournfully at Benjamin. Benjamin glaring back. Eddie mentally counting to a hundred and looking up and down the block for suspicious green Jaguars.

"How? How did he become my brother in the time it took me to pay off that old man? How?" Ace starts moaning and shaking his head.

"Keep it down, Ace. You don't want to get us arrested for making a public disturbance."

"Oh, Benjamin. Shit. Fuck. We're never going to get a break."

"Well, think about how I feel Ace."

"Benjamin, You've found me and you've lost me. What's worse, I've found you, but now, but now…" Ace can't complete his sentence.

Benjamin opens his mouth to reply, but Eddie cuts in before this can go on much longer.

"Oh for heaven's sake, Ace, go home. See your dad. You still have Dak. Go on. Take Benjamin."

"No. I don't want to. I don't want to go home. I don't want Dak. Didn't I already tell you that? I just want my J back. I'm parked blocks and blocks away, uphill, off Divisadero. I don't want to go. I don't want Benjamin to be my brother. I… I… Eddie, I don't know what I want. I don't know. I don't know."

"Go on. It'll do you good. Sometimes the not knowing is the best part. It's means you're starting over. It could be the beginning of starting something better."

"No."

"Ace…"

"No."

Benjamin pulls away from Eddie and ducks behind him, he positions himself front and center in front of Ace, plants both feet firmly on the sidewalk and puts both hands on his hips.

"One of us has to be practical, Ace. Look, let's just meet all over again. Let's take it from the top."

"What? What are you talking about? What do you mean, Jay, I mean Benjamin, no, I mean Jay? What? What?"

"Look. Here." Benjamin holds out his hand. "My name's Benjamin, what's yours?"

"Oh. That. I don't want to get to know you again, Benjamin. I don't want to do this."

"Well, Ace, you're just gonna have to. Shake it, mister."

Eddie pushes the two of them towards Divisadero and Ace's car.

The second to the last thing he hears as the two of them walk away, heading towards the corner, is Ace complaining with Benjamin listening. Benjamin smacks Ace in the back of his head, and stops him, holding him by his shoulders. Ace hunches over.

The last thing Eddie hears is Benjamin saying "Behave." Benjamin leads Ace around the corner. Eddie waits. He thinks somehow they're going to be all right.

He walks back towards the shop with the bread in the window. It's time for breakfast. Eddie's going to stuff himself with croissants. Then it's time to face the music. No more hiding and creeping. Alice is right. Eddie's done with all that. Eddie's headed back to the Periphanitides. To see Paul. And put an end to all this Eddie-bashing.

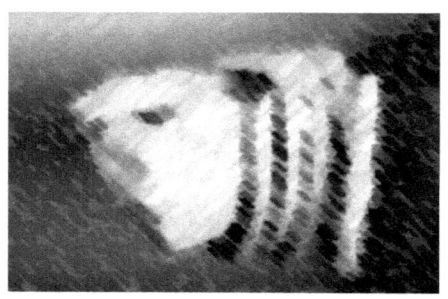

CHAPTER 24
(Sunday Afternoon 1:17 P.M.,
Eddie at Mr. P.'s House on Twin Peaks)

Eddie's yellow Vespa, The Great Banana runs out of gas at the halfway point between 18th and 19th going up Noe, which is to say, at the bottom of a very, very long and steep hill. When Eddie jogs to the top of the hill, and turns right to climb yet another hill, he's half dead and just barely breathing.

When he climbs finally to the top of that hill, and stands in front of Mr. P.'s house, he is sure he's lost a lung, and his legs feel like overstretched rubber bands. He almost passes the house, it looks like a parking lot up here. Ace's car isn't here yet, but there's and old red car in front, parked perilously close to Mr. P's green jaguar, and in front of that is Albert's scratched and faded blue Camry from the 1980's.

There's also a long black limousine type vehicle idling across the street. One window in the back mysteriously rolls one quarter of the way down as Eddie walks up the front stairs, gasping piteously at each step. When Eddie looks back at it, once he's in front of the door, the window is up again. Eddie doesn't watch much more because Mr. P. and Albert are talking loudly in front of an open window, standing in the big floor-to-ceiling walls of glass on the first floor overlooking the street and the city and all of the bay.

"All this running around, Paul, really, is it necessary? Does it accomplish something? Hmmm?"

"Eddie's made a fool of both of us. He must be stopped. To be stopped, he must be found. To be found, there must be running. Surely you can see that, Albert. He's made us both a laughing-stock."

"Well, maybe you. You're welcome to him. I think I'm getting too old to be doing all this spy business. You know I don't drive a stick very well. And that Jaguar is a terror to stop on an incline. I tell you, I won't drive around in it again. My nerves won't take it. It's the running that gets to you. And the dodging. And the steep hills. And the shifting gears. And the rolling backwards while you shift."

"And Eddie's milked me for thousands. I really don't want to say how much. But, a lot, Albert ."

"And the getting in and then the getting out of cars. The walking. Oh, the waiting. And, what about the missing meals? What about them, Paul? What about the meals? I'd forgotten about the food. Or lack thereof."

"What are you going on about Albert? We just had breakfast."

Albert mutters to himself under his breath "You had breakfast. I had air. I was running."

"Think, Albert, think, where could Eddie be? Right now? If I could only get my hands on him. He's probably halfway to Rio. If he is in Brazil, I wonder, there must be some diplomatic mechanism, some legal methodology for me to get my money back. There must be something. Albert, do you know if they torture people in Brazil? How about corporal punishment?"

Albert whispers to himself – "Where's Eddie? Where's Eddie? Where could Eddie be? Money, money, money, that's all you think about."

"Think, Albert, where do we look for him?"

Albert makes a show of looking over the side of the window, peering up and down the street, whispering to himself - "Look at the bottom of the bay, for all I care."

"What's that Albert? I can't hear a thing you're saying. You see him? Any signs of him? Anywhere? Where's that damned cell phone, maybe he'll answer by accident if I call him quickly."

Albert leans further out of the window and chews on his beard, muttering "Find it yourself."

Eddie ducks around the house. In less than a minute, Eddie, who snuck in by the back door using his security code, walks up behind Mr. P. who is looking over Albert's shoulder who is still gazing lackadaisically here and there out the window into the bright Sunday afternoon air. Eddie stands a few feet behind Mr. P. and talks in a very loud, but recognizably conversational voice – his normal voice for talking to Mr. P.

"Do you need your cell phone, Mr. Periphanitides?"

"What? Oh, no, Eddie, not now. Eddie! Eddie! Why, yes, Eddie, by all means give me my phone. I want to call the police. You've robbed me. I claim citizen's arrest. Albert, bind him."

Albert, who has pulled back in from the window, looks at Paul in wild surprise.

"What? Bind him? You want me to tie him up? With what, might I ask? The air?" Albert folds his hands over his substantial stomach and shoots a withering stare at Eddie and a scornful glance at Mr. P. Albert holds his empty hands up in the air. Obviously nothing to bind with. No binding implements anywhere to be seen. Albert seems to be thinking Paul will have to do without binding today. Poor, poor Paul. Albert is humming happily to himself, and smiling, looking at Mr. P., looking at Eddie, looking at his own empty hands, then looking back at Mr. P.

Mr. P. stops. He looks with concern at Albert.

"Are you quite all right, Albert? Feeling O.K.? You seem a bit... well... giddy. Like a schoolgirl."

"No. Fine. Not feeling unwell in the slightest Paul. Fit as a fiddle. That's me." Albert is still humming and smiling. Paul shakes his head.

"Oh. Well. Surely. Surely, there must be rope or something, somewhere, perhaps the basement, perhaps the kitchen. Just slip away down there, Albert, and..." Albert is shaking his head "no" furiously. Mr. P. looks puzzled. He stands, closes one eye, and puts his hand to his forehead. With his handsome face, mane of white hair, sensitive eyes, he looks the personification of foresight and prudence. Even Eddie is impressed. However, Mr. P. doesn't think of anything. Albert is content to be silent and smile. There is a quiet in the house.

Eddie breaks in, seeing the conversation beginning to flag somewhat, "Would, uh, this window sash do, sir?"

"What?" Mr. P.'s face immediately registers a very poetic righteous indignation. Again, as always, Eddie is charmed. It's very expressive, that face.

"What, Eddie? What's that you hold? A piece of my window treatment. The effrontery. Well. Oh. Yes. I see. Do you see, Albert? Do you see, now? That will do as a rope. I'm surprised you didn't' think of it, being in higher education for so many years. Surprised. Yes. Very. There you go, Albert. Tie away. You were a boy scout weren't you?"

Albert weakly wraps the velvety window sash a few times around Eddie's wrists and around Eddie's ankles and pokes and prods at it, making a desultory knot. He returns to the window and observes the two of them. Mr. P. nods sagely.

"Well done, Albert. Well done. Job one - incapacitate Eddie - check. Job two - inform the police. Albert?"

"Go ahead and call" says Eddie. "I'll find the cell phone, Albert can follow me and pick it up when I find it, since anyone can see I can't carry anything around in my current condition."

Eddie hops towards the center of the house and the stairs. Mr. P. watches, interested in spite of himself. Albert watches with a sour, worried expression. He moves closer to Mr. P. and talks in a voice loud enough to be heard across the street.

"Albert cannot follow. Look. Watch yourself Paul, he's planning something. I can tell he's scheming again." Albert follows Eddie to the spiral stairs.

"Come, Edward, you can't go down a staircase like that. I'd have to carry you. Paul, I will not carry Edward. Not down those blasted stairs from hell." Eddie starts hopping faster, Albert shuffles behind in a kind of gliding double time. There is a silence for a few moments again, punctuated only by Eddie's hops and Albert's unhappy shuffles, and the sound of Mr. P. anxiously pacing in front of the large front windows.

Eddie sees movement out of the side of his eyes, turns and first Thad appears, moaning softly to himself, then Ace, then Benjamin who is being led by the hand by Ace. Benjamin is holding his finger up to his mouth. Ace looks worried, Thad is squinting, like it's too bright and too loud and too early and he has a terminal, emergency room version of a headache – all of which are probably true.

The three of them creep up the staircase from the basement, in stocking feet, go past the first floor, keep right on climbing to the second floor. Albert stands open-mouthed, glaring at Eddie, like this is all part of some plot to deprive Albert of his reason and any opportunity for a future lunch.

Eddie forces himself to look at Mr. P. as he turns around, to face Albert and Eddie. Eddie shakes his head no at Albert. Albert says nothing, but continues to glare at Eddie. Mr. P. decides at that moment to call out to Albert.

"But, then, maybe I won't call, Albert. Later, certainly, but maybe not immediately."

Albert, alternating between smiles and frowns depending on whether he's facing Paul or facing Eddie is getting a little bewildered. And maybe a little nauseous.

"No, I insist, Mr. P., sir – I insist and I demand it. Call the police, let's get all this down on public record."

"Ah, yes. Public record. Hmmm. Well."

Mr. P. turns quickly towards Albert, who is tip-toeing for the front door, behind Paul's back. "Well, and what do you think, Albert?" Albert spins around and faces Paul. Albert takes in a deep breath. Exhales.

"So now we're not ordering Albert around, are we? We're asking Albert for advice? Now Albert is useful for something other than knotting and retrieving and running?"

Mr. P. waits in silence. He knows Albert has to run down before he'll answer a question when he gets like this.

"What do I think? What do I think? I'll tell you exactly what I think." Albert whirls around and points at Eddie. "Call them. Call the police, Paul. Put this troublemaker behind bars before he does more mischief. That is what I think, Paul. Do it. Do it now. What are you afraid of? Do it for the good of humanity. And for God's sake, let me get something to eat."

Mr. P. opens his mouth then closes it slowly. Mr. P.'s been halted in mid-response. He closes his mouth tightly and he rethinks his situation. A misty, far-away, contemplative look begins to fill his eyes. He reflects. Then he looks directly at Eddie. And Mr. P. smiles. He is the soul of sweet reason and rationality. What sensible man could oppose such a man as he? Eddie watches and shakes his head observing a true artist at work.

"Eddie?" says Mr. P.

Eddie wonders to himself as he admires that face and jumps in place to keep his balance – how does Mr. P. do it? How does he get his face so beautifully expressive? At his age? Was he an actor before he became an iron filings tycoon? Did he take lessons from someone? Was he the young able apprentice to an evil Grand Master of the Manipulative Arts? Is he a secret Knights Templar? What? Why? How? How does he do it?

"Eddie?"

Eddie at that very point in time, right then and there has an epiphany between hops. His second epiphany in 24 hours. He will never be free of the Periphanitides. He's bewitched by them - Mr. P., Ace, the whole crazy family of Periphanitides. And now there's Benjamin too. And can Filipa be far away? No. No. Unless he does something drastic - drastic and unexpected – he'll be working for these Periphanitides for the rest of his natural life. Eddie shakes his head and finds Mr. P. and Albert staring at him. Mr. P. seems to be talking to him.

"Eddie?"

Eddie nods, slowly.

"Yes, Eddie, Albert said I was afraid – is there anything else I should be afraid of?"

Eddie stops nodding.

"Uh..." Eddie can't think.

"Uh, well, sir..." Once again he has no idea what he's going to say next.

"Sir. Well, that is, well, uh, you know, I really couldn't say, sir. I might be able to help if I knew why, exactly it is, uh, we are calling the police, that is…"

Mr. P. looks at Albert raising his eyebrows and assuming an expectant expression. But Albert is finished with explanations. At least for now. No explanations on an empty stomach. Albert mutters to himself, crosses his arms, turns his back and looks out towards the distant glazing on the floor-to-ceiling windows and the sparkling blue sky showing beyond them

Albert is talking to himself "It's just within reach. I could be there. I could. In the space of a moment. Breakfast. Freedom. Tranquility."

What follows is a long moment of expectation in the House Periphanitides.

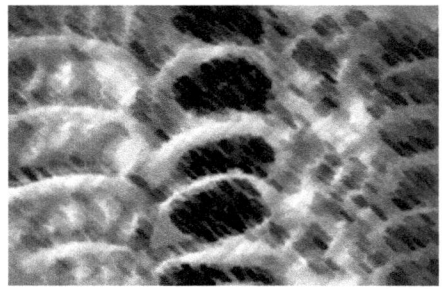

CHAPTER 25
(Sunday Afternoon 1:35 P.M,
Eddie at Mr. P.'s House on Twin Peaks)

After a moment, Mr. P. gives up on the unresponsive Albert. He looks at the ceiling, puts one hand up to his chin, and thinks again. Mr. P. even puts on a new and improved expression of thoughtful thinking. Eddie has got to stop watching Mr. P. with so much pleasure. Besides, Mr. P. is starting to look a little angry, a little upset.

"Well, we'll set aside what it is, exactly I'm afraid of. Time enough for all that later, right Albert?

Albert isn't listening, or at least he's wanting it to appear that way. Mr. P. continues, slightly exasperated.

"So, Eddie, first, what prompted you to say – well to say that the young man living in my house was actually my long lost son, since you knew he was not?"

"I chose to."

"You did it because... you chose to?"

"You got it. Five will get you ten, that young man *is* a son. I know he is."

Albert, who is, after all, overhearing the conversation, forgetting about breakfast, and getting interested again in spite of his desperate desire to escape this house, snorts loudly in what must have been an abortive guffaw. He smiles at Mr. P. and sidles up closer to Eddie, who's bouncing carefully on the toes of his shoes, and whispers to Eddie.

"I don't know where you're headed with all this, my boy, but watch yourself, Eddie. Don't say I didn't warn you. Paul is out for blood this time."

Albert has obviously changed allegiances. Mr. P. speaks forcibly in Eddie's direction. Albert assumes an innocent expression.

"Humph! A son the mother doesn't know?"

"Go ahead, bet me. He's a son of his mother." Albert rolls his eyes. Eddie jumps a few times forwards and backwards, so he doesn't tip over. The window sashes binding him are starting to work loose. Eddie tries to re-tie them by hopping in circles and jerking on them when he's facing away from everyone. Eddie rapidly gets dizzy. Mr. P. sighs.

"Well, yes, Eddie. That is, I mean no, Eddie. That is, this is getting us nowhere. Who *is he*, Eddie?"

Eddie slows down his spinning, but he sways this way and that, and the window sashes are falling off more and more.

"Excuse me, Mr. P.? What did you say?"

"Stop twirling like a dervish and listen to me. Who the hell is that young man?"

"If you must know, he's your son's boyfriend."

"His boyfriend? Already living in my house? I knew it. I knew it. Wait. Then why did I give you all that money? The first forty thousand, a couple of weeks ago? If he's not my son, who got that?"

"I actually did use that, to bail out the young man, Dak, and keep him from being shipped off to someplace while he was awaiting trial."

"I won't even ask for what crime. Why would you trick me like that, Eddie? Why? Are you opening up a private jail here in my house?

Albert stands behind Mr. P. now, breathing heavily. Mr. P. looks back with an annoyed expression and Albert mouths the words "Watch it" as Eddie finally bounces back into place in front of Mr. P. No one notices that his bound feet and hands are for all practical purposes free now. Eddie twists the sash around his limbs a couple of times, not bothering to hide his re-tying efforts anymore. He figures he should at least maintain the outward appearance of being a prisoner. But no, it all falls off the next time he moves his feet.

"Oh, never mind. And what about the last forty thousand? Where did that disappear to? Another young man who is not my son?"

"No. I gave that to someone that is your son."

"I have another son. What does that make? Three, no four. This is my day for gaining sons. How many does this make, Albert?"

He looks over at Albert, who is shaking his head, and counting something on his fingers. Albert goes over the same four fingers a couple of times. Mr. P. waits, watching Albert. Eddie clears his throat. Both Mr. P. and Albert look up with pained expressions, Eddie continues.

"Well, yes. But no. Uh, I don't know how many sir. I gave this money to the same son. The same son you already knew about. The one you have."

"The same son, you say?" Mr. P. looks at Albert. Albert shrugs, spreading and wiggling his fingers, looking at his hands.

"The same. We're talking about William. Ace."

"Oh." Mr. P. looks at Albert again. Albert is now staring patiently ahead of him, a stoic, resigned expression on his face. Mr. P. looks back at Eddie. "And you did that because…"

"Because I chose to."

Albert suppresses a giggle, doesn't suppress the snorting, and mutters to himself "I saw that coming."

Mr. P. looks at Albert, at Eddie, at Albert again. Then he raises his fist and looks for something to slam it down upon. Of course, his empty living room has nothing to break in it, at least not anymore. He slams his fist into his open palm, then bites his lip and curses "Damn, that hurt." Mr. P. looks fiercely at Eddie.

"Eddie, this has got to stop."

Eddie assumes a carefully hurt expression on his face. "Am I to be treated like a criminal here? Someone who only has the Periphanitides' family interests at heart? Am I?" Eddie has raised his hands at this point, and it's very clear he's no longer tied up as the sash is trailing behind him on the floor. No one notices. He's stopped hopping. He approaches Mr. P. freely walking.

"I deserve better, sir."

"Don't we all" says Albert, smiling and rocking back and forth on his heels, with his hands behind his back. He keeps glancing longingly in the direction of the stairs. He's licking his lips. He looks very hungry.

Albert suddenly makes a dash for it.

"Where are you going Albert?" says Mr. P. to the retreating form of Albert making for the back stairs. Albert stops as if he's been shot. He slowly turns around.

"Look, sir, Mr. P. All this is easily cleared up. Just go upstairs. Go up and check the second bedroom. Tell me what you see."

"Upstairs? Second bedroom? What are you up to Eddie? What do you know about this Albert?" Albert stares placidly ahead.

"More than I'd have liked to" mutters Albert. There is an uncomfortable silence. Albert's stomach growls. Mr. P. looks at Eddie, calculating.

"All right. I'll go."

"Well, Paul, if you're going upstairs, I'll just pop down into the kitchen for a few seconds. I'll be back. Directly."

"No, Albert. Someone has to keep an eye on Eddie. This could just be a trick. I don't want to take him with me. Since, apparently your knot-tying abilities are abysmal, you will just have to wait here and make sure he doesn't run off again. Not before we've cleared all this up."

Mr. P. strolls off to the spiral staircase. Albert rushes next to Eddie.

"Look, here, Eddie. What's all this about, anyways? And why do you always get me mixed up with your excessive plotting and your non-stop scheming? And where are you going to now? Stop. Stop, I say. Ah, bollocks." Eddie leaves Albert scowling.

Eddie jogs over the staircase and disappears downstairs, leaving Albert standing morosely at the head of the stairs. Eddie returns, holding something in his hands. Albert is still scowling, But now he is lying on the floor staring up at the ceiling. You can tell Albert has just about had enough of the Periphanitides for one day, or possibly for the remainder of the year. Eddie tries to help him to his knees. Albert refuses to get up. Mr. P.'s feet appear on the staircase, descending.

"What are you doing down on the floor Albert?", Mr. P. asks. Before Albert can answer, the two of them, Albert and Eddie hear a great many feet making their way towards them.

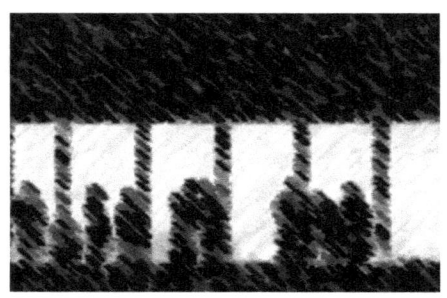

CHAPTER 26
(Sunday Afternoon 2:15 P.M,
Eddie at Mr. P.'s House on Twin Peaks)

Mr. P. returns down the staircase. He's not alone. He brings a young man in. It's Benjamin. More people follow. Filipa is fawning over Benjamin.

Ace is walking in behind Benjamin with Thad trailing behind Ace. Dak is walking behind all of them, a little sheepishly. Thad looks a little worse for the wear. Well maybe even a little worse than that. He must have had some night, caught in some man-stampede. Eddie can hear Thad's voice complaining from the next floor as the whole troop tromps down the stairs. Lucite groans in the process. Thad's pleasant whine fills the air.

"God, it's early. I haven't seen the morning sun on a Sunday for years. Or noon, for that matter. Who's up at this ridiculous hour? Why is the sun so incredibly bright?"

As if on cue, patches of fog begin to roll in. The sunlight blurs and falters, then fades out entirely. Shades of gray dance in front of the windows. Thad stands in front of one of them, and bows and spreads his hands out like someone getting applause on a stage.

"Ask and you shall receive" he announces, but frowns as he bows down "shit, my aching head. Does anyone have any aspirin around here? Or something stronger?" More fog falls over the house and the light weakens to its more natural, deep, habitual gloom. All you can see out the tall windows are the outlines of shadows, where houses and street at one time shone under the blazing noonday sun.

At that moment, an older man with black spiky hair, fierce gray sideburns and enormous aviator glasses marches in through the front door, of course, the one time Mr. P. forgets to lock it.

"All right, Periphanitides, all right. I saw people sneaking in here from the garage. What do you know? Spill it. What have you found out about Dak?" The man is brandishing a bundle of bills in one hand, waving them about. "I have the money. I've kept my side of the bargain. Paul! Tell me. Paul!"

Dak looks up with a shocked expression on his face. "R.L.?" The older man with the money almost falls backwards out the open door onto the porch. He catches himself at the last moment on the door jamb and rips a small piece off. Mr. P. winces.

"Dak?"

"Yes, it's Dak."

"Dak!. Dak! My boy! What have they done to you? Tell me! Dak!"

Mr. P., who has braced himself on the spider web coffee table, avoiding the splintered glass piled up underneath it, takes another step backward as this new stranger rushes in a second time, yelling at the top of his lungs. Then Mr. P. understands. Mr. P. knows. Mr. P. leans forward with a dazed, dizzy look in his eyes. "You. The pirate banker captain whoever you are. You. You know Dak? You know my son?"

Dak stares at Mr. P. in disbelief. "Oh, so now I'm your son again? Nothing doing. I'm leaving this nut house, for good."

Mr. P. can only look and nod. Dak and the Captain ignore him.

"Dak. Are you hurt?" - meanwhile the pirate captain has sunk to one knee - "Come home with me Dak. I'm sorry. I was wrong. You were right, all along. Come back home, Dak. Come home."

"R.L., stop it. You're embarrassing me." Dak smiles politely, looking at everyone, who is staring right back at him. Thad is still missing, searching the house, looking for acetaminophen or some other form of pain relief. Dak helps the Captain to his feet. He notices the money he's waving around for the first time.

"What's all this, R.L.?"

"I was going to pay Paul back for all the money he spent to get you out of jail."

"Oh. Mr. Periphanitides didn't pay for me. That man paid for me." Dak is pointing at Eddie.

"Then here, and much thanks, stranger. You do not know the good you do."

Incredulous, Eddie holds out his hand. The pirate captain deposits the cash. Dak smiles at Eddie.

The pirate captain doesn't see all this. He is looking at Dak. Dak looks deeply into R.L.'s eyes. They kiss. They walk out together, holding hands. Thad meanwhile comes back into the room, holding a glass of water and a pile of white pills. He also holds two beers. "So what did I miss?"

Everyone starts talking at once.

Mr. P. is talking to Filipa and Benjamin, "Of course you can stay here, both of you. Benjamin, my son. How you've grown. And Filipa, there's plenty of room on the fourth floor. Benjamin can have your room, Ace. No, you're going back to L.A. You have a job to do. No, you're working in Los Angeles. It's time you grew up."

Ace looks troubled and proud and very conflicted. All at the same time. "Sure. Sure. Anything J, I mean, B, I mean Benjamin - I mean, whatever he wants. Anything. Fine. Good. God, I'm so confused." He looks for a place to sit down in his father's living room. Albert smiles. Eddie can see him thinking - of course there is no place to sit down. Ace finally collapses on the floor.

Benjamin looks down at Ace's unshaven troubled face "You'll get used to it. It'll be easy. You'll see. I'll *help* you."

"You'll help me?" Ace looks weak.

"Get used to what?" says Filipa and Mr. P. at the same time.

Ace looks at Benjamin who smiles and looks at Filipa "Mom, just to life, get used to life."

Eddie watches the three of them with a satisfied expression on his face. He sees a small box-like object on the floor by the front door. He picks it up. It's Mr. P.'s cell. He looks directly at Mr. P. Its' getting darker in the house. The street outside is mostly gone, just the stray lamppost sticking up through the clouds. A fine white mist is curling in at the open front door.

"So, when do you take me in?"says Eddie to Mr. P.

"In? Into where?" says Mr. P..

"Into the police station, of course. I found your cell phone." Eddie holds it out to him.

"What is he talking about dear?" says Filipa "Is someone calling the police?"

"The police?" says Mr. P. "my cell phone?"

"You're taking me in. I think you should."

Ace, Filipa, Thad, and Benjamin watch Mr. P.. Albert looks longingly at the stairs and freedom and food.

"Uh, well, there's no need for that, Eddie. None." Mr. P. looks at Eddie closely. "Is there?"

"Sir, I don't know, sir. I think I deserve a reward. For all I've done."

"A reward? Well, I don't, that is, I mean to say, the money, a reward…"

"Yes, dear. You are very lucky to have someone like Eddie. He's worth his weight in gold" says Filipa.

"Everyone says that" says Eddie. Mr. P. briefly nods his handsome head. He tries to look severe. But it's not working. Mr. P. is looking too pleased with himself just now to be his usual harsh self. But he tries anyway.

"And a raise, sir."

"A raise?" Mr. P. gasps, looks around at the expectant faces around him, finds no harshness, just welcome and gives up. "All right. All right. All right, I said. You have a raise."

"And ask my pardon."

"Anything. Let's be done with it. Please pardon me Edward."

"I forgive you, Mr. P."

Mr. P. looks like he's about to explode, but Filipa pats him on the hand and calms him down. Eddie notices she's nodding a lot. Mr. P. is nodding back. Benjamin stands with his arms around his mother's waist, smiling and teasing Ace. Ace is trying to smile, sometimes successfully. Thad is holding his head and breathing deeply, watching Ace. You can tell he's trying to figure out how he can get all this to work out – somehow - in Thad's favor. Albert watches them all, like God on high and is pleased, mightily pleased.

Eddie watches them all too, and knows them all, and he guesses he loves them all. But he can't save them from themselves. They've got to do that on their own. From now on. Maybe they'd been doing it all along anyways, and Eddie just hadn't noticed.

Eddie closes the front door behind him, and a cold curtain of mist blows over Eddie's face as he gingerly steps down the steep stairs towards the street. Eddie remembers something, something in his coat pocket, and he jumps back inside to drop a bag filled with a napkin filled with a number of fresh croissants directly into Albert's hands. There's even some pats of butter in the bag and some honey packets. He makes eyebrows at Albert and then makes good his escape.

Eddie heads out, leaves the door open and turns around, standing on the porch. He steps back a few feet to the left and looks back in through the big front windows at the golden world inside. Filipa is turning on lamps. Albert makes very good speed for a man his age, head down, determined stride - focusing all his energy on moving his body towards the kitchen and presumably coffee. Thad sighs and asks someone to close the front door. Everyone starts to speak at once.

In a moment, Eddie is on the foggy sidewalk and safely down the steps, no injuries this time, and bam! he's on the street just as hears the front door closed and latched. They're getting along without him. Just like Alice said they would. He wanders off, heading down the sidewalk, allowing gravity to pull him downhill, on the lookout for The Great Banana (his oh so yellow Vespa) - not looking forward to pushing it around the Castro and filling it up with gas - but really, in no big hurry to get back home.

Eddie has nowhere he has to be. And that's fine with Eddie. Strangely, fine.

EPILOGUE
(A Few Months Later,
Eddie at Eddie's New Place)

It's hot out. So, Alice throws another beer Deb's way, then throws another two right after that, just to keep Deb busy. Janey, Alice's girlfriend sits on Alice's knee. Janey is getting her back rubbed by Alice and both of them are looking over at Eddie. Alice smiles her crooked smile in his direction.

"So, Eddie, whatcha call this place again? You gave it a name right? Like it's an estate or something. You calling it Graceland maybe?"

"Nah, Alice. It's called Rosy Beginnings."

"Nice, Eddie, nice." Alice kicks her feet up on a picnic table, pushes her chair back, leans into her leather jacket and just absorbs the whole scene in front of her. She has a quiet smile on her lips. Janey resettles herself down in the freshly cut lawn at Alice's feet and looks for some stray long stems of grass growing up through the chain link fence behind them, starts plaiting them carefully into a long belt in some complicated pattern.

Eddie's impressed. Janey's kind of shy, but she's direct. You'd have to be, living with Alice. Direct, that is. Janey looks down but speaks upwards in a clear voice towards Eddie "Yeah, real nice,

Eddie. Great place. I'm happy for you."

Alice winks at Eddie over Janey's head. She has a bigger smile on her face now. She takes a long chug on her beer. A bustling noise starts making its way towards them.

"So. So. So, where's this Rosy? Huh Al? This Rosy Beguptkis? And is she single? Oh, hell, what do I care?" says a slightly swaying Deb as she navigates back through the crowd, to get closer to the bar (which is just a red tablecloth draped over a few T.V. trays), "Is she cute? That's the question. And does she like older women? Sexy, older women? Sexy, drunk, older women?"

Deb throws one arm over Thad's shoulder, who's standing motionless by the beer tables. Thad's holding a nearly full manhattan. Thad has one of the blankest expressions on his face Eddie's ever seen on Thad. Thad hasn't been home at Eddie's trailer for 2 days and 3 nights in a row now.

Eddie's not sure what he thinks about that. Thad is a handful. Who knows why Thad does the things he does? Thad doesn't even know. When Thad first moved up north here, into Eddie's trailer, 34 eventful days ago, Thad turned Eddie inside out. Eddie was a house cat turned feral. The sex, it was non-stop. Now, well, Thad throws Deb's hand off his shirt, but doesn't look at her. He doesn't look at Eddie either. He just looks. Without looking at anything.

Eddie breathes in and out. The heat feels fine. He expected his asthma to get worse, being out in the country and all, and the new job, and the hard work, but so far, he's been doing pretty good. No, that's not true. He's been doing great. Eddie's been doing better now than he's done in years.

Ace pushes past Deb, then Ace pushes past Thad, then Ace races Deb to the bar. Deb beats him. Ace is talking over his shoulder at someone. Eddie rolls his eyes.

"I said no, Benjamin, no." Eddie looks, and sure enough, he sees a newly-bleached, platinum blond head following Ace. They're fighting again. As usual.

"Ah, c'mon, Acer, c'mon, you promised. You know you did."

"I promised before I morphed into your older brother. You are *not* going to a circuit party in Florida. Things happen. People happen. A lot of shit happens. Well, it's all going to happen to someone else, someone *other* than my kid brother. Get it? It will all have to go on and fucking happen without you fucking being there this fucking year. You are not fucking going, Benjamin. No."

Benjamin maintains a carefully neutral expression on his face. He knows it drives Ace wild. "Benjamin, I said no. No. Capische? No. Speeken Zee Das Angleesh?"

"You're so cute when you get mad, Ace."

"You can't call me cute anymore, Benjamin." Ace looks over at Eddie "Was I ever in my life as difficult as this? Ever?"

Eddie keeps his mouth safely shut. He doesn't venture to answer. Instead he smiles benignly, making his eyes as wide and as accepting as he can get them. There is a moment of silence.

Across the yard is the sound of Deb harassing two women who have just arrived in a very dirty, once-white truck. Deb is desperate to get them to do some unspecified thing, or series of things. To Eddie it sounds like the women are weakening. Deb sounds happier and happier.

Then Ace begins rationing Benjamin's beer intake. That involves more negotiations. The two of them, Ace and Benjamin, move off towards the back of the trailer where the volleyball net is strung up.

"Acer, you were a lot more fun when I wasn't related to you."

Their voices, somehow, do not grow softer, the further away they get. It promises to be quite the afternoon.

Now Thad is talking with Charley over by the mobile home's front door, by the deck. Charley's new boyfriend Harold, is off trying to re-hang the volleyball net, which has an unfortunate tendency to sag in the middle when unwatched. Harold's an engineer. He knows he can fix it. That's all right with Eddie. Charley looks happy when she's around Harold. Eddie likes it when Charley looks happy. And Charley isn't looking over at Ace, all the time, every five minutes like she used to. She looks calmer. Quieter. Like a cat that's landed on its feet.

Thad's face continues to radiate a disquieting blankness. Eddie thinks maybe he should talk to Thad, see what's what, so to speak, so Eddie walks over to the two of them, Charley and Thad, carrying some bottles of water. Charley's long legs are draped across the stairs leading up to Eddie's covered porch. Thad is leaning gracefully, intertwining his bare and bulging arms around a post at the base of the stairs. Charley's motioning with her hands for Eddie to hurry on over. Eddie hands Charley the waters. Thad observes the two of them, but doesn't move a muscle.

Charley gets up and hugs Eddie, waters in both hands. They feel delightfully cold against the small of his back. Pieces of ice skim down his skin and drip onto his legs. Then Charley steps back and looks him in the face - for a few seconds she doesn't say anything - just smiles and looks.

"You smile different Eddie. Slower. Deeper. I don't know. Different." Eddie blushes.

"Oh Eddie. And, thanks, Eddie. Thanks for inviting me. You're the best. And I love what you're doing to this place. Thanks for the pics in your emails too. Wow! The country. The wide open spaces. It's great getting out of the city and being with friends." Charley is beaming over at Eddie. Eddie beams back. Thad isn't paying attention. He's watching Benjamin walk off, thinking God knows what, fingering and pulling on his belt, slouching and re-slouching against the porch stairs railing. He looks bored. He looks perfect as usual. He's still carefully sipping the Maker's Mark manhattan Eddie fixed for him a thirty minutes ago.

"Don't you know any more guys than this, Eddie?" Thad looks out at Eddie out of the side of his eyes. Charley frowns slightly. Eddie shrugs. Thad looks him straight in the eyes for a minute, daring Eddie to say something. But Eddie's not biting. He's too smart for it now. Or maybe he just can't muster up the energy.

Charley's watching the two of them with a funny look on her face. She starts to say something, then she stops. Just then another pick-up pulls in, next to the trailer. It's got more girls in it. They all scream "Deb!" Deb screams back.

Eddie's started managing a bakery in a small town (really just the intersection of two highways) a few miles from the Golden Oaks Mobile Home Park – that's the place Eddie calls home now. It's way north of the city, away from all the excitement and agitation. But he's getting used to it. He almost likes it. It's growing on him. All he's been doing for the last 4 months is spend money, remodel the 40 year-old trailer, manage the store, eat and sleep. Oh, and lately, get wildly physical with Thad. Beyond that, nothing else.

Well, he was also treating himself to a dinner at the local diner on Sundays and Wednesdays. He kind of likes the food, but really he likes the cook, John, who's always talking about his wife Daisy, but never talks about her to Eddie. Typical. For Eddie. A decent, and unavailable man.

But Thad arrived, didn't like the food there, and Eddie stopped going. He and a couple of other people Eddie's met from the diner and the Farm and Ranch Supply Store said they were going to show up today for his inaugural barbecue. But so far no one local has. Except for women who know Deb.

But Eddie's content. He would've been content if no one had shown up at all. For the first time in his adult life, he's doing it all for Eddie. Well, not for him alone. He's making a new life that has a lot of room to spare for other people. Room to share. And if Thad doesn't want to share with Eddie anymore, well, no one's forcing Thad. No one's forcing anyone anymore, not around Eddie. Eddie's out of the forcing business. Hopefully, for good.

And when Eddie really ponders it, all he actually wants is to share, no forcing involved. And that includes Thad. Thad should be happy. Eddie wants Thad to be happy. Thad just has to want that too.

So, no, Thad, Eddie thinks to himself, Eddie doesn't know more guys. And Eddie's doing fine with that. Eddie's just great. Eddie's lucky, in fact.

Eddie yawns as another truck pulls into the line of others in the row forming in his driveway. Eddie's lucky, yeah, lucky to be awake right now, after working all night last night making bread and pastries. There's a big table of bread next to the beer. Another of long johns by the water. Eddie's proud of it, since it's all Eddie's work. Eddie hears a familiar voice coming from the front of the trailer, "Daisy!" He walks up front. So he gets to meet John's wife, after all. Everyone else is out back. Eddie wonders what she'll be like. Skinny? Energetic? Round and motherly? Wearing a print dress or decked out in overalls?

There's John. And a big red Irish Setter. John catches Eddie as Eddie rounds the side of the truck, and some large, oversized, long-haired, red paws jump up on his chest. Eddie leans back against the truck. Then the paws are off. And John's hands are on the truck's cab, one on each side of Eddie's head. And John leans in. Eddie holds his breath. Their lips meet, brush, and settle in for some more serious work. Daisy bounces around beside them, then sits down, then starts bouncing again. This goes on for some time. They're still kissing when Daisy goes off looking for people that are more interesting to bounce around.

Finally John breaks free. "I've wanted to do that for the longest time" he says to Eddie's half-closed eyes. Then he leans in for more.

Later, Charley, holding a deflated volleyball she's pumping up, gives Eddie a motherly smile and a look and a nod. Eddie's bringing more liquids back to the teams. He's the waterboy. Thad is gone with his car, missing in action. Alice and Janey are standing on one side of the volleyball net with Ace and John, Deb and Benjamin and about 5 girls are standing on the other side. Daisy's running around on both sides of the net, she can't decide which team to join.

Deb is teaching one of the girls how to serve the ball. It's requiring a lot of touching and close, physical work. Deb's smiling. The girl's smiling. Alice is yelling. "Ah, for Heaven's sake Deb, just hit it for her!"

John looks over at Eddie, smiles. Eddie smiles back. Eddie thinks to himself "John. Who knows? Maybe?" He stops for a second, not knowing if he's mumbling again, but, really, he doesn't care if he's talking out loud or not. He doesn't care who hears him talking to himself. What the fuck, Eddie owns the place.

Eddie's carrying some trash out back when he notices it. He stops, not really all that surprised and lets the trash bag drop into the tall weeds by his fence line. Next to Thad's Camaro car tracks, deep ruts peeling out in the dust and the mud, there's a long, deep, jagged scratch all the way down the side of Eddie's black Ford pickup. It ends with the words "Two Timing Mother Fucker" written in caps from his radiator to his driver's side door. Eddie waits to feel something. Nothing. He waits some more. Nothing. Then more nothing. Then it hits him.

Eddie feels free. Eddie can be Eddie. He can be himself. And he can throw himself. He can throw Eddie out on the universe, spread himself around some, and he isn't afraid anymore to see what parts stick and what parts don't. He's got himself. Right in his own hands. It's an odd feeling. It was a long time coming. But Eddie figures, hell, he was worth the wait.

He picks up the trash, tosses it in the big construction dumpster he still has sitting at the end of his lot. Daisy runs back to check on him. He hears people yelling and laughing by his trailer. Someone's asking loudly for more beer. He stops in the trailer on the way back to grab a couple of cold six packs and Daisy waits for him outside. He emerges, moves heavily down the trailer front steps with his precariously balanced load of alcohol and a volleyball flies over the end of the trailer, bounces, and rolls up to his feet. Daisy noses it around some, then looks up at him, expectantly, pink tongue out, panting and smiling at him.

"Should we go, Daisy? Huh? Should we go back and play? Huh? Daisy? Should we? Huh? Should we? Daisy? Yeah! Let's do it. Let's do it, Daisy. Let's go back and play. That's right Daisy. Let's go. Let's go. Here we go, Daisy. Here we go."

Eddie throws the ball back over the trailer, there's some general noises of surprise as the ball appears out of nowhere. Daisy bounds off after it, Eddie shoulders his beer burdens, follows the dog and walks towards his backyard and the loud, raucous sounds of his rowdy guests.

AUTHOR'S NOTES

OF PLAUTUS AND THAD

I. Plautus and *Epidicus*

Thad Says Parts is Parts (and Thad is Right) comes straight out of the Roman playwright Plautus's comedy *Epidicus*. Many are the writers who have stolen from (borrowed from, been inspired by) Plautus over the last couple of millennia, including the likes of Shakespeare, Molière, and Sondheim, to name a few. And now that list of "thieves" includes me.

Not that I'm grouping myself with the likes of Molière. Not at all. Maybe I just share with them a weakness for the same predictable, quirky, obvious, low brow, slapstick, pun-filled humor that Roman audiences couldn't get enough of – humor that made Plautus a very successful man, and the father of Latin comedic theater.

Who was Titus Maccius Plautus? Plautus's first name, Titus, was a fairly common first name for Romans. He took his middle name (Maccius) from the name of a silly stock character found in the folk-comedy of his day, and got his last name (probably) from a reference to the flatness of his feet, or possibly his ears – thus his public name in Republican Latin was something like Tim Groucho Flatfoot.

So Groucho (Plautus) was apparently a carpenter who fell into the pseudo-religious, but still highly disreputable world of actors and plays at an early age. Having somehow gained enough money to allow him time to write, he brought Greek-language comedy to Rome in Latin translation, where it was a slightly scandalous affair. The Romans didn't build an actual permanent building for such a filthy place as a theater for another century and a half after Plautus wrote and produced his plays. Not that the plays were unpopular. Nobles and peasants, patrician and pleb, everyone flocked to his temporary platform and stood around the stage to watch his theatrical productions (well, the patricians probably sat). If you want to know more about Plautus, he's easily accessible in

Wikipedia – the place I found most of my information.

This play, *Epidicus*, was reportedly Plautus's favorite. That's one reason I chose it. The Roman Plautus, of course, stole his plot (probably) from the New Comedy Greek playwright Menander, who (probably) wrote almost the same play (or a similar set of plays) 200 years earlier in Athens. Where Menander may have pulled his plot(s) from, well, no one knows that for sure.

With Menander (or Menandros) we're right back at the start of theater itself, when putting on a mask and declaiming lines in front of an audience was still a religious act, but only just. Theater was becoming a civic behavior – something people in a city or polis might do – a *political* act. That was the Old Comedy in Greece, done by playwrights like Aristophanes: instructing the citizenry, improving society, inculcating excellence through humor – all done through satire – jokes about current political situations, something along the lines of a monologue on the Tonight Show. But theater was still very religious. It took place during a festival or set of games honoring a god and began and ended in ceremony and sacrifice.

However, Menander, Plautus's source, wrote New Comedy, not Old Comedy. The New Comedy of Menander was Old Comedy minus the politics. It was a Charley Chaplin or a Buster Keaton film – all humor, no overt education, maybe slight political subtext as long as it was nearly invisible and not blatantly preachy.

And Plautus was writing 200 years later in Republican Rome, not in Athens. A completely different society. The years around 200 B.C.E were a time of social and political upheaval for the city of Rome (the Second Punic War with Hannibal). And since the upper-class patricians (who paid for the production of Plautus's plays) were not accustomed to laughing at their own political shortcomings, Plautus wisely chose politics-free Greek New Comedy as the model for his productions. Thus, Plautus successfully became one of the first of the Romans to port Greek theater into the brave new world of the rapidly expanding Latin Republic – a republic that would grow, in another 200 years, into the Roman empire.

But, oddly, theater still had a religious aspect to it (re-ligio: Latin for a re-tying of earth to heaven) an act, or a public ceremony meant to please the formidable and mysterious powers that ruled men's lives and (as an afterthought) warn and instruct mortals in the proper way to behave themselves. Theater was part of the process of sacrificing. An awe-ful act. Comedy was a release from awe – turning society upside-down, making fun of social classes and conventions, celebrating sex and excess and trickery, making light of forces so terrible and powerful you couldn't face them in any other way. Comedy sprang from a very serious purpose. Something the serious Romans would appreciate. And Plautus knew that.

Now, having said all that. *Epidicus* is none of those things, really. *Epidicus* is what we would call a screwball comedy, a comedy of errors, a play full of stock characters and predictable, but staggeringly complicated and improbably intertwined plot lines. And it is a joy to behold, if somewhat difficult to follow at times.

Rome grew over the next 600 years, after Plautus. From a city, to a city-state Republic that covered the entire Italian peninsula, to an empire that encompassed the entire Mediterranean basin. And theater, and Plautus were there the whole time (well, for most of it).

Then Rome fell. Plautus, and theater and the idea of theater in general were almost all of it, lost, within the next 700 years or so. When the empire evaporated in the West, Plautus himself almost didn't make it. The best text we have of Plautus is due to the laziness of a medieval monk who only half-erased a previously used manuscript (all of Plautus's works) before writing something else on top of them (the technical name for an erased and re-used vellum manuscript is a palimpsest - interestingly - the title Gore Vidal gave to his autobiography, but I digress). If that monk had had a stricter supervisor, the play *Epidicus* would be unknown, Plautus would be only the name of an otherwise little-known Roman writer, and this book un-written. Which some might say, might have been a blessing.

So, after the fall of Rome, in the West, and the rise of Christian Rome in the East, theater was successively discouraged, marginalized, then forgotten entirely. Medieval European society had to run through the whole cycle again of a theater-less existence, religion, religious plays (for example passion plays and morality plays), culminating in a non-religious theater once more – theater for the sake of theater, theater for the sake of itself. When we get to the 1500's and beyond, we have playwrights once again too. And people stealing from Plautus - just like I did – and that brings us full circle, right back to Shakespeare, Molière, and Sondheim.

And that's what interested me in Plautus from the very beginning. That and the movie *Something Funny Happened on the Way to the Forum*, which if you like Zero Mostel, and Sondheim is fantastic. I highly recommend it.

The version of the play I used as the basis for *Thad Says Parts is Parts* was translated into English in 1912 (The Comedies of Plautus, Henry Thomas Riley, London. G. Bell and Sons, 1912), and is online at the Tufts University Perseus Hopper (http://www.perseus.tufts.edu/hopper/text?doc=Perseus:text:199 9.02.0100).

II. *Thad Says Parts Is Parts* and *Epidicus*

There is, actually a method behind my madness, if anyone is interested. What follows is how the two works: Thad and Epidicus line up if compared – by characters, and by chapters/acts.

1. THE CHARACTERS

Figure 1

Comparison Between the Characters in "Thad Says Parts Is Parts" and the Characters in Plautus's "Epidicus"

Thad Says Parts is Parts		Plautus's *Epidicus*	
"Eddie" Edward Stone	*Personal Asst. to Paul Periphanitides*	Epidicus	*Slave to Periphanes*
Paul Grigor Oinomaos Periphanitides "Mr. P."	*Rich father of Ace Periphanitides*	Periphanes	*Rich father of Stratipoccles*
"Ace" William Periphanitides	*Son of Paul Periphanitides*	Stratipoccles	*Son of Periphanes*
"Thad" Thaddeus Tucker Tavoularis	*Best friend of Ace*	Thesprio	*Best friend of Stratipoccles*

Thad Says Parts is Parts		Plautus's *Epidicus*	
Filipa	*Ex-extra marital affair of Paul, Ace's dad*	Philippa	*Ex-amour of Periphanes, Strat.'s dad*
Charley	*Friend (female) of Ace*	Chaeribulus	*Friend (male) of Stratipoccles*
"Dak" Dakota	*Fake son of Paul, 1st ex-boyfriend of Ace*	Acropolistis	*Fake daughter of Periphanes, 1st ex-girlfriend of Stratipoccles*
Benjamin "Jay", "Dak-Benjy", "BJ"	*Boyfriend of Ace, son of Paul and Filipa*	Telestis	*Girlfriend of Strat., daughter of Periphanes and Phillipa*
Albert Barnard "Al"	*Friend of Paul*	Apaecides	*Friend of Periphanes*
R.L., Investment Banker	*Rich man enamored of Dak*	The Pirate Captain	*Rich man enamored of Acropolistes*
Fulk Faulkner	*Imaginary boyfriend of Ace*		
Alice	*Friend of Eddie*		

Thad Says Parts is Parts		Plautus's *Epidicus*	
Adam	*Friend of Eddie*	Flute Girl	*Person sent to fool Periphanes*

2. THE STRUCTURE

Figure 2

Comparison Between the Chapters in "Thad Says Parts Is Parts" and the Acts and Scenes in Plautus's "Epidicus"

Thad Says Parts is Parts		Plautus's *Epidicus*	
Chapter		**Act**	**Scene**
Prologue	A Few Weeks Before, Eddie by a Body Shop in the Bayview District	–	–
1	Saturday Morning 9:15 A.M., Eddie in The Castro	I	1
2	Saturday Night 9:03 P.M., Eddie on the Corner of Castro and Market	I	1

Thad Says Parts is Parts		Plautus's *Epidicus*	
Chapter		**Act**	**Scene**
3	Saturday Night 9:08 P.M., Eddie on a Staircase Leading Down	I	1
4	Saturday Night 9:09 P.M., Eddie on the Floor of the Castro Muni Station	I	1
5	Saturday Night 9:26 P.M., Eddie Almost Back on the Corner of Castro and Market	I	1
6	Saturday Night 9:42 P.M., Eddie by the Lamp Post on the Corner of Castro and Market	I	1
7	Saturday Night 10:04 P.M., Eddie Going Down Seventeenth Street	I	1
8	Saturday Night 10:18 P.M., Eddie by Some Garbage in the Castro	I	2
9	Saturday Night 10:46 P.M., Eddie on a Street in the Castro	I	2
10	Saturday Night 11:15 P.M., Eddie Still on a Street in the Castro	I	2
11	Saturday Night 11:45 P.M., Albert at Paul's New House on Twin Peaks	II	1
12	Saturday Night/Sunday Morning 12:15 A.M., Eddie Under a Tree on Twin Peaks	II	2
13	Saturday Night/Sunday Morning 12:34 A.M., Eddie at Mr. P.'s House on Twin Peaks	II	2
14	Saturday Night/Sunday Morning 12:48 A.M., Eddie at Mr. P.'s House on Twin Peaks	II	2

Thad Says Parts is Parts		Plautus's *Epidicus*	
Chapter		**Act**	**Scene**
15	Saturday Night/Sunday Morning 1:09 A.M., Eddie at Mr. P.'s House on Twin Peaks	II	2
16	Saturday Night/Sunday Morning 1:37 A.M., Eddie Walking Down From Twin Peaks	II	3
17	Saturday Night 11:45 P.M., Thad, Ace & Charley at Charley's Flat	III	1
18	Saturday Night/Sunday Morning 2:57 A.M., Eddie in Front of Charley's Flat	III	2
19	Sunday 11:22 A.M., Paul and Albert at Paul's House on Twin Peaks	III	3
20	Sunday 11:47 A.M., Paul at His House on Twin Peaks	III	4
21	Sunday 12:16 P.M., Paul and Filipa at Paul's House on Twin Peaks	IV	1
22	Sunday 12:34 P.M., Paul and Filipa Still at Paul's House on Twin Peaks	IV	2
23	Sunday 12:00 P.M., Ace and Eddie on Market Street in the Castro	V	1
24	Sunday Afternoon 1:17 P.M., Eddie at Mr. P.'s House on Twin Peaks	V	2
25	Sunday Afternoon 1:35 P.M, Eddie at Mr. P.'s House on Twin Peaks	V	2
26	Sunday Afternoon 2:15 P.M, Eddie at Mr. P.'s House on Twin Peaks	V	2

Thad Says Parts is Parts		Plautus's *Epidicus*
Chapter		**Act Scene**
Epilogue	A Few Months Later, Eddie at Eddie's New Place	– –

ABOUT THE AUTHOR

There's really not much to tell. Anders lives a fairly routine-filled, somewhat solitary, very ordinary life. He'd like to say he regularly goes spear-fishing-scuba-diving - parachuting backwards out of vintage WWI biplanes into shark-infested stretches of the mid-Pacific armed only with his trusty toe-nail clippers clenched carefully between his molars. But he doesn't. The clippers would most likely only chip the enamel on his teeth, or he'd end up swallowing them (and wouldn't that be interesting), and all the fish would probably be schooling 1000 miles away near five star resorts enjoying the white sandy lagoons of Fiji.

Mostly Anders stubbornly carves a life out of the 24 hours he's been given each day, sometimes painfully and with great effort, sometimes ludicrously easily and without even knowing he's doing it. But, he supposes, that could be said of anybody.

And then there's the writing, which is a relatively new thing, and the jury is out on what, if *any*, future there might be in that department.

In the past, there's been the burger-flipping, the accounting, the landscaping, the delivery-van-driving, the Medieval History teaching, the computer programming, and a brief stint around the turn of the century turning countless boxes of mortgage papers and documents into spreadsheets that he was told were to form the backup for a new type of stable international financial product, a kind of security – the bundled mortgage (who knew?).

The truth is, this author has had the incredible luck to find integrity and honesty much more common than he was led to believe, that even though the world is a dangerous and scary place, you don't have to become dangerous and scary yourself to live in it, and that sometimes, if you're persistent, you can find love in all the wrong and in all the right places.